THE HUNTER BECOMES THE HUNTED

Tone woke to darkness, all of his senses suddenly alert. He rose, and on cat feet pulled on his nightshirt, then stepped into the shadows to the left of the window. Outside, the fog was thick and there was little light in the room. Fighting to control his rapid breathing, he raised the Colt and waited.

The door crashed into the room with such force, it was torn from its hinges.

On the bed, the woman shrieked.

Tone saw a bulky body directly in front of him. The man fired into the bed, fired again. The woman screamed louder.

Tone had waited to see how many assailants he was facing. There were two of them.

He fired at the man who'd shot into the bed. He heard a grunt and the huge body turned toward him. The man fired and the bullet crashed into the wall a few inches from Tone's head. Tone blasted another shot at his assailant and the man staggered back, slamming into his companion. The second would-be assassin made an attempt to get to the doorway, but Tone shot twice, very fast, and the man went right on through, then tumbled down the stairs, slamming and crashing his way to t

Ralph Compton

Bounty
Hunter

A Ralph Compton Novel
by Joseph A. West

A SIGNET BOOK

SIGNET
Published by New American Library, a division of
Penguin Group (USA) Inc., 375 Hudson Street,
New York, New York 10014, USA
Penguin Group (Canada), 90 Eglinton Avenue East, Suite 700, Toronto,
Ontario M4P 2Y3, Canada (a division of Pearson Penguin Canada Inc.)
Penguin Books Ltd., 80 Strand, London WC2R 0RL, England
Penguin Ireland, 25 St. Stephen's Green, Dublin 2,
Ireland (a division of Penguin Books Ltd.)
Penguin Group (Australia), 250 Camberwell Road, Camberwell, Victoria 3124,
Australia (a division of Pearson Australia Group Pty. Ltd.)
Penguin Books India Pvt. Ltd., 11 Community Centre, Panchsheel Park,
New Delhi - 110 017, India
Penguin Group (NZ), 67 Apollo Drive, Rosedale, North Shore 0632,
New Zealand (a division of Pearson New Zealand Ltd.)
Penguin Books (South Africa) (Pty.) Ltd., 24 Sturdee Avenue,
Rosebank, Johannesburg 2196, South Africa

Penguin Books Ltd., Registered Offices:
80 Strand, London WC2R 0RL, England

First published by Signet, an imprint of New American Library,
a division of Penguin Group (USA) Inc.

First Printing, October 2009
10 9 8 7 6 5 4 3 2 1

THE IMMORTAL COWBOY

This is respectfully dedicated to the "American Cowboy." His was the saga sparked by the turmoil that followed the Civil War, and the passing of more than a century has by no means diminished the flame.

True, the old days and the old ways are but treasured memories, and the old trails have grown dim with the ravages of time, but the spirit of the cowboy lives on.

In my travels—to Texas, Oklahoma, Kansas, Nebraska, Colorado, Wyoming, New Mexico, and Arizona—I always find something that reminds me of the Old West. While I am walking these plains and mountains for the first time, there is this feeling that a part of me is eternal, that I have known these old trails before. I believe it is the undying spirit of the frontier calling, allowing me, through the mind's eye, to step back into time. What is the appeal of the Old West of the American frontier?

It has been epitomized by some as the dark and bloody period in American history. Its heroes—Crockett, Bowie, Hickok, Earp—have been reviled and criticized. Yet the Old West lives on, larger than life.

It has become a symbol of freedom, when there was always another mountain to climb and another river to cross; when a dispute between two men was settled not with expensive lawyers, but with fists, knives, or guns. Barbaric? Maybe. But some things never change. When the cowboy rode into the pages of American history, he left behind a legacy that lives within the hearts of us all.

—*Ralph Compton*

Chapter 1

Big John Tone rode a sorrel horse out of the Chocolate Mountains of southern California, then swung due north, riding parallel to the Colorado River.

Ahead of him lay Milpitas Wash, which at this time of year, high summer, was as dry as mummy dust. On the south bank of the wash stood a sprawling cabin with a corral, barn, other outbuildings and a few smoke-colored ironwood trees growing here and there.

Apart from the dozen horses in the corral and the pigs and chickens rooting around in mud near the screeching windmill, Tone saw no sign of life.

But John Wesley Stillwell and his three sons were there. Tone was ready to bet the farm on that. And their womenfolk, a thorny complication that all too often shaped up to trouble.

Tone drew rein on the sorrel, swung out of the saddle and slid a .44-40 Winchester from the scabbard. He slapped the horse away from him, then stood straddle-legged in front of the cabin.

The heat was intolerable, and sweat trickled down

Tone's back. Flies buzzed around his head and the
thick air smelled of dust, pig shit and creosote bush.

"John Wesley Stillwell," Tone yelled, his voice loud
and commanding in the quiet. "Come out. We have
business to attend to, you and I."

Silence. Then a chair overturned, thumping onto the
cabin floor as though someone had brushed past it in
some haste.

The door opened and Tone levered a round into his
rifle.

A gray-haired, careworn woman stepped outside,
probably years younger than she looked. The arid cli-
mate of the southern California plains country played
hell on the fairer sex.

"I'm Martha Stillwell," she said. She had her hands
hidden under a linen apron. "What do you want?"

Tone acknowledged the woman's presence with a
slight incline of his head. "My business is with John
Wesley, ma'am, not you. Tell him to step out and take
his medicine."

"My husband is not home."

A curtain twitched in the window to the left of the
door. Tone noted the movement and would remember it.

Martha spoke again. "What business do you have
with my husband?"

"I think you already know my business, ma'am.
John Wesley is wanted dead or alive for murder and
cattle stealing. The price on his head is five hundred
dollars, and I can take him in alive or dead. The choice
is his."

"We have womenfolk inside, and children."

"They can come out after John Wesley."

The woman took a step toward Tone, her mouth

working. "Mister, we have so little and don't foresee nothing but hard times comin' down. We don't need more misery heaped on misery."

"John Wesley should have studied on that before he lifted cattle and murdered a drover, ma'am."

Tone's ice blue eyes ranged across the front of the cabin. Did that damned curtain move again?

"The drover fell off his horse and broke his neck," Martha said. "John Wesley had no hand in that."

"The vaquero died trying to stop your husband from running off his *patrón*'s cattle. If there had been no rustling, the man would still be alive." Tone motioned to the cabin with his rifle. "The day is waning fast and my patience grows thin. Tell John Wesley to get out here."

The woman shook her head. "My God, man, have some pity."

"I have none to give, ma'am."

"Who are you? Or are you a devil in the guise of a human being?"

"My name is John Tone." He touched his hat brim. "Your servant, ma'am."

Martha looked like she'd been slapped. "I've heard of you, John Tone. You're the Nevada gunfighter all the men talk about."

"Get your husband out here, ma'am, or I'll go inside for him." Tone's cold eyes chilled the woman like winter wind. "If I am forced to do that, I'll kill anyone, man, woman or child, who gets in my way."

But the woman was no longer hearing words. Instinct had taken over, transforming her into a she-wolf protecting her brood. "You heartless son of a bitch!" she screamed.

As Tone had known they would, when Martha took

her hands out from under her apron, they were holding a gun. As she thumbed back the hammer on the old Dragoon Colt, her eyes fixed on him, Tone fired. The impact of the heavy bullet slamming into her chest drove the woman backward. Amid a flurry of white petticoats, she tumbled into an empty zinc water trough and lay still.

A bearded man ran out the door, carrying a Greener shotgun. He took in the scene at a glance and cried, "Martha!" with an agonized shriek of despair and loss.

John Wesley Stillwell's lips curled back from his teeth in a snarl of rage and he fired the scattergun from his hip.

A clean miss!

Tone fired, did not wait to see Stillwell drop, but levered the Winchester again and sent a shot crashing into the window. A man's scream wrenched out over the racketing echo of the rifle fire and the shiver of shattered glass.

Stillwell was up on one elbow, clutching at his blood-soaked belly. The Greener had fallen just beyond his reach, but he ignored it, his eyes hot and furious on Tone.

"Just lay quiet, John Wesley," Tone said. "There's been enough killing here."

A young towhead stumbled through the door, a rifle in his hands. His right cheekbone had been shot away and his face was a scarlet nightmare.

The man screamed curses, wild sounds bubbling out of his bloody mouth. He raised his rifle and Tone shot him, fired again. His first round took the towhead high in the left shoulder, but the man rode his second bullet into eternity.

As a hog and a flock of terrified, squawking chickens scampered past him, Tone fed shells into the Winchester from his cartridge belt, his eyes on the cabin door.

In the quiet that followed the panicked flight of the chickens, his senses alert to any sign of danger, he heard the soft scrape of wood on wood.

A door had just opened at the rear of the cabin.

Stillwell was dragging himself along the dirt, his right hand reaching for his shotgun. Tone ignored him and stepped on cat feet to the corner of the cabin. Just behind him, Martha Stillwell was sprawled in the trough, her face slack in death, eyes half open.

Tone watched and waited, and after a few moments the youngest of the Stillwell sons stuck his head around the corner. Tone's snap shot was immediate and on target. His bullet took the youngster between the eyes, and he fell without a sound.

Turning, Tone saw John Wesley's fingers scrabbling in the dirt close to the Greener. He closed the space between them in a few long strides and kicked the shotgun away.

"You, out there!" A man's voice.

"What do you want?" Tone asked. He looked at Stillwell, who was dying hard and angry.

"We're coming out." A pause. "We're done."

"Step out with your hands empty, you and the women and kids. I'm not a trusting man."

The surviving Stillwell son led the way, his arms stretched out from his sides, fingers splayed. Two young women and three children followed.

Under a sky the color of steel as the day faded, the women threw themselves on the bodies of the dead, their sobbing, shrieking lamentations scraping the twi-light raw.

Tone glanced at the young man, who was now kneel-ing beside Stillwell. "Is he dead?" he asked.

The man nodded, not looking at Tone.

"What's your name, boy?" Tone asked.

"Tom. Tom Stillwell."

"Well, Tom, bridle your father's horse and bring it out here."

"Damn you! I told you, he's dead!"

"So you say, but I'm still taking him to the law in Yuma."

The man raised a tearstained face to Tone, his voice unbelieving. "My mother, father, brothers . . . You killed them all." He shook his head, stunned, like a man who has just been read a bad-news telegram. He looked around him. "Two widows . . . orphans . . . all my brothers . . . dead."

"Sometimes the cost of doing business comes high," Tone said. He dug into his shirt pocket for the makings and rolled himself a cigarette. He thumbed a match into flame and through a cloud of smoke said, "Now bring that horse out here like I told you."

As the undulating cries of the women rose in pitch and volume, Tom Stillwell rose to his feet and looked at Tone. He had brown eyes that were made soft by long black lashes.

"Pa talked about you, John Tone the man hunter. When the kids wouldn't go to bed, he used to tell them, 'Better get to sleep soon or John Tone will get you.' We thought it was funny. The thing is, it was not funny. Not then, not now."

Tone glanced at the sky. It would be dark soon

and he'd have to ride. "I'm in a hard, unforgiving business," he said absently.

"I know what you are, Tone. You're a dangerous, heartless animal, a man without a conscience or a soul."

"I'm all of those things, and worse. But I sleep well at night." Almost casually Tone lifted the muzzle of the Winchester until it was in line with Stillwell's belly. "Now you git, and bring out that damned horse."

The man opened his mouth to speak but thought better of it. He turned on his heel and walked toward the women, who had removed his mother's body from the trough and laid it out on the ground.

He stopped and glared at Tone. "Get your own damned horse."

Tone glanced around him, at the wailing women and children and the pale dead, pondering with detached interest on the mayhem he had wrought in just a few minutes of hell-firing violence.

If John Wesley had taken his medicine and come quietly, none of this would have happened. That's what Tone told himself. And that was what he believed.

He did not consider himself a cruel man and he harbored no ill will toward the men he hunted. When possible, he preferred to bring them in alive, but when guns were drawn, all bets were off.

Tone walked to the corral, bridled a gaunt old buckskin and led it back to Stillwell's body. A tall man, and strong, he effortlessly lifted the dead body and draped it facedown across the horse's back.

"What are you doing?"

A young blond woman strode toward Tone, her infuriated eyes the color of flames in smoke. "Leave him be," she snapped. "I won't have my father-in-law lie in foreign soil."

Tone gathered the reins of the buckskin, stepped into the saddle of his sorrel and looked down at the woman. "You can retrieve his body and the horse in Yuma from the Territorial Vigilante Committee." Tone touched his hat. "Good evening to you, ma'am."

"You coldhearted son of a bitch, you murdered him! And his sons!"

Tone shrugged. "I'm sorry you take that attitude, ma'am. But John Wesley was notified."

He swung his horse around and led the buckskin with its grim burden out of the yard. Something smelly splattered against his shoulder and a rock flew past his head. He turned. The women and their kids were throwing pig shit and anything else that came to hand at him.

John Tone glanced up at the violet sky, where the first stars hung like lanterns, lighting his trail.

He needed a bath and a hot meal. All in all, it had been a long, wearisome day.

Chapter 2

"Mr. Tone, there's someone at the front desk asking to see you, sir."

The morning hour was late and Tone was the sole patron of the Riverbank Hotel's dining room, where he had been enjoying his ritual breakfast—when he was home in Reno, at least—of coffee, three fingers of straight Kentucky bourbon and his first cigar of the day.

Irritated that his tranquility had been disturbed, Tone nodded to the desk clerk. "Very well. Show him in, Lawson."

The clerk bowed and glided away. He returned a few moments later with a small, wizened man who looked like a molting bantam rooster dressed in expensive broadcloth.

The man's smile died somewhere between his thin lips and his eyes. "Mr. Tone, I presume."

Tone carefully placed his cigar in the ashtray and rose to his feet. "I don't believe I've had the pleasure."

"Luther Penman, attorney-at-law, of San Francisco town." The man gave a quick, birdlike bow. "At your service, sir."

Tone waved Penman into a chair. "Please be seated."

Penman perched on the edge of the chair, his glittering black eyes darting like an inquisitive crow, taking in the younger man's expensive tailoring and snow-white linen.

"I'm happy to see you are prospering, Mr. Tone."

Tone smiled. "I've had better times, and worse."

"Not much better, I'll be bound. I was about to say that your elegant and expensive suit is by Brooks Brothers of New York, but now, on closer inspection I believe it was tailored farther west, perhaps by Marx and Cohen of Silver City. Your diamond ring and stick-pin are, of course, of local manufacture. The workmanship is slightly crude, but the stones are of excellent quality."

Penman glanced over his shoulder, then leaned forward in his chair. "Are you armed, Mr. Tone?"

Tone nodded. "A .44-40 in a shoulder holster." He grinned. "By Sam Colt of Hartford, Connecticut."

"Yes, a clever little quip to be sure," Penman said, flashing a grimace that may have been a smile. "But, you understand, I have enemies in Reno and they could quite soon become yours."

Tone raised an eyebrow in surprise, but said only: "Coffee?"

"Tea, if you please."

The waiter, a sad-looking man wearing a black claw-hammer suit, was eyeing the table, wringing his hands. Whether he was eager to leave or fearful of interrupting, Tone could not guess.

"Henry, tea for the gentleman."

The waiter seemed relieved. He smiled and bowed, then returned a couple of minutes later with a china teapot, cup and saucer.

Tone poured tea for Penman. "Cream? Sugar?"

"Neither, thank you."

"Cigar?"

"I don't indulge."

"Bourbon?"

The lawyer shook his bald head.

"Then perhaps you should state your business." Tone sipped his whiskey, then picked up his cigar. "I must admit, the idea of your enemies all of a sudden becoming mine intrigues me."

"I will talk plainly, Mr. Tone. No beating about the bush, but I will be circumspect of speech."

"Yes, please do."

Penman tried his tea, holding the cup in both white, blue-veined hands. He peered over the rim. "I'm here to make you rich, Mr. Tone."

Speaking through a cloud of fragrant blue smoke, Tone said, "Now you interest me even more."

"I can't reveal all the details of my proposition. That will be done by my principal. But it involves the deaths of six men, I can tell you that." Penman set his cup on the saucer without a sound. "Ah, the elimination of, shall we say, six business rivals is your line of work, is it not?"

"There are bounties on these men?"

"Yes."

"Enough to make me rich? That seems hardly likely."

"You are correct—you will not make a lot of money

from the bounties. In fact, none at all. But, as you will learn, my client will pay a bonus, a very large bonus, for each of the dead men."

"Who are these . . . business rivals?"

Penman's back teeth nibbled the insides of his cheeks. Finally he said, "Come now, Mr. Tone, be circumspect. Remember, curiosity killed the cat. Be assured, all will be revealed in the course of time."

Tone drained his glass. "When do I meet this client of yours? I'm meeting a lady of my recent acquaintance for a late lunch and I expect to spend the evening with her."

"That will be impossible, I'm afraid. We leave on the one-thirty cannonball for San Francisco."

Tone shook his head. "No. What you suggest is impossible. If you knew the young lady in question, I'm sure you would understand why."

"I realize that courtesans don't come cheap in Reno, Mr. Tone, but is she really worth many thousands of dollars?" The lawyer's hard obsidian gaze razored into the younger man's face. "Give me an answer to that question and be quick. If you prefer riding a sweating, grunting whore to earning a fortune, then I must find someone else."

"The lady is not a whore, Mr. Penman," Tone said, his voice edged.

"All women are whores, Mr. Tone. The sin of Eve condemned them to eternal damnation and they use their wicked feminine wiles to drag men down to hell with them."

Penman sat back in his chair, allowing his shoulders to just touch the upholstery, and spoke above steepled fingers. "I can see the answer to my question in your eyes, Mr. Tone. You desire the woman, yes, but you want the money more."

Tone made no answer, and the lawyer said, "I want you, above anyone else, for this task. I sense a stillness in you, Mr. Tone, but it is the calm before the storm. Handsome, elegant, right now you look like any other prosperous businessman in Reno, but we know better, you and I, don't we? You're a killer, Mr. Tone, and the job I'm offering you requires just that: a man who will kill without hesitation."

Tone attempted to explain that he was a bounty hunter, bound to the letter of the law, but Penman talked over him. "I heard about your desperate shooting scrape with the Stillwell gang. That was well handled."

"There was no Stillwell gang. John Wesley Stillwell would dab a loop on a few slick-eared calves now and then and nobody much minded. But when a cowboy got killed chasing him, for fun probably, everything changed. It seems the cowboy was well liked—at least that's what folks claimed after he was dead. I don't know what they claimed when he was still alive."

"Whether he was a calf poacher or not, you killed Stillwell anyway, and a couple of his sons."

"The local ranchers had the Yuma vigilantes put a price on Stillwell's head, dead or alive. I went to collect it."

"I say again, you killed him."

Tone nodded. "He was notified, but he ignored me."

"Come, Mr. Tone, a straight answer to a simple question: will you accompany me to San Francisco on the one-thirty train?"

"Yes, since at the moment I have no other pressing business, except lunch with my lady friend."

"I'm sure she'll get over it. I hazard that by ten o'clock tonight some other young buck will have his head between her thighs."

"Penman, did anyone ever tell you that you have the soul of a poet?"

"Mr. Tone, I have no soul. I am an attorney, a very successful one, and poetry is no part of me." The little man consulted the gold watch he'd taken from his vest pocket. "It's now noon. I suggest you throw a few things in your bag and meet me in the lobby in half an hour."

"You're allowing us a lot of time. The station is only a ten-minute walk away."

"Mr. Tone, we may need that time. I am convinced someone will make an attempt on our lives before we even reach our destination."

Chapter 3

"I should be back in a couple of days, Lawson," Tone told the desk clerk.

The man smiled. "I will see that your room is undisturbed."

Tone nodded, picked up his key and climbed the stairs to the second floor. His room lay at the end of the hallway and he unlocked the door and stepped inside.

After throwing a few items of clothing in a carpetbag, Tone opened a dresser drawer and removed a .44-40 Colt with a seven-and-a-half-inch barrel. It had once been a match for the revolver he wore in the shoulder holster under his coat, but he'd had the barrel of his hideout gun shortened to three inches and the ejector and front sight had been removed. It was a weapon modified for close-up, personal work, but he might also need the long-barreled Colt's longer reach.

Tone tossed the Colt into the bag, removed his gray top hat and checked himself in the mirror. Staring back at him was a handsome, black-haired young man with a long, faintly melancholy face and eyes the color of ice in a mountain crevasse. His mouth under the sweeping dragoon mustache was wide and generous and had once, in another time and place, been quick to smile.

Tone dropped his hands from his cravat and gazed at his reflection, unsettled by the coldness of his eyes. He detected no hint of humanity, no songs still to be sung. Rather he saw the eyes of a predatory animal, ruthless, merciless and calculating.

Women looked at him, he knew, and their bold stares lingered, wondering. And so did men. But most would glance away quickly, not liking what they saw.

The others, the ones who would meet his eyes and not look away, were men like himself, wolves among sheep, those who lived by the Colt and had long since accepted the hard lessons it taught and its violent tyranny.

Tone continued to stare into the mirror, like a man in a deep trance. He remembered another face, not unlike the one in his reflection, but twenty years younger and much less hard and uncompromising. And he recalled a voice, the good-natured bellow of big, laughing Michael O'Rourke.

Suddenly he was in another time and in a more ancient, greener place . . .

"Ah, my lad, 'tis a wonderful tenor voice you have and no mistake," O'Rourke said, slapping seventeen-year-old John Tone on the back. "You must turn the angels sick with envy."

"Sing us another, John," a man yelled from the bar.

The pub in the village of Ballenlake, deep in the Wicklow Mountains, was crowded that day in the bitter winter of 1867, as Ireland licked her wounds and nursed her festering grievances. With great brutality, the British had crushed the Éirí Amach na bhFiann, the Irish Fenian revolt, a few months before, and many of Erin's heroes had danced their last jig at the end of a hangman's noose.

The men present, and the few crooning grannies huddled by the fire, took whatever solace they could find in whiskey and the auld music. As it had been for hundreds of years, the British would write the history of the '67 revolt and the Irish would write the songs.

"Give us 'The Old Fenian Gun,' John," the man at the bar called out, to an instant chorus of approval.

"Sing, is it?" young Tone asked. "And with me pipes as dry as sticks."

The man at the bar yelled, "Hey, Molly, get the boy a pint of porter."

"He can have a glass of cider," Molly O'Hara said, tossing her glossy black mane of hair. "John is too young to be drinking porter and ale with the rest of you sots."

"Ho, John, when you marry Molly, she'll put a ring through your nose and lead you around like Tom Flaherty's bull." The man laughed.

Molly was the pub landlord's daughter, a quick, lively girl who was the same age as John. They had been walking out together for a year, and everyone expected their nuptials to be announced soon, this despite her being the daughter of a wealthy pub owner and John the poor son of a poorer widow.

John adored Molly with the hot, ardent fervor known only to the very young and, as far as he was aware, she returned his love in equal measure.

The girl set the glass of cider on the table before John and flashed him a dazzling smile that was both warm and affectionate.

Then, from the bar: "Come now, John. 'The Old Fenian Gun,' it is."

Molly rounded on the man. "He won't be singing that rebel song, Tom Doyle! If the British hear him he'll be hung. They're hanging men and women for less these days."

"Aye, what you say is true, Molly O'Hara," the man called Doyle said. "And, by Christ, more will swing before these troubles are over."

"That will do, Tom," said a small man dressed in black, a clerical collar at his neck. "'Tis a mortal sin to take the Lord's name in vain."

"And indeed it was not a curse, Father," Doyle said. "I used the Lord's holy name as a prayer for all the poor martyrs the English government will hang this winter."

A gloom settled over the bar as the banshee wind howled outside and rain hammered against the pub windows.

"I don't fear the English," Tone said with a youngster's reckless bravado. "I'll sing the song for you, Tom Doyle."

"Good lad," Doyle yelled, and the others cheered.

Tone threw back his head and in a fine tenor voice began the old rebel song, written to commemorate failed rebellion.

It hung above the kitchen fire, its barrel long and brown,
And one day with a boy's desire, I climbed and took it
*   down.*

Me father's eyes in anger flashed. He cried, "What have
* you done?*
"I wish you'd left it where it was, that's my old Fenian
* gun."*
I fondled it with love and pride, I looked it o'er and o'er.
I placed it on my shoulder, and I marched across the floor.
My father's anger softened, and as he shared my boyish
* fun,*
"Ah, well," he said, " 'tis in your breed, that old Fenian
* gun."*
I remember—

The pub door crashed open and four British soldiers
swaggered inside, led by a huge, burly sergeant, his
veined face the color of fired brick. Dripping rain, the
men strode to the bar and the sergeant slammed the
palm of a beefy hand on the polished mahogany.

"Four pints of porter, and be quick about it," he demanded.

James O'Hara, as big as the sergeant and angry,
slapped away the man's hand. "We serve no redcoats
here, so be off with you."

"You serve no redcoats 'ere, is it? You'll be serving us
or I'll burn this place down around your bleedin' ears."

"You'll get no porter in my pub. Now be off with
you or I'll report you to your officer."

"Like he cares?" The soldiers around the sergeant
laughed. Suddenly the man reached out, grabbed O'Hara
by the shirtfront and slammed his ham of a right fist
into the landlord's face. The blow shook O'Hara and he
would have fallen had not the soldier kept him on his
feet. The sergeant hit him again, and everyone in the
bar heard the bones of his nose shatter.

Suddenly Molly was on the Englishman like a tigress, screaming her rage as her small fists hammered into his face and head. "Leave my father alone, you bastard!" she yelled.

The big soldier ducked his head against the blows raining down on him. He tried to push Molly away. "Get off me, you papist bitch!"

John sprang to his feet, but immediately two of the privates leveled their Enfield rifle muskets at his chest.

Opposite Tone, Michael O'Rourke, who had fought in the recent rebellion, also rose, but he laid a restraining hand on the boy's shoulder. "Not yet, John," he whispered. "They'll kill you. Not yet, lad."

O'Rourke, a left-handed man, was furtively reaching into the pocket of his coat.

Then Tone saw Molly O'Hara die.

The big sergeant had grabbed the girl by the shoulders, and his bearded, open mouth sought hers. "Give us a kiss, darlin'," he said with a grin. "I'll wager you've already been done enough times that you won't miss it."

Molly spat in the man's face and her fingernails taloned his cheek, drawing blood as scarlet as his coat.

The sergeant cursed and backhanded a vicious slap across the girl's face. She stumbled away from him and fell, the back of her neck slamming into the corner of a heavy oak table on the way down.

Later, men said Molly O'Hara must have been dead when she hit the floor.

O'Rourke roared in fury and pulled a .442 Tranter revolver from his pocket. If the British soldiers had been militia, recruited for the duration of the rebellion, the big Irishman might have stood a chance. But they were regulars and well trained.

Before he could even level the Tranter two heavy balls crashed into O'Rourke's chest. The big man yelled, "They've killed me, lads," then dropped, the revolver falling from his suddenly nerveless fingers.

The gun thudded onto the table and without a thought, Tone picked it up. The soldiers who had shot O'Rourke were reloading, and the boy ignored them. The third private had been pinned between his sergeant and the bar and was trying to extricate himself. The man wriggled free and his rifle came up fast.

Tone fired. Hit hard, the soldier slammed against the bar and slid to the floor. The sergeant turned, his face shocked and Tone shot him.

He did not wait to see the effect of his bullet on the man, but fired at the two privates who had reloaded and were bringing their rifles to bear. Both men were hit, one discharging his rifle into the ceiling as he fell.

The huge sergeant, his face a mask of fury, had not been carrying a rifle, but he'd drawn the bayonet from the frog at his side and was advancing on Tone, cursing. This time the boy took careful aim, holding the big Tranter at eye level in both hands. The bullet hit just under the polished brim of the man's shako, driving into the bridge of his nose.

The sergeant screamed, staggered, then crashed face-down onto the pine floor.

Through a thick gray mist of powder smoke Tone jumped over the fallen soldier and ran to Molly's side. The faces of the old women kneeling beside the girl told him all he needed to know. Death shadows had already gathered in the girl's face and her half-open eyes were staring into her eternity.

Racking sobs shook the boy's slender frame as he

bent over Molly's still body, but the luxury of grief was not for John Tone that day.

Strong hands were pulling him to his feet and James O'Hara's bloody face swam into his view. The big man's expression of sorrow and shock had been carved into his features like lines on granite and they would remain there for the rest of his life.

O'Hara pressed notes into Tone's hand. "That's forty English pounds there, John. Use it to get out of Ireland. Go to America, lad, where the British can't reach you." The man's blue eyes bored into his own. "Now get ye gone into the hills or you'll hang at Dublin Castle before the week is out. There are informers all around us who would sell their own mothers for ten shillings."

Behind him, Tone heard a gurgling shriek as a wounded soldier's throat was cut. He shoved the money into the pocket of his pants as O'Hara's words finally got through to him.

"Molly . . . ," he said.

"She knows what's happening, John," O'Hara said. "Trust me, she knows. Now go before it's too late."

John Tone blinked, the face in the mirror again his own, older, harder. Lines of time and life and the living of it had engraved the corners of his eyes and mouth. It was a face from which all the songs had fled. Since that day in the pub at Ballenlake he had never sung another.

He turned away, a small grief in him for youth's lost innocence and his love for a girl whose face he could no longer remember.

Chapter 4

Tone and Penman made their way through crowded, noisy streets and reached the Central Pacific railroad station without incident.

"So far, so good," the lawyer said, his eyes darting this way and that like those of an inquisitive sparrow. "But we must remain on guard at all times until we reach San Francisco."

Before he settled into the cushions, Tone stashed his bag in the net rack above his seat along with a heavy coach coat. Penman had advised him to bring the coat because the nights could get chilly in a city surrounded on three sides by water.

After the train pulled out of the station, Penman began to relax.

"When we reach our destination, we'll take a cab to the waterfront," he said. "We'll be met at the dock by a boat that will take us out to my client's steam yacht."

"You still won't tell me his name?"

Penman ignored that and said, "The dock is in a dis-

trict called the Barbary Coast. Have you ever been
there?"

Tone shook his head. "No, but I've heard of it."

"And no wonder. Its infamy is known all over the
world. The place is home to murderers, footpads, burglars and hoodlums of all kinds. Thousands of whores
and their pimps prey on the poor, foolish sailormen
who frequent the dives along Front and Pacific streets
and all too often end up robbed, drugged and shanghaied."

"Seems to me your client could have chosen a safer
place to meet," Tone said.

"He has many business interests along the Barbary
Coast," Penman said. "And from time to time it is his
home."

The little lawyer looked out the window, signaling
that any talk about his client was over for now. "The
mountains of the Sierra Nevada are beautiful at this
time of the year, are they not?" he asked.

"At any time of the year," Tone answered.

"Indeed, yes."

Tone sat back and tipped his top hat over his eyes.
"Wake me if we run into trouble," he said.

A heavy mist curled through the dark streets of the Barbary Coast as Tone and Penman's cab threaded through
traffic toward the dock on Pacific Street.

The horse's hooves clattered and clanged over slick
cobbles and every so often the driver would vent his
lungs, unleashing a string of curses as a drunk staggered into his path.

"Over there to our right is Shanghai Kelly's saloon
and boardinghouse, in which my client owns a consid-

erable interest," Penman said. "Kelly is a violent man and the most notorious runner in the city."

Tone's face was in shadow, but Penman, with a lawyer's acumen, noticed the question in his eyes. "There are hell ships out of New York City commanded by captains under whom no sailorman in his right mind would sail." In the gloom Penman's smile looked like the grin on a yellow skull. "Runners provide those crews."

"I guess business makes for some strange bedfellows," Tone said.

"Ah, you mean my client and Kelly? Well, my client got his start here along the coast, working for a runner named Johnny Devine. After Johnny was hanged for murder, my client inherited his saloon and boardinghouse. He's now rich, but still looks back with fondness on the days when he was reckoned to be the best man with the blackjack, slingshot and brass knuckles along the entire Barbary Coast."

Tone smiled. "I'm looking forward to meeting this paragon of virtue."

"Be circumspect, Mr. Tone, be respectful," Penman snapped. "Remember, times change and so do men."

The cab horse clashed to a stop and the hansom creaked on its springs.

"The Pacific Street dock, gentlemen," the cabbie said. "In this fog I can't get any closer or I could drive right over the seawall."

Tone pulled the lever that opened the doors, picked up his bag and stepped outside. The air was chill, heavy with dampness, and the night smells of oily, stagnant water, filthy ships waiting to be scrubbed out and the nearby dives were more pungent than polite.

The saloons lining the street were doing a roistering

business, their gas lamps glimmering like stars through the mist. With his far-seeing eyes, Tone could make out a few of the painted signs hanging over the front doors: THE ROARING GIMLET, THE COCK OF THE WALK, BULL'S RUN, THE RAMPANT ROOSTER, BELLE OF THE UNION. He could also see one particularly disreputable dive that laid its main attraction on the line—THE HAPPY HARLOT.

As Penman stepped to Tone's side, the cabbie, a black man wearing a greatcoat and top hat, peered through the drifting fog at them. "Are you sure you want dropped off here?" he asked. "If you don't mind me saying so, this dock is no place for two gentlemens of your quality. Why don't I bring you back tomorrow in the daylight?"

"We'll be fine, cabbie," Penman said frostily. "Now, be off with you and mind your business."

The man shrugged. He touched his hat, then drove into the gloom, the cab's orange side lanterns bobbing until they were swallowed by darkness and distance.

The mist curled around Tone and Penman like a gigantic gray cat, the topmasts of the moored sailing ships just barely visible above the murk. Somewhere far out in the bay a buoy bell clanged, a lonely, melancholy sound.

"Where is that damned boat?" Penman said testily. "It should have been here waiting for us."

"The fog?" Tone suggested.

"There's always a damned fog in the bay. Any boatman worth his salt won't let a little sea mist hamper him."

Tone shivered and wrapped his heavy coach coat closer around him, glad of the triple cape that gave him some protection from the evening cold. Penman wore only a light tweed topcoat, but the night was no chillier than the man himself and apparently brought him no discomfort.

Heading in their direction, footsteps thudded on the cobbles and voices were raised in drunken song. As Tone watched, three men staggered out of the mist. Two of them were supporting a third, who was so hopelessly drunk the toes of his boots dragged along the street behind him.

"Tone," Penman said, quietly but urgently.

"I see them."

"Be on guard."

Though the three were big, rough-looking characters, Tone had been willing to give them the benefit of the doubt. But the alarm in Penman's voice, a man not easily scared, had him on edge.

Suddenly the three men separated, the one in the middle now squarely on his feet. The guns came out of their pockets fast.

But Tone had already drawn and fired.

One of the men went down, and the others looked at him, hesitating for just a moment as they were stunned by Tone's speed. In a gunfight any pause can be a fatal mistake.

Tone fired again, another hit. The man who'd been playing the drunk staggered back a step, then crashed onto his back. The third ruffian, scared now, turned and tried to flee. Tone aimed between the man's shoulder blades and fired. All at once the tough's legs seemed to be made of rubber. He lurched forward, taking a few ungainly steps, then sprawled his length on the ground.

Gun smoke drifted with the mist as Tone swung his Colt on men who were running from the nearby dives.

" 'Ere, you bloody toffs, what are you up to, then?" a man cried in an English-accented voice that even after twenty years set John Tone's teeth on edge.

"Those footpads attacked us," Penman said. "We were forced to defend ourselves."

The Englishman was big, walked with a sailor's rolling gait and had chosen to be belligerent. The two dozen or so others with him were no friendlier and Tone and Penman were surrounded by a sea of hostile faces.

"That there is Long Tom Piggott," the Englishman said. "And over there is Billy Maitland." He looked at a man in the crowd. "You, go see who our other dead shipmate is."

The man stepped to the body and turned it over with the toe of his boot. He looked across at the Englishman and yelled, "It's Cod McNear, Sam."

"Three of the finest sailor lads to ever walk the streets of the Barbary Coast," the man called Sam said. "They was all good shipmates, but Cod was gold dust."

"Aye, an' always good for a drink when a poor sailorman was down on his luck," another man yelled.

There was a muttering among the crowd, which had swollen by the addition of a score of eager-eyed whores. Fists clenched and curses were thrown in Tone and Penman's direction.

Sam turned, obviously enjoying being the center of attention. Now he played to the crowd. "Lads—an' ladies"—that last brought a ribald cheer from the whores, as the man knew it would—"I say it's coming to it when honest men can't walk the streets without being gunned down by toffs out for a night on the town."

Men cheered and a whore spat in Tone's direction and screamed, "I say we tar an' feather them and run them out of the waterfront on a rail."

The crowd was eager for any diversion and cheered wildly.

A tarring and feathering often resulted in death, but Sam, basking in his sudden glory, had something even more radical in mind.

"Or we can string 'em up, lads. What do you say?"

This time the cheering was louder. A man yelled, "I'll get ropes!" He turned and ran toward one of the dives, his feet growing wings as the crowd urged him on.

Tone was aware that he had only two rounds left in his Colt. With a wild recklessness in him, partly driven by his hatred for Englishmen, he took two long paces and was suddenly in front of Sam.

He jammed the muzzle of the revolver into the man's forehead, thumbed back the hammer and smiled. "You first, Sammy boy. As soon as your man shows up with a rope I'm going to scatter your goddamned brains."

The Englishman was suddenly so terrified that he pissed his pants and everyone saw it. At least temporarily, it took the wind out of the crowd as they saw their hero so humiliated.

"That won't be necessary, Mr. Tone."

Tone took a quick glance behind him. A tall man wearing an officer's rings on the sleeves of his uniform coat was watching him. He was backed by four tough sailors armed with Winchesters.

The officer looked at Penman. "Sorry we're late. The fog out in the head of the strait is thick as molasses in winter."

"I'd say, Mr. Brown, that you arrived in the nick of time," the lawyer said, flashing his wintry smile.

Brown looked over at Sam, who was standing as still as a stone statue, his eyes crossed as he fixed his horrified gaze on Tone's gun. Clubs and brass knuckles he knew, but guns and the gunfighters who used them had not been any part of his education.

"Sam Wilkins, go back to your rum and your whores," Brown said. "There will be no more talk of hanging, or tarring and feathering either."

Wilkins' throat worked for a few moments, and then, standing stock-still, he said, "He's going to shoot me, Mr. Brown."

"I doubt it, Sam. Why would he waste a bullet on the likes of you?"

Tone eased down the hammer of his Colt. "You're lucky, Sammy," he said. "I really don't like you." He laid emphasis on the statement by driving his left fist into Wilkins' belly. Then as the man bent over, retching green bile, Tone slammed the barrel of his revolver on the back of his head. He stepped aside to let Wilkins fall, then walked around him and picked up his bag.

"Shall we get on board, gentlemen?" Brown asked, looking emotionlessly at Wilkins, who was groaning on the damp cobbles. "It's a long ways out to the strait."

Brown's cold eyes swept the crowd. "I'd advise you people to get off the street. If you have any more mischief in mind, let me warn you that my men will drop a dozen of you before you cover a couple of yards."

The mob was surly, still on the prod, but the sound of levering Winchesters convinced them that this was not a good night to die.

Brown watched them go for a few moments, then

called out, "When Sam Wilkins recovers tell him to bury the recently departed, since he was so fond of the dear, honest souls."

Penman stepped to Tone's side. "Not a man to forgive and forget, are you?" he asked.

"Live longer that way," Tone answered.

Chapter 5

The yellow fog pressed around Tone as he sat on a thwart at the stern of the rowboat, Penman huddled beside him. There was no sound but the creak and thud of the oars in the locks and the slap of water against the sides.

Tone was no judge, but Brown seemed to be a capable sailor. He stood in the stern and constantly checked the compass he held, now and then altering course a degree or two.

The rowers were a rough-looking bunch and most showed scars, probably from past violent encounters in dockside dives all over the globe.

Brown turned and peered at Penman through the gloom. "How are you holding up, Mr. Penman?" he said.

"As sick as a pig, Mr. Brown. Need you ask?"

Brown nodded. "The sea is picking up as we get closer to the strait, starting to roll some." His teeth gleamed in the darkness. "Once you get on board the *Spindrift* you'll be as right as rain."

"I doubt that, Mr. Brown. Speaking to you as a dying man, I doubt that very much."

"And you, Mr. Tone?" the officer asked.

"I'm all right, just thinking how good some fried salt pork and beans would be about now."

One of the rowers guffawed, and Penman turned his green face to Tone. "Sir, your cruelty knows no bounds, does it?"

Tone grinned and opened his mouth to reply, but the little lawyer was already retching over the side.

Brown looked quickly away, but not before Tone saw that he too was grinning. It seemed that the abrasive Mr. Penman had few friends on land . . . or sea.

Fifteen minutes later, as Penman sat hunched and miserable beside him, Tone saw a long black shape emerge from the gloom.

"The *Spindrift*," Penman said, gulping as he fought to keep down what little was left in his stomach. As though it was something he'd memorized, he added, "She's an iron three-masted steam schooner, one hundred and seventy feet long, built in 1880 by Ward, Stanton and Company of Newburgh, New York. My client made certain modifications to her deck a few years ago."

Tone had little interest in boats, but from where he sat in the rowboat, the craft looked enormous, graceful and beautiful.

"How much does something like that cost?" Tone asked.

"A small fortune, Mr. Tone," Penman said brusquely. "No questions. Be circumspect, now."

After Brown identified himself and his passengers to a seaman on deck, ladders were lowered and grinning sailors helped Tone and Penman clamber ungracefully from the pitching rowboat and climb on board.

An officer saluted smartly and said, "Welcome to the *Spindrift*, gentlemen. I'm instructed to take you below to the owner's stateroom."

A voice called out from the bridge, a glass-covered structure forward of the raked funnel. "Mr. Tyler, are the gentlemen aboard?"

"Aye, sir."

Through the drifting fog, Tone could make out a shadowy, squat figure leaning out of the port side of the bridge. "Then let us get under way, Captain Tyler, and head for open water. I don't want to get trapped in the strait."

The officer saluted. "Aye, aye, sir." He looked at Tone and Penman apologetically. "Duty calls, gentlemen. I will have a seaman show you to the stateroom."

After the man left, Tone turned to the lawyer. "What did he mean 'trapped'? Trapped by what?"

"All will be explained presently, Mr. Tone," Penman said. He looked sick, weak and miserable, like a man who desired only a quick, merciful death.

The ship thrummed into life and the stern dipped as the screws bit into the water. Burly seamen thronged the deck, performing mysterious tasks that Tone couldn't even guess at, but one detached himself from the rest and picked up Tone's bag. "This way, shipmates," the man said, motioning with his head.

The sailor led the way down a steep, almost vertical ladder into a narrow passageway with doors along each side leading to the galley, officers' quarters and storerooms. Though the ship had been built as a pleasure craft, the overhead was so low that Tone had to remove his top hat and stoop to clear the supporting deck beams.

He and Penman followed the sailor to a door that marked the end of the passageway. The man knocked, got no answer and opened the door wide. "Inside, ship-mates," he said. "The cap'n said to make yourselves comfortable and the owner will be with you shortly."

Tone followed Penman into the stateroom and the sailor set the bag on the floor, then quietly closed the door behind them.

To call the small spartan cabin a stateroom was a gross overstatement. An oak desk stood in the middle of the carpeted floor and an iron cot was jammed against the starboard bulkhead. A few straight-backed chairs and a liquor cabinet displaying a variety of crys-tal decanters and glasses completed the furnishings.

The overhead was as low as the one in the compan-ionway and Tone was grateful to take a chair and straighten out his back. Penman also perched on a chair and sat hunched and forlorn, gulping now and then as his seasickness threatened to rebound on him. As the *Spindrift* made her way through the Golden Gate to the open sea, she rolled like a wallowing sow and the little lawyer's distress grew more and more evident.

After a few minutes the door opened and a short, stocky man stepped inside. Penman immediately got to his feet, and Tone, deciding that was what protocol demanded, also rose, only to bang his head hard into a deck beam.

"Be seated, gentlemen," the stocky man said. He sat behind his desk, making no attempt to shake hands.

Despite his aching head, Tone studied the man. He was short, heavily muscled in the arms and shoulders and dressed in the rough wool and canvas garb of an ordinary sailor. His skin was as dark as mahogany, the weather-beaten face deeply lined. Stark white against his dark complexion, a terrible scar ran the length of his left cheek, close to the mouth. The scar had drawn the corner of the man's top lip slightly upward, as though he was wearing a permanent sneer. His eyes were bright blue, lively and not devoid of humor.

The man looked at the lawyer. "Not puking your guts up, Penman? This is a change. Of course, the seas are calm at the moment—maybe that explains things."

"I did it earlier—puke, I mean. I've got nothing left in my belly."

"Well, you're not spewing now, so I say we'll make a seaman of you yet—lay to that."

"Never," the lawyer spat. "I'm more than happy to take care of your business interests without ever leaving dry land."

The man looked at Tone for the first time. "Penman doesn't like ships, or sailors or me." His blue eyes went to the lawyer again. "Is that not so, Luther?"

"Sir, you pay me to conduct your business affairs. Likes or dislikes do not enter into it."

As though he hadn't heard, the stocky man said to Tone, "Luther doesn't like women either, though a plump and rosy-cheeked young cabin boy will turn his head fast enough."

Penman scowled, but retreated back into his own nauseated misery, drawing what was left of his dignity around him like a tattered cloak.

"And you, I presume, are John Tone," the man said. Tone allowed that he was.

"My name is Lambert Sprague. I own this craft."
He rose to his feet and crossed to the liquor cabinet.
"Drink?"

Tone nodded and Sprague said, "Does Old Fitzger-
ald suit your taste?"

"That's just fine."

Sprague poured three fingers of bourbon into each of
two glasses and handed one to Tone. "As you probably
know, Luther doesn't drink." He grinned and looked
over at the lawyer. "What else don't you do, Luther, apart
from women?"

Penman made no answer, but Sprague had decided
to needle him. "I tell you what you don't do, Luther—
you don't live. You're a pathetic, dried-up old mummy
who is only happy when he's in the tomb he calls an
office, surrounded by mice and dusty lawbooks."

"I take care of your business from that tomb, as you
call it."

"I know, and that's the only reason I keep you
around, you puking old turd."

Tone realized that there was a sadistic streak in
Sprague that he apparently had the wealth and power
to indulge, and its roots would run deep, all the way
back into the man's murky past. He was an hombre to
be watched and reckoned with.

Sprague raised his glass. " 'May no son of the ocean
ever be devoured by his own mother,' as the Limey
sailors say." The man drained his glass and Tone followed suit.

Sprague replenished their bourbon, then said, "How
old were you when you killed your first man, Mr.
Tone?"

"Seventeen. It was back in the old country." Tone believed what was left of his brogue identified the country he was talking about.

"And how many since?"

"I don't know. I've never counted them."

"Including the three men you killed earlier tonight, I make it an even score."

Tone shrugged. "Some men need killing."

Sprague nodded, then said, "Come over and sit at the desk."

Tone did as he was told and Sprague opened a drawer and laid six separate bundles of bills on the desk in front of him. He added a seventh, considerably thicker than the rest. Tone was aware of Penman struggling to his feet. Pale and sick, he stood behind his client.

"Each of these six stacks contains a thousand dollars," Sprague said. "You will receive one of these every time you successfully perform a certain task for me."

"And the seventh?"

"That stack is higher than the others, as you can see. That's because it contains twenty-five thousand, the amount you will get from Luther when all six undertakings have been brought to a conclusion satisfactory to all concerned."

Sprague opened a cedar box on his desk and proffered it to Tone. "Cigar?"

Tone took one, bit off the end and Sprague lit it for him. Through a cloud of smoke he said, "What are these tasks?"

"Each stack of bills represents one man. You will seek out and kill all six of them."

Tone's chair creaked under his weight as he leaned

forward. "Mr. Sprague, I'm a bounty hunter, not a hired killer."

Sprague smiled. "I don't quite see the distinction."

He opened a drawer again, brought out a slip of paper and slid it across the desk to Tone. "Those are the six wanted men and there on the desk are their bounties."

"They're not wanted by the law."

"No, but they are wanted by me. You said earlier that some men deserve killing, and those six do. Each of them, many times over, is a murderer, robber and rapist. Vicious, dangerous cutthroat rogues, every man jack of them."

"Why do you want these men dead?"

"That is my business."

"And killing men is my business, is that it?"

"Surely you know the answer to that question better than I do."

Tone picked up the list. "Where do I find these men?" he asked.

Chapter 6

Lambert Sprague waved an indolent hand, as though he was already getting bored. "Tell him, Luther."

"All six of the names on your list currently reside in Virginia City," Penman said. "They grew rich off the sweat of the Comstock miners—"

"The hell they did," Sprague snapped, suddenly angry. "They grew rich from blackhearted piracy on the high seas. Many a fine ship and brave sailor lad they sent to the bottom, aye, and wench too if the truth be told." The man shook his head, a small act of contrition for past sins. "And God help me, for seven long, bloody years I was one of them."

Tone looked up from the list of names he'd been memorizing. "Then these six men were your friends."

"Friends? No, not my friends. I was their captain."

Sprague turned his head to look at the lawyer. "Luther, bring the decanter."

"I'll get it," Tone said, half rising to his feet.

"You stay there," Sprague said. Then louder: "Luther, the decanter!"

As the lawyer stepped to the liquor cabinet, Sprague said to Tone: "As long as you are on board this ship, don't ever countermand an order of mine again. Why would I keep a dog like Luther Penman and do my own barking?"

Again Tone sensed the latent cruelty in Sprague, and the steel. Sitting behind his desk, his iron gray hair cropped closed to his great nail keg of a head, he looked indestructible, a hard man to kill.

Sprague was talking again. "We got our start in the late War Between the States after I bought the twenty-gun sloop *Devonshire* from the British navy. She was laid up in ordinary at the time in a dry dock at Portsmouth and her masts, rigging, sails and guns had been removed. I had a crew, but no money to refurbish her."

Penman poured bourbon for Sprague, then refilled Tone's glass.

"Luckily, that first year of the war, British sympathies were with the Confederacy," Sprague said. "I had a letter of marque as a privateer signed by Jefferson Davis himself, and that convinced the Admiralty to refit the sloop, provided I changed her name. That I did, and when we finally sailed she was the *Tuscaloosa*."

As though warming to his story, Sprague sat forward in his chair. "We ran the Union blockade for two years, carrying arms and goods from England, doing our bounden duty for the South, you might say. Then, in the spring of 1863, we chanced on a fat French merchantman loaded to the gunnels with wine and cognac, bound for Boston town.

"Well, we took the ship, cut the throats of the crew and tossed them overboard. Then we loaded the cargo onto our own ship and scuttled the Frenchman in the middle of an empty ocean and not a soul the wiser.

"It was then, Mr. Tone, that we decided there was more money to be made from piracy than blockade running. The risk was less, so long as we stayed out of the way of Union frigates, and the rewards were enormous."

Sprague looked behind him at Penman. "Isn't that so, Luther?"

He turned to Tone again. "Luther handled our first cargo, then all the others. He invested heavily in San Francisco and the Barbary Coast and by the time the war was over I was a rich man, and so was Luther. He always made sure to take his pound of flesh."

"As the Bible says, the laborer is worthy of his hire, Mr. Sprague," Penman said.

"Aye, and you've been worthy, Luther, a born crook like me and the six on my list. You can tie up to that."

"I'll ask you again, Mr. Sprague," Tone said. "Why do you want these men dead?"

"The short answer is because they want me dead." He nodded to the paper in Tone's hand. "Those men were my ship's officers, and like me, they were rich when the war ended. Luther is right—they moved to the Comstock and bought saloons and hotels, providing what the miners wanted: gambling, whores and whiskey. All six of them are good with guns, and very few other hard cases in Virginia City were willing to challenge them. Those that did ended up dead.

"They also sank money into the Barbary Coast, and now that the Comstock mines are played out and the miners moving on, their San Francisco holdings have suddenly become very important to them. They want more of the liquor and prostitution business along the Barbary and the one person standing in their way is me, their old cap'n. I already own most of the waterfront and I'm not selling and I won't be pushed out."

"So you want me to kill them before they kill you, is that it?"

"Exactly. And you're being well paid for your trouble."

Tone smiled, the bourbon helping him mellow. "There's law in Virginia City. At least five police precincts as I recall. You just don't walk up to six men in the street and gun them."

"You won't need to go to Virginia City, Mr. Tone," Sprague said. "Once the word gets around, and it will, that you're working for me, the six will come after you." The man's smile was wintry. "Depend on it."

Sprague looked at Tone, his face like a hunk of hewn granite. "Well?"

"Well, what?"

"Damn your eyes, man, will you take on the task I've offered ye?"

Tone nodded. "It's my business, and money talks."

"Aye, it does. It speaks every tongue on earth." Sprague turned to Penman. "Get Blind Jack and tell him to bring Tom McGill. Then administer the oath."

After the lawyer left, Tone said, "Administer the oath? To me or to Blind Jack?"

"It is you who will take the Pirate's Oath, Mr. Tone."

Tone smiled. "I'm not a pirate."

"Nor am I, at least no longer. Being a gentleman of fortune was an honest trade once, but now it's gone forever. The oceans are full of ironclads carrying guns that can shoot for miles and there's nowhere left, on land or sea, for even a lively pirate lad to hide. You'll meet Black Tom McGill soon. He was one of the greatest pirates of them all, until a Brazilian ironclad blasted his sloop out of the water east of Barbados not a dozen years since. Black Tom couldn't see that his day was over, and in the end it done for him.

"But the oath remains, an unbreakable bond between men."

The door opened and Penman stepped inside, followed by a giant of a man, a narrow black band wrapped across his eyes and tied at the back of his head. Blind Jack topped Tone's six-four by several inches and his massive shoulders were an axe handle wide, his huge hands the size of shovels.

"Jack lost his lights when a cannon breech burst on him," Sprague said. "But he can see more than most men, in light or in dark. Set Black Tom on my desk, Jack, will ye?"

His shoulders bent under the low overhang, the big man opened the velvet drawstring bag he was carrying and removed a skull. With unerring accuracy, he laid the skull in front of Sprague, then stepped back.

Sprague poured a full glass of whiskey and held it out toward the giant. "A drink with you, Jack, to wet your pipe, like."

"Thank'ee, Cap'n," the giant said. He took the glass from Sprague's hand as easily as would a sighted man.

"You'll witness the oath, Jack," Sprague said. "We have a new recruit on board, Mr. John Tone of Reno town."

"Aye, Cap'n, a tall man who's sitting down at the moment, young, and he has a revolver with him, recently fired."

Sprague looked at the startled Tone and smiled. "He heard your breath from where you sit and gauged your height. Your breathing is strong, so you are young and healthy. He smelled the revolver."

"I could be a short man standing," Tone said.

Sprague shook his head. "Jack heard the chair creak. I didn't, nor did you, but Blind Jack heard it."

Tone's attention was drawn to the skull on the desk. Its entire yellowed dome was covered in a fine golden filigree depicting ships at sea and bare-breasted mermaids. The lower jaw was bound to the rest of the skull with gold wire and rubies had been set into the few teeth it still possessed.

The skull, Tone decided, was a work of art.

"Tom McGill, I presume," he said.

Sprague nodded. "All that's left of him. After he was shot by the Brazilians, I managed to acquire his head after it hung from their mainmast for a six-month. I needed to call in a lot of favors, but it still cost me a pretty penny."

"And you did the gold work?"

"Had it done in San Francisco. It's the least I could do for the last gentleman of fortune to freely sail the Seven Seas."

"I'm sure he was a fine man," Tone said with a straight face.

Sprague looked at him sharply, but the younger man's expression revealed nothing. He reached into a drawer, produced a scuffed, leather-bound Bible and slid it across the desk. "Luther, administer the oath," he said.

Penman told Tone to rise and approach the desk. "Take the Good Book in your left hand, place your right hand on Black Tom's skull," he said.

Slightly drunk, wholly bemused, Tone did as he was told.

"Jack," Penman said.

For a blind man, Jack moved easily and with incredible speed. Before his alcohol-dulled senses could react, Tone's head was bent back and the keen edge of Blind Jack's knife was at his throat.

As though nothing unusual had happened, Penman said, "Do you, John Tone, in the presence of this assembled company, pledge your undying loyalty to Captain Lambert Sprague?"

Aware of the knife, imprisoned in the rough embrace of Blind Jack's steel hawser arms, Tone said nothing. Penman told him to say: "I swear it."

"I swear it."

"Do you, Jack Tone, swear your willingness to be bound with chains, branded with irons, lashed with whips, hung by a noose or have your carcass left to rot in a cage rather than betray the sacred trust of Captain Lambert Sprague?"

"I swear it."

"Do you, Jack Tone, swear on the skull of Black Tom McGill and the Bible to carry out all lawful orders, commands, directives, mandates, prescriptions and assignments as Captain Lambert Sprague deems necessary?"

"I swear it."

"Now, after due consideration, if you wish to renege on the terms of your service, speak up at once, though be warned that your life will immediately be forfeit."

The blade of the knife pressed deeper into Tone's throat.

Penman told him to say that after all due consideration, he did not wish to renege on his sacred oaths.

Tone said the words and the knife blade was taken away from his throat. He looked around him, ready to smile, expecting the three other men to laugh, slap his back and tell him he'd been a good sport.

It did not happen.

The faces of Sprague, Blind Jack and Penman were solemn, like broadcloth-wearing bankers in church. Tone had thought the oath silly. He knew now that if he broke it Sprague wouldn't rest until he was dead.

With great reverence, the skull was placed in the velvet bag again. The Bible got shorter shrift. Sprague picked it up and threw it back in the drawer.

He looked at Tone. "You will return to the coast tonight. I've arranged for you to take a room at one of my own places, a tavern called the Rose Garter. It's better than most dives along the waterfront. The rum is good, the beds clean and the poker fairly honest. The Rose Garter is run by a man who took the same oath as you did. His name is Simon Hogg and Penman will instruct him to supply you with anything you need—food, liquor or women. And he'll stand by you in a fight."

"Hogg will supply your needs within reason, of course," Penman said. "You should try to keep your expenses as reasonable as possible."

"There speaks the bookkeeper," Sprague said. He studied Tone from head to foot. "Until you know your way around the waterfront and my six old shipmates make their move, best you look like an ordinary sailorman. Those fine clothes you're wearing will draw unwelcome attention."

Sprague turned to Penman. "Find him something from the slop chest."

He looked at Tone again. "For safety's sake, I stay to

sea as much as possible and let Luther handle my affairs on land. But I'll be back in the Barbary Coast in a few weeks and I fully expect you to have some successes to report by then. Any questions?"

"None," Tone said.

"A word of warning to ye, then. You've sworn a scared oath, Mr. Tone. If you betray any part or parcel of that oath, the punishment is to be marooned on an island with your eyes burned out and your blue guts tied to a tree." Sprague paused, then: "Do you understand?"

Tone nodded. "I catch your drift."

"So be it. I believe you're a good man, Mr. Tone. You've already proved you're a hand with a gun. Now prove yourself to me." He shook his head. "Don't disappoint me."

There was no note of encouragement in Sprague's last statement.

It was a warning.

Chapter 7

John Tone sat at the window of his darkened room, staring at the street below, where the white fog twined. Men came and went, their footsteps loud on the cobbles, and from the bar downstairs a piano competed with the drunken roars of men and the high-pitched, false laughter of whores.

"Come back to bed, darlin'," the woman said. She introduced a practiced little-girl pout into her voice. "Jennie's getting lonely."

Tone smiled and said without turning, "It must be a long time since you were lonely in bed."

"You say cruel things to me, John. Why do you say cruel things?"

"I don't know. Because you're a whore. Why do you care?"

"Because I like you, John. You're not like the other men I meet. You don't beat me or try to cheat me."

"You're Irish, huh?"

"From Donegal. I came over on a British ship. It was terrible, bad food and storms every mile of the way."

"I knew a girl in Ireland once. Her name was Molly and she had beautiful black hair."

"Not like mine."

"No, nothing like yours."

"What happened to her?"

"She died."

Tone's attention went back to the street. It had been a week since he'd taken the oath on Sprague's ship and since then he hadn't seen the man, or Penman either.

He'd spent his time exploring the waterfront, realizing just how far he was from his natural element, the wild western lands. Here, along the Barbary Coast, the arroyos were dark, rank alleys, the mountains the high, rickety buildings that rose on all sides of him, and the only streams were the rivers of bad whiskey and rum that flowed in the taverns.

And the sea was always there, making its presence known by sight, sound and smell, as alien to John Tone as the landscapes of the moon.

"What are you thinking about, John?" the woman asked.

"Nothing."

"You must be thinking about something. Me, maybe?"

"Yes, you. I'm thinking about you."

"What are you thinking? Do you want to try something new?"

"I'm thinking you're the gabbiest whore I've ever met."

"See, you're being cruel again. Why do you never get far from your guns?"

"Because I may need them in a hurry."

"Why would someone want to kill you, a poor sail-orman?"

Tone smiled again and turned. "You ask too many questions."

The woman was lying on top of the tumbled bed, naked as a seal, the coral tips of her breasts just visible in the darkness. She had a wide, inviting mouth that was smeared with scarlet and her eyes were half shut, languid with awakening desire.

Tone lay beside her and cupped a breast in his hand, caressing the silken skin with the ball of his thumb.

"You like sleeping with me, John, don't you?"

"Sure I like sleeping with you."

"Tell me why. Tell me why you like sleeping with me."

"Because I don't have to love a whore."

Tone woke to darkness, all of his senses suddenly alert.

There it was again!

A soft creak on the shoddily built stair outside his room. Then another.

He reached out to the bedside table and picked up the long-barreled Colt. Beside him the woman was breathing softly, lost in dreams.

Tone rose, and on cat feet pulled on his nightshirt, then stepped into the shadows to the left of the window. Outside, the fog was thick and there was little light in the room. Fighting to control his rapid breathing, he raised the Colt and waited.

The door crashed into the room with such force, it was torn from its hinges.

On the bed, the woman shrieked.

Tone saw a bulky body directly in front of him. The man fired into the bed, fired again. The woman screamed louder.

Tone had waited to see how many assailants he was facing. There were two of them.

He fired at the man who'd shot into the bed. He heard a grunt and the huge body turned toward him. The man fired and the bullet crashed into the wall a few inches from Tone's head. Tone blasted another shot at his assailant and the man staggered back, slamming into his companion. The second would-be assassin made an attempt to get to the doorway, but Tone shot twice, very fast, and the man went right on through, then tumbled down the stairs, slamming and crashing his way to the bottom.

Now Tone moved to his left, aware that he had only one shot left. He heard a groan and through the gloom saw that the man he'd shot was down on his hands and knees, coughing up blood.

"Stay there, you son of a bitch," Tone said, "or I'll blow your damned head off."

He stepped to the bed, ignored the shrieking woman and found a match. He lit the gas lamp above the fireplace and a ghostly, pale blue light spread through the room.

Tone crossed the floor, hooked his bare foot under the wounded man's chin and raised his face to his own. "Who are you?" he asked.

Blood filled the man's mouth and his eyes were bright with pain. He tried to speak, but could not.

"Who sent you?" Tone said, anger flaring in him.

"You're talking to a dead man, Mr. Tone. He can't speak."

Looking around, Tone saw Simon Hogg in the doorway. "You blowed his damned liver out," Hogg said.

"Recognize him?"

Hogg, a big, bearded man with a mottled patch of blue skin on his right cheek where he'd once gotten too close to a firing gun, shook his head. "Never seen him afore, or the one at the bottom of the stairs either."

"Is he dead?"

"As hell in a parson's parlor."

Tone kicked the kneeling man on the side of his head. His assailant fell on his side, coughing up blood. "Look at his feet," Tone said.

"Texas, by God," Hogg said.

Tone nodded. "He dressed himself like a sailor, but you can't get a Texan to give up his boots."

"Drover?"

"At one time, but look at his hands. This man hasn't done any punching in years."

The man on the floor rolled on his back. His breath rattled in his throat and his eyes turned up in his head as he died, a sight that made the woman scream and reach for her clothes.

"I'm getting out of here," she yelled, jiggling into her dress. "John Tone, you're not only cruel, you're crazy."

She flounced past him and walked out the door, assisted by a grin and a slap on the rump from Hogg. "She'll be back," he said. "Jennie Burns has seen worse."

He looked at Tone. "Do you think he and the other one were sent by the six men who plan to kill the cap'n?"

"I'd bet on it, unless . . ." Tone hesitated. He nodded in the direction of the dead man. "Hogg, are you sure he's not one of the six?"

"I'm sure. By all accounts they're dangerous men, but they can afford to have their killing done for them. Besides, that man was way too young to have been in the war."

"But how could they have known—"

"That you're Cap'n Sprague's sworn man?"

"Yes. How would the six men know?"

"Beats me, Mr. Tone. I sure as hell didn't tell them. I'm a sworn man me ownself."

Heavy footsteps sounded on the stairs and a huge man dressed in San Francisco police blue filled the doorway. He looked around him, his icy blue eyes missing nothing. "This your doing, Hogg?" he asked finally.

The innkeeper shook his head. "Not this time, Sergeant Langford. This man and one other attacked Mr. John Tone here, one of my guests."

"I saw the one other on the landing downstairs. He'd been shot, but it was a broken neck that killed him." He looked at Tone. "You've got some explaining to do, young man."

As Hogg would tell Tone later, despite his weathered face and iron gray hair, Sergeant Thomas Langford was a police officer to be reckoned with. Like every officer assigned to waterfront duty, he'd been handpicked for his bravery, strength and huge size. He carried the regulation nightstick, heavy revolver and in a large outside breast pocket within easy reach of his hand, a bowie knife with an eight-inch blade.

At one time or another, Langford had used all three of his weapons, but he was an expert with the knife. A year before, after he was attacked by three burglars in a used-clothing store on Pacific Street, he'd drawn his knife and charged the men in the face of their revolver fire. Despite several wounds, Langford had decapitated one, cut the hand off another and sent the third man, badly slashed, screaming into the night.

Now he listened patiently while Tone recounted the attack and his desperate fight for his life.

When Tone was finished, Langford said, "Where is your ship?"

Tone looked helplessly at Hogg, and the man said quickly, "At the moment he's between ships, Sergeant. Resting on the beach, you might say."

"Do you always answer for him when he's asked a question, Hogg?" Langford said.

"Ah, well, he's a shy lad an' no mistake. But he's gold dust, Sergeant Langford, pure gold dust."

"And if he's a sailor, I'm the queen of England," the big officer said. His cool eyes fell on Tone. "A week ago, probably in the late afternoon or the early evening, three men were shot to death down by the Pacific Street docks. Would you know anything about that?"

"He's been here in his room the whole week, Sergeant, quietly a-reading his Bible an' thinking pious thoughts, God bless him," Hogg said, smiling at Tone like a pleased parent.

"You do answer his questions for him, don't you?" Langford looked at Tone again. "Do you know anything about that?"

Tone caught Hogg's imperceptible shake of his head. He shrugged. "Not a thing, Sergeant."

"The man who killed those men knew how to use a gun exceptionally well," Langford said. "I've been a police officer for a long time, Mr. Tone, and to me, you look like a man who can use a gun exceptionally well."

"I get by," Tone said.

"Uh-huh," the big cop said. He lifted his nose and sniffed. "You've had a woman in here. Was she reading the Bible with you?"

"Instruction," Hogg said quickly. "Mr. Tone was instructing a poor fallen woman, as you so rightly observed, on the Christian virtues."

"Hogg," Langford said, "don't answer another question for Mr. Tone." His face hardened. "Not one." And to Tone: "Is that right? You were instructing a whore on the finer points of Christianity?"

Tone's expression did not change. "I was instructing her, yes."

Langford looked around the room. "Where's your Bible?"

"The poor soul took it with her," Hogg said. "She was that grateful, like."

Hogg saw Langford's scowl and said quickly, "Beggin' the sergeant's pardon, but I'm just so happy when I see a sinner return to the good Lord."

"Then maybe you should practice what you preach, Hogg," the cop said. He got down on one knee, then looked up at the two other men. "Did either of you search him for identification?"

"Not us," Hogg said.

Langford went through the dead man's pockets and then hefted five double eagles in the palm of his hand. "Nothing, except this. Same for the one downstairs." He rose to his feet. "I'm confiscating the money as evidence. I'll send someone to pick up the bodies."

"Please do, Sergeant," Hogg said. "Bless ye, it's bad for business, having stiffs lying around all over the place."

"You should know, Hogg," Langford said. "We've

carried enough of them out of this dive. As I recall, at least one with your knife between his ribs."

"Ah yes, all unfortunate circumstances, Sergeant, and no mistake."

"Mr. Tone, it would be another unfortunate circumstance and a big mistake if you should try to leave San Francisco. We have more talking to do, you and me." His eyes bored into Tone's. "And I do plan to find out who John Tone is, what he does and where he comes from."

"He's just a poor sailorman, to be sure," Hogg said, smiling.

"That's the one thing I know he isn't," Langford said. "I have the feeling in my gut that he's one of Lambert Sprague's sworn men. I also have a suspicion that a war is brewing along the waterfront, and I don't intend to let that happen. I may have to break some heads before all this is done."

For that, Hogg had no answer.

Chapter 8

After the bodies had been taken away and Hogg had had a swamper mop the floor, Tone lay on top of the bed, sleepless in the dead of the echoing night.

The attempt on his life had not been a case of mistaken identity. He had been targeted. But who had given him away? Only Simon Hogg and Luther Penman knew who he was and why he was living on the waterfront, and he trusted both of them implicitly.

Then who?

Tone had no answer for that question and it troubled him deeply.

Restlessly, he rose to his feet and looked out the window. It was four in the morning and the maelstrom of vice and sin that was the Barbary Coast was winding down for the night. Discordant music still came from the Chinese gambling houses where a sailor could rent a thirteen-year-old girl from Canton or Shanghai for a couple of dollars a night or buy her outright as his slave for four hundred, cash on the barrelhead.

A few whores still patrolled the misty street, among them stately Spanish American women in solemn black, wrapped to the eyes in their rebozos, who gave passing men bold, promising glances but said nothing

In a couple of hours the first blue light of dawn would stain the sky over the Contra Costa hills to the east and the whores, Chinamen and sailors would vanish, melting into the day like enchanted villagers, to reappear again only after darkness fell.

Tone moved away from the window, lit the gas lamp and retrieved an oily cloth wrapped around cleaning patches and bore brushes from his carpetbag.

He cleaned and oiled the long-barreled Colt and reloaded five chambers with ammunition he had specially made for him by a Reno gunsmith. The powder charges were slightly less than in regular rounds, but he was willing to give up some hitting power in exchange for reduced recoil.

He laid the revolver on the bedside table and turned out the lamp.

After a while he slept and he dreamed of Molly O'Hara. She was in her father's pub, but she was wearing a rebozo and he could not see her face.

Daylight was streaming through Tone's window when he was wakened by a pounding on his door. Instantly alert, a habit of men who live by the gun, he grabbed his Colt and yelled, "Who's there?"

"Me, Simon Hogg, as ever was."

Tone told the man to step inside, and when he was certain that his visitor was in fact Hogg, he eased down the hammer of the revolver.

"Damn your eyes, Hogg, what the hell time is it?"

"Beggin' your pardon, but it's gone noon and I bring news."

Tone shook his head. "Coffee first, then your news."

"Ah, a wise decision, Mr. Tone. Coffee soothes a man's soul, an' no mistake."

The big innkeeper vanished and when he returned after a few minutes he carried in a tray with a coffeepot and a cup.

Tone was sitting at the table, already dressed. He lit a cigar as Hogg passed the steaming cup to him. The man watched anxiously as the level in the cup lowered; then, when he considered Tone had drunk a sufficient amount, he said tentatively, "Are you ready for my news now?"

Tone nodded. "News away, and be damned to you for getting a man up at this time of the morning."

"Ah, well, yes, it is early as you say, but my news can't wait, lay to that." Hogg rubbed his hairy hands together. "I was speaking to Officer Frank Welsh this morning, he's one of Sergeant Langford's right-hand men, you might say, and he claims he knew one of the men you shot last night." Hogg pointed at the floor. "The one who lay right there, a-coughing up his liver, poor soul."

Now, despite his irritation, Tone was interested. "Who was he?"

Happy to be the center of attraction, Hogg beamed. "His name was Mason Tucker."

The name came as such a shock to Tone that he almost dropped his cup. "You mean Mason Tucker, the El Paso gunfighter?"

"That's what Frank Welsh says."

"How would he know?"

"Frank was a deputy sheriff in El Paso before he quit and signed on with the San Francisco police. He says when he saw Tucker's body he recognized him right off."

Lost in thought, Tone absently refilled his cup. Mason Tucker had been a named man, a gunfighter who had killed more than his share, and his services didn't come cheap. The hundred dollars Langford had found in the man's pocket was probably a down payment on his fee, the balance to be paid when the job was done and Tone was dead.

Only the six men on Sprague's death list had those kinds of funds.

"Seems obvious who hired Tucker," Hogg said. "It could only be the men who want the cap'n dead."

Tone rose, reached into his coat hanging in the armoire and returned to the table. He spread out the list and told Hogg to sit opposite him.

"I'll read out a name and you tell me what you can about the man," he said.

"It won't be much, Mr. Tone. The cap'n don't confide in me like he does you."

"Just try your best, Hogg." Tone's eyes dropped to the paper and he read: "John T. Moylan."

"He owns the Bucket of Blood saloon here on the waterfront and has shares in some of the Chinese opium and whore businesses. He lives in Silver City, but I don't know what he does there."

"They all live in Silver City," Tone said. He read again: "Mickey Kerr."

"He strong-arms for Moylan. That's all I know, 'cept he's a bad 'un."

"Edward J. Hooper."

"He owns a couple of boardinghouses along the Barbary and specializes in shanghaiing sailormen and importing opium and young Chinese gals as whores. He can buy a girl for four dollars in Canton and sell her for hundreds along the waterfront." Hogg brightened. "I know what he does in Silver City. He owns a bank and he's a church deacon. The cap'n told me that."

"Luke Johnson."

"I don't know nothin' about him except I've seen him with the others."

"Joseph Carpenter."

"Joe Carpenter owns a couple of waterfront dives and he has a small steam yacht he keeps at the docks. He's real good with a gun. About a year ago he shot two of his customers dead for roughing up one of his whores."

"Last, but probably not least, Maxwell Ritter."

"He owns as much of the waterfront as the cap'n and he's just as rich. He doesn't go anywhere without two or three bodyguards."

Tone sat back on his chair, lilac cigar smoke curling over his head. "It's not much to go on, but at least I know where to find . . . what's his name?" He looked at the paper. "Edward J. Hooper. How many churchgoing bankers can there be in Silver City?"

"You're going there?" Hogg asked, surprised.

"Better than staying here and making myself a target for any two-bit gunman who wants to earn fifty dollars."

"Mr. Tone, I don't think the cap'n—"

Knuckles pounded on the door. Luther Penman shoved it open and stepped inside. He seemed to be in an evil temper, his death's head face set and scowling.

He ignored Tone and looked at Hogg. "Simon Hogg," he snapped. "What an unpleasant surprise."

"I was just leaving, Mr. Penman," the innkeeper said, almost bowing to the man who represented all the wealth, authority and power of Lambert Sprague.

"Then go, and be about your business, nefarious though it no doubt is."

Hogg shuffled his feet, suddenly uncomfortable in his own crawling skin. "Begging your pardon, Mr. Penman, but Mr. Tone here says he plans on leaving for Silver City. That's what we was about to discuss, like."

"If Mr. Tone wishes to discuss his future actions, he'll discuss them with me and me alone." His empty eyes fell on Hogg and the man squirmed worse than before. "Why are you still here?"

Hogg knuckled his forehead and headed for the door, a man relieved to be anywhere but in Tone's room.

"Coffee?" Tone asked after the man was gone.

Penman shook his head and took the chair recently vacated by the innkeeper. "Why did you tell Hogg you were leaving for Silver City? Be brief now, and to the point."

"I'm tired of making myself a target. Do you know what happened here last night?"

"I heard about it." Penman let his shark eyes rest on Tone. "The whole point of your agreement with Mr. Sprague is that you do make yourself a target. You will remain on the waterfront, draw the six men to you that you've been contracted to kill and then deal with them."

"I think—"

"Don't think, Mr. Tone; it doesn't become you. We hired your gun, not your brain."

"I want to take the fight to the men who paid to have me killed last night."

"You will let them bring the fight to you. Those are your orders and you will abide by them." There were pinpoints of flickering blue in Penman's eyes. "A word of warning: don't take the Pirate's Oath lightly, Mr. Tone. The last man who did was taken to an island off the coast, his belly was ripped open and his intestines were strung out and tied around a tree. I have it on good authority that he screamed for three days before he succumbed."

Penman smiled with all the warmth of a python regarding a wounded rabbit. "That man's name was Jim Riley, one of Mr. Sprague's most trusted crewmen. I recall that he was a stout, jolly fellow. He was not so jolly when he tried to tear loose from his own guts."

"I won't break the oath," Tone said, angry that he heard a catch in his voice.

"Good, it's settled. Mr. Sprague will be in San Francisco in a week, and you can report to him personally then. Like me, he's going to say that it's high time you earned your first thousand dollars. And speaking of money"—Penman pulled a slip of paper from his pocket—"this is Hogg's bill for your keep, and quite frankly your expenses are horrendous.

"Five dollars a night for whores ... champagne ... Havana cigars ... it goes on and on. For instance, here—why did you feel the need to buy five dozen roses?"

Tone shrugged. "To go with the whores, champagne and cigars."

"My dear fellow, this can't continue. I've instructed Hogg that your per diem allowance for bed and board will be three dollars a day. Anything above that amount must be cleared by me or met out of your own pocket." The lawyer sniffed. "Who buys roses for whores?"

"I do." Tone smiled.

"Well, no longer. Roses for whores . . . pearls before swine, indeed."

As Penman rose to his feet, Tone smiled and said, "Anyone ever tell you that you're a likable man, Luther?"

"No."

"Then I won't either."

"Remember," the lawyer said as he stepped to the door, "Mr. Sprague will be here in a week."

"I'll do my best to stay alive until then," Tone said irritably.

Chapter 9

Night fell on the Barbary Coast and the gas lamps were lit in the streets, illuminating another long orgy of intoxication, fornication and homicide.

The dance halls, concert saloons and gambling dives were open for business, already filled to the walls with sailors, miners, slack-jawed rubes from the hills, whores, pimps, robbers and cutthroats of all kinds. Everywhere could be seen licentiousness, debauchery, pollution, disease, insanity from bad liquor, dissipation, misery, grinding poverty, great wealth, profanity, blasphemy, death . . . and here and there pale-faced preachers, Bibles clutched to their breasts, warning the few who would listen that hell was yawning open to receive the whole putrid mess.

Into this maelstrom of sin that came easy but never cheap walked John Tone, his short-barreled Colt in a shoulder holster under his navy blue peacoat. Penman had told him that he was being paid to make himself a target, and he'd decided that anything was better than waiting in his room for another assassin to strike.

Pacific Street was crowded with humanity and few people paid Tone any attention, intent as they were on their own pleasures.

The alleys leading off the street were mysterious canyons of shadowed darkness, except those where the Chinese lived, which were bright with paper lanterns, teeming with male and female Celestials wearing gaudy red, yellow and blue silks.

Jostled by the crowds, Tone strolled along the street, his restless eyes everywhere, the weight of the Colt bringing him a measure of comfort. He passed a saloon where sailors were singing a popular waterfront song about the used-clothing dealer Solomon Levy.

After a couple of minutes Tone passed Levy's store, conveniently located between Montgomery and Sansome streets, and open for business twenty-four hours a day. In front of Levy's door were huge piles of worn blankets and old clothes and shoes, chained and padlocked to large iron staples driven into the front of the building.

Every customer who bought a dollar's worth of goods received from Levy's own hand, with great ceremony, a card on which he'd painstakingly penned a composition of his own making:

My name is Solomon Levy,
And I own a clothing store
A way up on Pacific Street—
A hundred and fifty-four.
If you want to buy an overcoat,
A pair of pants or vest,
Step up to Solomon Levy,
And he'll sell you all the best.

The sailors considered Levy's verse first-rate poetry and they sang it to every tune they could bend to the words.

Beyond Levy's store the crowd thinned a little, but there were more Chinese in evidence. Small men hurried past Tone, each carrying heavy burdens on the ends of a supple bamboo pole slung across a shoulder. Others balanced huge bundles of soiled clothing on their heads. None spared Tone a glance as they trotted past, chattering to each other in a language he could not understand.

Tone walked by another alley, this one dark, and his hand strayed to his gun. His instinct for danger clamoring a warning, he saw nothing. Then he heard a short, sharp scream from somewhere ahead of him. Here there were few streetlamps and the fog drifting in from the bay reduced their light to hazy blue and yellow orbs.

It had been a girl yelling out; he was sure of that. But women's screams were heard often along the waterfront and he was inclined to walk away and let the whore and her pimp work things out for themselves.

Another little shriek, then a man's harsh voice, followed by the hard crack of a backhanded slap. Tone sighed and walked toward the disturbance, cursing himself for being a meddling fool.

He was coming up on an alley, and he slid his Colt from the leather. As he stepped closer he saw black shadows move against the lesser darkness of the alley. Then he heard the man's growl again.

"Get her on the ground, Clem. We'll do her there. And rip them damn Chink pants off'n her and we'll see what she's got."

On cat feet, Tone stepped into the alley. A man had his back turned to him and Tone tapped him on the shoulder. "Excuse me," he said.

The man swung around, his face frozen in shocked surprise. Tone hammered the barrel of his Colt across the man's nose, hearing bone break. Sudden blood streaming into his mouth, the man squealed and staggered back. Tone ignored him, aware of the second man jumping up from between the girl's naked thighs. His pants and long johns were down around his ankles and he tripped, staggered a step and fell. Tone drew back his right foot, then kicked the man full in the face. The kick should have stopped him. But it didn't. This would-be rapist was big and mean and full of fight.

He sprang to his feet, quickly stepped out of his pants, and a knife suddenly appeared in his right hand, held low and sharp blade uppermost for a slashing belly cut.

"Damn you." He snarled. "I'll gut you from balls to navel, I will."

It was an English voice. Tone fired, fired again. Hit twice dead center of his chest, the Englishman groaned and sank to the ground, his right cheek scraping down the rough brick of the alley wall.

Tone looked down at him. "This was to be a gunfight, Englishman," he said. "I'm real surprised you didn't notice."

The man with the broken nose got to his feet, cast a pained, terrified glance at Tone, lurched into the street and took off in a staggering run. Tone let him go.

As the dying man's last breath rattled in his throat, Tone kneeled by the girl. She was very young, her black eyes huge and scared. Her legs were open and a small dark triangle pointed the way to the portal where all the mysteries of womanhood began.

He spoke to her, trying to make his voice calm and reassuring, but he knew the girl, a child really, did not understand a word he said.

After Tone helped the girl to her feet, she found a scrap of white handkerchief in a pocket of her *pien-fu*, the silk knee-length tunic worn by Chinese women along the waterfront. She carefully wiped off the top of her thighs, then grimaced in disgust and threw the handkerchief away. She pulled up her baggy silk pants and tied them at her waist and stepped to the two baskets suspended from a bamboo pole that she'd been carrying when she was attacked.

The baskets were filled with burlap sacks that leaked a black powder. Tone tested the stuff between his thumb and forefinger and nodded to himself.

He'd heard somewhere that Celestials were much given to fireworks of all kinds and the sacks contained the raw material for such displays, gunpowder.

The girl bent to pick up the pole, but Tone lifted it himself and hefted it on his shoulder. It was a balanced load but surprisingly heavy, too heavy for the slight girl who'd carried it.

He smiled. "Allow me to escort you home, ma'am."

The blank look on the girl's face told him she didn't understand, but she walked out of the alley and turned left and Tone followed.

They passed Solomon Levy's store, where a couple of drunk sailors were laughing and slapping each other on the back as they tried on silk top hats, and then the girl led the way into one of the Chinese alleys, ablaze with paper lanterns and gaslit shop fronts.

Tone's nerves were stretched as taut as fiddle strings and what happened next came at him too fast, and for a moment he felt a surge of panic.

The girl threw herself into the arms of an older woman with a dark, deeply lined face, and began to shriek words between sobs. Immediately Tone was surrounded by a hostile crowd of Chinese men, some of them wielding wicked-looking knives, all of them yelling, their black eyes glittering with rage.

He took a step back, burdened by the bamboo pole on his shoulder. He had three rounds left in the Colt . . . three more men dead on the ground . . . then he'd be chopped to pieces.

Chapter 10

The older woman saved John Tone's life.

Her yell was almost a scream, a torrent of Chinese that had no meaning and held no emphasis, good or bad, for Tone.

But the effect of her words was almost magical. Instantly scowls and angry yells turned to smiles and the knives disappeared. Men stretched out and touched Tone, whether for luck or out of a sense of gratitude, he had no idea.

A handsome younger man, tall for a Chinese and well built, wearing tailored Western clothing, pushed his way through the crowd. He went immediately to the sobbing girl and spoke to her for several minutes.

The young man stepped in front of Tone. Without a word he took the bamboo pole from his shoulder, then stared intently at Tone's face, as though memorizing his every feature.

Finally he said, "Thank you. Best you leave now."

Tone nodded. "I hope the girl is all right."

"She is my sister and she will be all right." He hesitated a heartbeat, added, "Her honor is still intact."

By the flat expression in the man's eyes, Tone judged that this conversation was now over. He nodded again, then turned and walked to the mouth of the alley. When he looked back, the young Chinese man was watching him.

By ingrained habit, Tone sat at the table in his room and cleaned and oiled his revolver. More than one man had died in a gunfight because of a dirty weapon.

He reloaded, then looked at the gun on the table in front of him, his mind racing, considering the Colt's implications.

He had deliberately made himself a target, but ended up shooting the wrong man. The Englishman needed killing, or so he told himself, but his death didn't bring him a profit and no closer to settling with the six men on his list.

He would not walk the street again at night. There were so many robbers and killers along the waterfront that by making himself a target he could kill men every night. Where was the sense in that? There was none. He was a businessman, not a killer.

Unbidden, another, more disturbing thought, came to him: did the Englishman die only because of his nationality?

Tone picked up the Colt, enjoying its balance, the cool look of blue metal, the warm glow of the mahogany handle.

The Englishman came at him with a knife, threatening to gut him. It was a justified killing. Self-defense as ever was. But he'd fired twice, making sure the man would die. No, that wasn't true. He wanted only to put him down and have him stay down.

Tone laid the Colt back on the table. He hadn't murdered the English sailor. He'd killed the man in a fair fight. Even Blind Jack would be able to see that.

The Fenian rebellions, the Troubles, Molly O'Hara's death—that was all behind him, a life he'd led in a different time and place. Ireland was a forgotten memory, like a beautiful fairy gift that had vanished in the morning light. . . .

Someone tapped lightly on the door. Tone asked who it was, his hand on the revolver.

"It's me, John. Jennie Burns."

Tone told her to come in, but he didn't let go of the gun until the woman stepped inside. She was carrying a bottle. "A peace offering for running out on you like that," she said.

"I guess you had good reason," Tone said.

"Glasses?"

"By the bed there."

Jennie brought a couple of glasses and set them on the table along with the whiskey, and she sat opposite Tone.

"A couple of drinks first, then I'll give you a riding lesson you'll never forget. I'm a bucker, remember?"

Tone smiled. "I remember."

The woman filled two glasses and handed one to Tone. She raised her drink and smiled. "Slainte!"

"Slainte!"

Tone drained his glass and stretched out a hand for

the bottle to pour another. He never reached it. Suddenly the room was cartwheeling around him and Jennie was smiling . . . a smile of triumph.

The door burst open and Simon Hogg rushed inside, a couple of big men right behind him. Despite his reeling head and blurred vision, Tone was aware of a fourth man standing back in the shadows, gaslight wobbling in the little pince-nez glasses perched at the end of his nose.

"That's him!" Hogg yelled.

Tone struggled to his feet. "Hogg, you traitorous bastard!" he shouted.

The big man's face seemed to be submerged in a tank of turbulent water. "You're only a traitor if someone finds out about it, Mr. Tone," he said. "And no one will, because by this time tomorrow you'll be on the high seas bound for Canton."

Tone staggered across the floor, trying to reach his gun. He tripped over his own feet and fell flat on his face.

"Pick him up, ye swabs," the man with the pince-nez said harshly. "Kill the whore, then let's get him on board."

His cheek on the rough floorboards, Tone saw the glittering arc of a descending knife blade, then heard Jennie's terrified scream. Hogg stabbed again and again, and finally the girl fell silent.

Strong arms lifted Tone to his feet and he was carried out the door and into the street. As he was dragged toward the misty docks, his mind closed down and he no longer knew what was happening.

Like his captors, he was unaware of the burdened

Chinese coolies trotting past him, their eyes looking at nothing but seeing everything.

Tone woke to darkness, his head threatening to split open from pain.

He could see nothing, but he heard the soft lap of water and smelled the dank stench of ancient piss, vomit and rotten slops. Rats scurried everywhere in the gloom and squealed and squeaked and gnawed.

Tone was lying on his back on heavy timbers and he rose to a sitting position, a movement he instantly regretted as white-hot pain bladed into his skull.

He tried to take stock of his situation by piecing together what had happened. He had been drugged, he remembered that. Jennie and her bottle! Her smile as his head spun . . . but now she was dead. Hogg had stabbed her. That damned blackhearted traitor. "You'll be on the high seas, bound for Canton. . . ." He tried to think. Where was Canton? In China . . . yes, that was it . . . a long, long ways from San Francisco. . . .

Something hairy with wet feet scurried across Tone's hand. Then another. He cried out in panic and lurched to his feet, only to bang his head hard against a deck beam. He didn't remember falling because he was already unconscious.

"Damn it, did the whore's drink kill him?"

"He's alive. Look, his eyes are opening." Simon Hogg's voice.

Yellow lantern light spiked into Tone's vision, blinding him. He blinked and tried to focus on the shadows surrounding him.

A man spoke, his words hard-edged, meant to wound.

"Wake up, Tone. You'll be needed on deck soon. Them soft hands of yours will soon get hardened by the rope."

"And so will his back, I warrant," another man said, and Tone heard Hogg laugh.

"Water," he croaked.

"Give him water," the hard-voiced man said. "No point in killing him all at once."

A ladle of water was pressed to Tone's lips and he drank deep. Then he said, "Where am I?"

A man's face swam into Tone's sight, the pince-nez at the end of his thick nose glittering orange in the lantern light. "Why, matey, you're aboard the good ship *Lady Caroline* out of New York town, soon bound for Canton with five hundred tons of cotton cloth and yarn."

"She's a hell ship to be sure, Mr. Tone," Hogg said. "Cap'n Silas Muller loves nothing better before breakfast than seeing the cat flay the skin off a poor sailorman's back. He says it gives him an appetite for his salt pork, like."

"I guarantee you'll get well acquainted with the cat before too long," Pince-nez said.

Anger flared in Tone. "Who are you, apart from a lousy son of a bitch?"

The man smiled, then backhanded Tone hard across the face. "Watch your lip, matey. As to who I am, why, I'm Edward J. Hooper, large as life."

"The church deacon and slaver."

Hooper shook his head and Tone could feel the force of his anger. "Now I regret not putting a bullet into you, Tone. In my day I've slid a cutlass into the bellies of a dozen just like you, swabs who fancied themselves hard cases. Aye, church deacon and slaver, if you consider Celestials to be human. As far as I'm concerned, I import monkeys, that's all."

"Why did't you kill me and get it over, Hooper?" Tone asked.

"Excellent question!" The banker turned to Hogg. "Is that not an excellent question, Mr. Hogg?"

The big man shrugged. "If'n you say so."

"But I do say so, Mr. Hogg. Indeed I do." Hooper pushed his face closer to Tone's. "It seems that Sergeant Thomas Langford has taken a keen interest in you, damn his eyes. Now, normally this would not trouble me overmuch. Langford can die like any other man. But if your body was found, in an alley perhaps, or washed up by the tide, it could cause"—he waved his arms helplessly as he sought to find the right word— "complications."

"Complications indeed, Mr. Hooper," Hogg said, nodding, as though the man had fairly stated the case. "Sergeant Langford is a curious man."

"Indeed, Mr. Hogg." Hooper agreed. "I said that Langford can die like any other man, but killing a San Francisco sergeant of police can get messy. The law starts poking its nose into places where it's not wanted and that can be bad for business."

The man sighed. "No, I thought the matter through and decided this is the best way. The good Captain Muller will work you to death, Tone, then bury you at sea. Langford will shortly find the body of a dead whore in your room and deduce that you killed her in a fit of rage, then fled the city for parts unknown. The case will be then closed as far as the police are concerned."

Lantern light shadowed the white mask of Hooper's face. "Truth to tell, Tone, you are so very unimportant I wonder that I'm even talking to you. All you are is an annoying little fly that Muller will soon swat for me."

He turned to Hogg. "When will the captain have his full crew?"

"Another couple of hours at most. Most of them will be drugged, but he'll have enough able-bodied seamen to sail on the tide."

Hooper nodded. "See that it's done."

"Aye, aye, sir," Hogg said.

Tone's eyes sought the big man in the gloom. "Hogg," he said, "I'll come after you. I'll hunt you down and I'll kill you."

Hogg laughed. "Talk comes cheap, Mr. Tone. By this time next week you'll be food for the sharks."

He and Hooper and the others with them who had been silent and invisible in the darkness climbed out of the hatch, then let the heavy cover slam back in place.

Once again Tone was imprisoned in a dank tomb where only the blind rats were thriving.

Chapter 11

A man in absolute darkness has no sense of the passage of time.

Sometime earlier, Tone had tried to explore his prison, had tested the hatch, then went back to his place, a sense of defeat weighing heavily on him.

The drug, whatever it had been, had mostly worn off, but his head still ached, whether from the laced drink or from banging his head on the deck beam, he did not know.

The rustling, gibbering rats, some of them as large as cats, had become bolder, running over him, nipping at his exposed hands and neck. Tone fought them off as best he could, lashing out blindly in the crowding, stinking gloom. Patient as death itself, by sheer force of numbers the rats would win in the end and devour him to the bone.

Was he to be left here, or brought up on deck? He had no chance of escape from the bilges, but once out in the open, he could jump overboard, or go down fighting. Better to seek a man's death than be slowly eaten by rats.

Above Tone, feet thumped on the deck. He guessed that Muller was getting the first of his shanghaied crew, trained seamen and country rubes who had been drugged in sleazy waterfront dives. By 1887 at least forty gangs along the Barbary Coast were engaged in the runner trade, providing unwilling crews for the notoriously savage New York ships.

More footsteps thudded along the deck, and even in his closed prison Tone thought he heard a man scream in mortal agony.

Captain Muller was a sadist, and his hellish discipline was starting early.

Suddenly the hatch cover was lifted, and Tone rose to his feet, being careful to avoid the beams. He clenched his fists at his sides, prepared to fight.

A man appeared in the hatchway and whispered: "You come, quick!"

It was a Chinese voice.

Tone asked no questions. He stumbled to the ladder and climbed. A few lanterns glowed around the ship, enough to see the bodies of several sailors sprawled on the deck, their throats cut. He hoped Muller was among them.

"Quickly now," the Chinese man said. "You follow."

He led the way down the gangplank and onto the dock and Tone stayed close to his heels.

Wreathed in a twisting fog, a hansom cab stood near the dock, the driver's face concealed by a heavy coat and muffler.

"Inside, go now," the Chinese man said. He held the door open and Tone quickly stepped inside. The door shut behind him.

A man sitting in the shadows called to the driver in

Chinese and the cab lurched into movement. "Take this," the man said. He shoved a British .476 Enfield revolver into Tone's hand. The weapon was bulky, almost a foot long, and lacked the fine balance of a Colt, but Tone found its weight reassuring.

He turned and his eyes tried to penetrate the gloom. "Whoever you are, thank you," he said finally.

The man turned as a gas lamp reflected on his face. "You saved my sister. Now I'm repaying the favor."

Recognition dawned on Tone. It was the young Chinese man with the wide shoulders and European clothes he'd seen in the alley.

"How did you know where to find me?" Tone asked.

Even in the gloom Tone saw the white flash of the man's teeth as he smiled. "All those little coolies that run around with burdens on their backs, the ones you don't notice or even consider human, they see everything that happens along the waterfront." The man nodded. "They know."

Tone's inclination was to deny that he thought as so many others did, that the Chinese were one step below blacks, who were, God knows, on the very bottom rung of the ladder. His protestation would have sounded hollow and he let it go.

"Where are we headed?" he asked.

"Chinatown. You'll be safe there until the hue and cry dies down."

"And then what?"

The man's black eyes glittered in the darkness, reflecting the passing lamplight as they clattered through the shadowed night. "That will be up to you, Mr. Tone." Seeing the other man's surprise, he added, "Yes, I know your name. In fact, I know a great deal about you and why you are in San Francisco."

Suspicion dawning on him, Tone asked, "Are you a detective?"

A small laugh in the creaking, hoof-clacking quiet. "Hardly that. I am Tong."

"That's your name?"

The man hesitated. He seemed amused. "No, that is not my name. The Tong is a business organization, set up to protect the interests of the Chinese people in San Francisco. We also control a few commercial enterprises along the waterfront." Another pause, then, "As for my name, you may call me Weimin. In Chinese, it means 'one who brings greatness to the people.'"

"You can call me John," Tone said. "I don't know what it means."

"So be it. You are John I Don't Know What It Means."

"John will do just fine," Tone said.

After thirty minutes of negotiating narrow, winding streets, the cab clattered into the outskirts of Chinatown, where thirty thousand poverty-stricken people were crammed into just twelve city blocks.

Despite the darkness Tone could make out dirty streets and alleys crowded with flimsy shacks and ramshackle storefronts, an alien, dangerous land where no policeman ever ventured.

Unlike the waterfront, here the alleys were not bright with paper lanterns lighting the traveler's way, and the smell from their large underground cellars where as many as five hundred men, women and children lived their entire lives, was a cloying stench that found its way into the cab.

Even at this late hour of the night, the streets and alleys were thronged with people, a teeming mass of coolies, artisans, whores and men on the make. Some of the rich Chinese merchant princes who enjoyed slumming in Chinatown walked around with as many as ten concubines and twice that many bodyguards.

The noise was incredible, a constant babble of shrill voices and hawkers' cries, overlaid by bawling children, barking dogs and the clamor of caged chickens and pigs.

Slowed by the crowds and hundreds of hand-drawn carts, the cab traveled on for another fifteen minutes before stopping at a timber building set back from the street.

"We're here, John," Weimin said. "You will be among friends, Tong like me."

Eager hands opened the door of the cab and Tone shoved the Enfield into the pocket of his peacoat before he stepped into the street. Weimin followed and the cab clattered away.

A man in traditional Chinese dress stood at the door of the house. He bowed low as Weimin approached, then indicated that the two men should step inside.

Tone walked into a long hallway, lined on both sides by a dozen almost-naked women. Their entire bodies were shaved and they stood at the doors of their cribs, displaying what they had on offer. Obviously this was a house of prostitution aimed at Americans, because a sign tacked to a low beam of the roof read:

Two bits lookee
Four bits feelee
Six bits doee

The air inside was thick and cloying, heavy with the smell of perfume, incense and warm woman flesh.

"This way, John," Weimin said.

The man did not even glance at the women as he and Tone passed, and they in turn bowed their heads and averted their eyes. Chinese women were considered chattel, and whores were valued much less than that, worthless playthings to be used for a while, then tossed aside.

Whoever he was, Tone decided, Weimin was a man of such considerable power and influence in Chinatown that no fallen woman dared to look at him directly.

There was a stairway at the end of the hall and Weimin beckoned Tone to follow him. Yet another hall, this one with fewer rooms on each side, and the Chinese man walked to the last door on the right and opened it wide.

"This is where you will stay for a few days," Weimin said. "When I think it's safe, I'll get you out of San Francisco. In the meantime, you will be supplied with food and drink and I'll get someone to wash your clothes." The man smiled. "You stink like the bilge of a ship."

"Well, thank you very much for that," Tone said, laying on his sarcasm like frosting on a cake.

If Weimin noticed, he didn't let it show. "One more thing, John: don't use the women. They are diseased, all of them." He waved a hand around the room, expensively furnished in the overly ornate Victorian style then in fashion. "In the meantime, make yourself comfortable."

He nodded to a filled bookcase. "I'm sure you'll find

books to your taste that will help pass the time."
Weimin smiled, a rare occurrence for him. "The last
gentleman I sheltered here occupied this room for six
months. He read so many books, he told me he'd gotten an education. He also got a dose of the clap. So be
warned."

"I'll bear that in mind," Tone said. Weimin turned to
leave, but Tone's voice stopped him. "Thank you for
what you did tonight. You saved my life."

"And you saved the life of my sister. The men who
attacked her would have cut her throat after they'd
finished with her."

Tone smiled. "Then we're even."

"Not yet. When I get you out of San Francisco safe
and sound, then we will be even. Not before. I'm a man
who pays my debts in full. That is the way of the
Tong."

Without another word Weimin turned on his heel
and left, closing the door behind him. The only sound
in the room was the tick of the grandfather clock in the
corner and the crack of the log fire in the grate. But the
smells of Chinatown filtered through the windows,
strange, exotic, alien . . . playing their own lost music.

Chapter 12

By the third day of his confinement, John Tone decided he'd had enough.

Despite excellent food and the congenial company of Mr. Dickens and Mr. Scott, Simon Hogg's treachery chafed at him like a pair of cheap britches.

It was time for a reckoning.

As night fell on Chinatown, Tone dressed in freshly laundered clothes and shoved the Enfield into a pocket of his peacoat. He stepped into the hallway, looked around, then made his way downstairs.

Only a couple of women were in evidence, but the rhythmic squeals of cot springs and the salivating grunts of bucking men told him this was a busy evening in the whorehouse.

The Chinese man who had first bowed Tone through the door stepped out of a room, saw the big man dressed for outside and threw up his hands in alarm.

"No! No! You stay! Mr. Weimin no like."

Tone smiled. "I'll be back."

"No! I send you woman, two woman, all for free. You stay, doee all night."

The little man looked genuinely scared. Weimin owned the dive and he was not a man to cross.

Tone grabbed the Chinese man by his shoulders and looked into his alarmed black eyes. "I'll be back, I said. Mr. Weimin need never know."

The man shook his head. "Many mens after you, hunting blood. If you die, Tong lose face. Bad things happen then, to me, to all in this house. You go back to room, jiggy-jig pretty girls, no be big dumb son of a bitch."

Not inclined to spend any more time arguing with a Celestial in the lobby of a brothel, Tone again assured the man that he would return before first light. Then he stepped past him, opened the door and entered the teeming street.

As Tone walked away, the angry little man stood at the door, hurling after him what he guessed was a string of Chinese invective. That was confirmed when the man ended with a heartfelt, "You big bassard! Rotten son of a bitch!"

No one in the passing crowd paid the least attention. A brothel keeper yelling curses at a sailor was nothing new in Chinatown.

It took Tone an hour to reach the waterfront, partly due to the crowds but mostly because he continually lost his way in a tangle of misty streets and alleys.

When he reached Hogg's place he stood at the entrance to a passageway and watched the building for a few minutes, trying to form a coherent plan. He was mainly motivated by revenge, enraged by Hogg's cold-blooded betrayal. In return for money, thirty pieces of silver from the fat banker Edward J. Hooper, the man had turned his back on his solemn pirate's oath.

Simon Hogg deserved to die. But Tone would leave that pleasure to Lambert Sprague.

His immediate concern was to get Hogg to tell him where he could find Hooper and start earning his bounty money.

His mind made up, Tone left the shelter of the alley and stepped into Hogg's place. The tavern on the ground floor was crowded with sailors and women, and the air was thick with pipe smoke, cheap perfume and the smells of sweat, spilled beer and urine, the pervading odor of every dive along the waterfront.

His watch cap pulled down to his eyebrows, collar up around his face, Tone pushed through the noisy throng, his eyes searching for Hogg. The man was nowhere in sight.

He made his way to the bar and when he caught the bartender's attention, he asked in a gruff tone: "Hogg?"

"Who wants to know?" the man asked suspiciously,

"Mr. Hooper sent me."

The bartender's face cleared and he nodded to the hallway outside the tavern's side door. "Try the kitchen."

Tone retraced his steps, his hand on the butt of the gun in his pocket. The kitchen lay at the end of the corridor, its door ajar. Quietly he stepped inside. A gray-haired woman was at the burdened stove and when she turned and saw him, Tone jerked a thumb over his shoulder. "Get out," he said.

The woman had spent too many years on the waterfront not to recognize trouble when she saw it. She threw Tone a frightened glance, then dashed past him, closing the door behind her.

Out of the corner of his eye, Hogg had seen the woman leave. He came from behind a counter and yelled, "Hey, Maria—" He stopped dead in his tracks, his face draining of color. "You!"

"Yeah, Simon, me. Now we're going to have a few words, you and I."

"Damn your eyes, Tone, who got you off the ship? Was it Sprague?"

"I reckon Mr. Sprague will answer that question for you very soon."

"Captain Muller and five of his men murdered, throats cut, every man jack of them," Hogg said. "Damn him. Only Sprague kills like that."

Hogg had been at the counter carving slices of beef from a roast. Tone picked up a slice and chewed on it. His eyes hardened to the color of blue steel. "Hogg, I'm going to ask you a question. Whether I let you live or not depends on how you answer it."

"Ask, and be damned to ye. And leave my meat alone. It ain't for the like o' you."

Tone helped himself to another slice. "Where can I find Hooper?"

"Ah, that be your question, Mr. Tone. The answer is you can't. But he will find you, lay to that." Hogg's eyes grew crafty. "I can tell you this: he's close, and I am under his protection."

Tone drew the revolver from his pocket. The Enfield was a self-cocker, a style of weapon he had never used. He thumbed back the hammer for a shorter trigger pull and said, "Not doing a good job of it, is he, Hogg? I could blow a hole in you right now."

"Maybe, but you'd never get out of this place alive. I have friends here."

It was a standoff and Tone knew it. There would be much satisfaction to be gained by putting a bullet in Hogg, but the noise of a shot would bring the innkeeper's men running.

In the end, it was Simon Hogg who decided his own fate.

He was wearing a shabby coat over a filthy white apron. His hand blurred as it dived under the coat for his waistband. He threw the knife with a quick backhand motion, a technique much practiced among blade fighters.

But Tone had the gunfighter's fast reactions. He moved his head to the right, only an inch or less. But it was enough that the blade missed his left eye and cut a bloody groove across his temple.

Tone fired and Hogg, hit square in the chest at a distance of three yards by the big .476 bullet, lurched back, his face unbelieving, mystified at the manner of his death. The man plunged into eternity with that expression on his face, dying as miserably and uselessly as he'd lived.

Feet pounded in the hallway outside. Tone fired a couple of fast shots through the door that brought the charge to a sudden halt.

There was a back entrance to the kitchen and Tone plunged through the door into an alley, the air vile from the smell of the outhouse and a huge pile of stinking garbage.

Tone looked around, then moved to his left into a canyon of darkness. Behind him men were yelling and a shot rang out. But the bullet came nowhere near Tone and he figured it was some drunken rooster firing at phantoms.

He flattened himself against a wall, his gun up and

ready, and waited a moment, planning his next move. He did not relish returning to the silken prison of the Chinatown brothel, but he could not remain on the waterfront.

He had only one choice and he knew it: he must find Luther Penman's office and let the shrewd lawyer plan his strategy.

The man would consider him a failure, since all six men he'd been contracted to kill were still alive and seemingly more powerful than ever. It was a bitter pill, but all Tone could do was swallow it.

Moving farther along the alley, shrouded in inky blackness, he took a narrow passageway between two warehouse buildings and walked into a parked wagon, cursing when he banged his shin on an iron-rimmed wheel.

He stopped and rubbed his aching leg as he listened to the night. There was no sound of pursuit. It seemed that the threat of his dangerous gun and the darkness had taken all the fun out of the chase.

Walking carefully along the arroyo between the soaring warehouses, Tone finally emerged onto a busy street, jammed with horse-drawn vehicles of all kinds and constant foot traffic.

He'd left the waterfront behind him. Ahead lay the residential, commercial and financial hub of San Francisco with its fine, tall buildings, tree-shaded streets and row on row of bright electric arc lamps.

But where, in a city of three hundred thousand people, could he find Luther Penman?

Away from the waterfront, sailors were rare enough in the city, and Tone's watch cap and peacoat drew more attention than he would have liked. He tried a couple of saloons, asking after Penman, but a sailorman with no money to buy drink garnered little response.

Finally a friendly bartender told him there were some law offices on Washington Street and gave him directions to get there.

Unlike the denizens of the Barbary Coast, most people in downtown San Francisco paid their taxes and went to bed early. The streets were fairly quiet as Tone followed the bartender's directions, walking under streetlamps that turned the falling drizzle into a shimmering cascade of shining needles.

Head bent against the rain, Tone almost bumped into a tall, burly man in blue.

"Here, watch where you're going, boyo," the big cop said.

Tone mumbled an apology and tried to walk around the man, but an arm as big and solid as a pine trunk shot out and stopped him in his tracks.

"Not so fast," the officer said. "What are you doing so far from the waterfront, and you a sailorman as all can see?"

Tone decided on two things: to tell the truth and revive his brogue.

"I'm looking for my lawyer's office, your worship, and that's a fact."

The policemen had a face as red and round as a ball and small, twinkling blue eyes that showed a deal of humor. "And what would a poor mariner be wantin' with a lawyer, I ask meself."

Tone lied easily. "An inheritance, a small one, just a few hundred pounds left to me by an uncle in Ireland."

If the cop doubted that story he didn't let it show. "And what would your name be, boyo?"

"John Tone, from County Wicklow."

"Tone is an honorable name, to be sure." The cop's face hardened. "Why did you leave the auld country? Or did you jump ship? Answer that question, then answer another: if you did jump ship, why would you have an American lawyer?"

Again Tone settled for the truth. "I left because of the Troubles. The rebellion of sixty-seven was crushed and the English were hanging men and women all over poor Ireland. I killed some British soldiers and had to flee to America."

The big cop was silent for a few moments, then said, "So, you didn't jump ship, then?"

"No, I didn't."

"And I'll wager you're not a sailorman." The man's face brightened. "Maybe you still fight for the cause from afar?"

Tone let a significant silence answer the question, and it seemed to be confirmation enough for the officer. "Walk with me, John Tone," he said.

"As far as Washington Street," Tone said. "I was told there are law offices there."

The cop smiled. "And what if I told you I was running you in?"

"For what? Being on the street?"

"Vagrancy. Loitering with intent. I could find something."

"Are you running me in?"

This time the officer laughed. "No. I'll walk with you to Washington Street. Auld Ireland has lost enough of her heroes as it is."

A few people hurried past in the street, most sheltering under umbrellas that glided through the rain like gigantic bats. Cabs rattled by on the wet road, the flames of their oil side lamps fluttering, drawn by blinkered horses that looked underfed and overworked.

Washington Street was a wide boulevard, lined with plum trees, its residential and commercial buildings built in the Second Empire style, inspired by the opulent architecture of Paris.

Polished brass plaques were affixed to many of the doors Tone passed, announcing that the occupants were physicians, architects, engineers and attorneys. But none bore the name Luther Penman.

"Then here's what you do, John," the cop said. "No, wait, let me ask you first if you have money for a hotel room."

Tone smiled and shook his head. "I have money in a bank in Reno, Nevada, but not here. I didn't expect to spend so much time in San Francisco."

"Then you'll sleep in the doorway of one of the offices, and come morning when the attorney shows up for work you'll ask him where you can find your lawyer friend." The man winked. "Lawyers know other lawyers. And so they should, given the time they spend bickering with each other in court."

The cop put his hand on Tone's shoulder, a friendly gesture he had not expected. "I'll be sure to pass this way several times tonight to check on you. Footpads are always about, and so too are the Hoodlum Gang, a nasty lot of young thugs, female as well as male, who rob and kill all over the city. I'll be watching for them most of all, and so should you. Sleep light and be on guard. If you see them, you'll know who they are. They wear hoods, the scoundrels, and add 'lum' to every word that comes out of their lying mouths."

Short of getting arrested, Tone had no better suggestion than a doorway to offer, and the rain was falling heavier, fat drops ticking from the branches of the plum trees. He found the deep portico of a lawyer's office that offered shelter and settled into a corner.

He looked up at the cop. "You haven't told me your name."

"Ah, me name is Thomas O'Brien, so it is."

"An honorable name."

O'Brien nodded. "And I should think so, since it was the one borne by the high kings of Ireland." The big cop raised a hand. "Now I'll bid ye good night, John Tone. I must be about my duties."

"Thank you," Tone said.

"No thanks needed, since it's little enough I've given you, a doorway to sleep in on a cold, rainy night."

"It's enough."

O'Brien waved again, then walked into the splintered darkness, light from the arc lamps gleaming on his wet shoulders.

Cramped and stiff, Tone eventually found an uneasy sleep. He dreamed of dead whores and Hoodlums.

Chapter 13

Someone was shaking his shoulder. John Tone woke up with a start, his hand reaching for the gun in his pocket.

Officer Thomas O'Brien saw the motion and smiled. "The British are not at the gates. It's only me."

Tone rose to his feet, stretched and groaned the kinks out of his back. "What time is it?"

"Almost seven, and time I was getting home or Mrs. O'Brien will take a stick to me, fine woman that she is." The cop held out a thick ceramic mug. "A dish of hot tea. And here"—he reached into his pocket and produced a bread roll—"it's got butter and a nice slice o' ham. As good a breakfast as any and better than most."

For a few moments O'Brien watched Tone eat hungrily, then asked, "Did you sleep well?"

"I dreamed that Hoodlums were chasing me."

"Better to dream of Hoodlums than meet them for real."

Tone smiled. "I guess so."

O'Brien sounded apologetic. "I have to wait for the

mug, since I took it from the station and I'll have to return it. They count them, you know."

Tone drained his tea and finished off his sandwich. He handed the mug to O'Brien and thanked the man again.

"Ah, well, it's me for my bed," the cop said. "I expect the lawyer"—he peered at the plaque on the door—"Mr. Matthew Petty, Attorney-at-Law to the Gentry, will be here shortly to point you in the right direction." O'Brien stuck out his hand. "Well, good luck to you, John Tone. And when you return to Ireland, stay well clear of an English noose."

Tone said he'd bear that in mind, and when the cop left he huddled in the doorway again. It was still raining.

The lawyer showed up an hour later, a small, bent man with white hair and a sour expression. He was startled when he spotted Tone, and then frightened.

"Who are you, and what do you want with me?" he asked, his voice quavering.

For his part, Tone understood the man's anxiety. A huge, unshaven and rough-looking sailor blocking his doorway was not a thing Mr. Mathew Petty, Attorney-at-Law to the Gentry, would encounter every day.

Tone stood where he was, not wanting to alarm the man further. "I'm looking for a lawyer," he said quickly.

The old man threw up his hands. "No, no, I can't take on any new cases for at least a twelve-month."

"His name is Luther Penman," Tone persisted.

Recognition dawned on the lawyer's crabbed face. "I know him. He's a shady character and a sodomite who should have been run out of San Francisco on a rail years ago. What business do you have with Penman?"

"It's a private matter."

"His establishment is on Grant Street." Petty pointed to the west. "Two blocks that way." He managed a smile. "If I were you, I'd count my fingers after I leave his office. And my toes. Now, will you step aside and give me the road?"

"I'm obliged for the information," Tone said, stepping down to the sidewalk.

Petty's harsh voice stopped him. "Remember what I told you, young man—to his everlasting shame, Penman is a damned sodomite."

Luther Penman's office was one of four businesses crammed into a two-story brick building huddled behind a hostile spiked iron fence. His door was to the left of the lobby, a wooden sign affixed to its front that said only:

L. PENMAN, ATTORNEY

Tone knocked, then pushed on the brass handle. The door, locked from the inside, didn't budge. He rapped the heavy oak with his knuckles.

After a few moments a small, timorous voice asked, "Who is it?"

"Tell Mr. Penman it's John Tone."

Tone waited, then heard footsteps scuttle behind the door. It swung open and a small, worn-looking man with thin black hair and sad brown eyes waved him inside.

Having recently read Mr. Dickens' *A Christmas Carol*,

Tone grinned at the man and said, "Your name wouldn't be Bob Cratchit, would it?"

The little man either missed the reference or thought it wasn't funny because he didn't crack a smile. "No, sir, my name is Barnabas Dale. I'm Mr. Penman's clerk."

He almost bowed. "This way, please."

Dale led Tone into a dusty office, every available surface piled high with books and legal briefs. There was an oil portrait of a stern Civil War officer on one wall and for a reason known only to Penman, an oval print of old Queen Vic, looking even sterner, on the other.

The lawyer rose from behind a parapet of legal tomes, the morning light gleaming on his glasses and the scalp of his skull head. "Barnabas," he said, "find Mr. Tone a chair. Then shut the door, but stay close. I will need you later."

The clerk did as he was told, and when he'd quietly shut the door behind him, Penman said, "Why are you here?"

The office was cold, the lawyer chilly and rain trickled down the windowpanes like a widow woman's tears.

"By this time I think you probably know."

"Don't speak to me of probabilities, Mr. Tone," Penman said, baring his yellow teeth. "I don't deal in probabilities. Give me the facts. Now, I ask you again: why are you here?"

Tone fought to overcome his dislike for the man, then recounted how he'd been kidnapped by the banker Edward J. Hooper and later rescued by a Chinese Tong leader. Then he told how he'd been forced to kill the traitorous Simon Hogg.

Penman listened in silence. When Tone was finished,

he waved a dismissive hand. "Hogg was of no importance, but the fact that Hooper can now recognize you is." The man looked at Tone over his steepled fingers. "All six of the men you've been contracted to kill are now in the Barbary Coast, and they've already moved to take over Mr. Sprague's business interests along the waterfront. Unless he's changed his plans, Mr. Sprague is scheduled to arrive two days from now and he is determined to fight for what is his. Consider the revenues from opium, prostitution, slave running and gambling alone and you will comprehend that a vast fortune is at stake. There will be war and Mr. Sprague will need your gun."

"I can't go back to the waterfront," Tone protested. "As you said, Hooper knows who I am and his men will be on the lookout. I won't get near him, or the others."

Penman nodded. "Not in your present . . . ah, persona. But you can go back as a Chinese coolie."

The lawyer's words were so shocking, so unexpected, that Tone laughed. "Damn it, man, I'm six foot four inches tall and weigh about two hundred and fifty pounds!"

"Then you'll be a rather large Chinaman, that's all." Penman shook his head irritably. "Mr. Tone, nobody notices Celestials. To the toughs along the waterfront they're just little brown, harmless people who come and go. Despite your imposing stature, you will be invisible, trust me."

Tone opened his mouth to protest again, but Penman's upraised hand stopped him. "You will not be alone. You'll have someone else by your side, a person of the same profession, a bounty hunter."

"Who is he?"

"He is a she."

"A woman!" Tone was scandalized. "Hell, there are no women bounty hunters. That's—that's an abomination."

"Maybe so. But nonetheless, that's exactly what she is. She was one of the first lady Pinkerton detectives and later a successful outlaw hunter. That is, until I lured her away from her wild frontier ways by pointing out that she could make more money working for Mr. Sprague than she could gunning badmen."

Now Tone was angry. "Penman, I'm not going to put my life on the line and depend on a . . . a . . . petticoat to help me out in a shooting scrape."

"You might change your mind when you see her."

"Yeah, I bet I love her mustache."

Penman consulted his watch. "She'll be here shortly. I put her up at a hotel nearby and asked her to step round to be briefed. Of course, her first task would have been to find you."

"What's her name?" Tone asked stiffly.

"Miss Chastity Christian."

"Oh my God," Tone said with a groan.

"Names, like appearances, can be deceiving, Mr. Tone," Penman said dryly.

Chapter 14

Barnabas Dale scratched on Penman's door.

"Enter," the lawyer said.

"Miss Christian is here, sir."

"Send her in."

Chastity Christian was a pretty brunette, dressed in the latest New York fashion, the bustle of her gray silk morning dress huge, the hat perched on top of her mane of dark, upswept hair tiny. She had large, expressive brown eyes and a wide, full-lipped mouth, little arcs at the corners revealing a quickness to smile. Her waist was tiny, her bust large, firm and high.

She was, Tone admitted to himself reluctantly, a very desirable woman. But she was not what she claimed to be—of that he was equally sure.

Penman made the introductions, then said, "I briefed Miss Christian earlier on what she must do at the waterfront, Mr. Tone. She will disguise herself as a Chinese woman and assist you in any way you require. Of course, her task has been made easier since she no longer has to find you first."

"It will be an honor, Mr. Tone," the woman said, her small white teeth flashing. "I've heard of you, of course. You are much talked of in Texas." Her smile grew wider. "And other places. Oh, and please call me Chastity."

Horrified, Tone looked past the woman to Penman. "Get rid of her," he said. "She'll be nothing but trouble, and totally useless besides. Maybe at one time she did some nice ladylike detective work, but she's never hunted a dangerous outlaw in her life."

He didn't expect what happened next, although it did serve to confirm his suspicions about the woman.

Looking like she'd just been slapped, Chastity's eyes misted and she opened her drawstring purse and pulled out a lacy white handkerchief. Tone didn't see the derringer wrapped inside until the muzzle was jammed hard between his eyes.

"Mister," she said, her voice suddenly cold and flat, "even a woman can scatter your goddamned brains at this distance." The sound of the hammer being pulled back was loud in the office. "In the past eighteen months I've killed three men and wounded two others. I don't know where you've stashed your hogleg, but go for it and see what happens next."

Penman seemed amused. "Now, now, Miss Christian, no unpleasantness, please. Mr. Tone is a little overwrought and didn't mean what he said. Did you, Mr. Tone?"

Tone kept his head very still, but dropped his eyes to Chastity's. "You're sudden," he said.

"Yes, Mr. Tone, and really quite good with a gun." She thumbed down the hammer and let the derringer drop to her side. "Now, you were saying something about me being useless? I'll let the trouble part go, because for some men that's exactly what I am."

Tone nodded, iron in him. "I'm impressed, and I see how you work. Get a man to believe that he has nothing to fear and everything to gain by getting close to a pretty, harmless young lady. Then blow his damfool head off." Tone had been smiling, but now his face was stiff. "But a word of warning: You ever pull a gun on me again and I'll put a hole in you, woman or no woman."

"Don't count on it, Mr. Tone," Chastity said. "You'll live longer that way."

Tone and the woman were standing as close as lovers, but both knew that something had come aborning between them that was far from love, a dangerous thing that could one day demand a reckoning.

Penman, a perceptive man, knew he had to end it. "This is getting us nowhere," he snapped. "Your fight is with the enemies of Mr. Sprague, not each other. Mr. Tone, Miss Christian is now your partner in this endeavor and that's my final word on the matter."

He looked at the woman. "You remember my instructions?"

Chastity stepped back from Tone and nodded. "We get to the house of Chang in Murder Alley. He will supply us with suitable clothing and tell us the whereabouts of our targets."

"Mr. Chang is in my employ and he has spies all over the waterfront," Penman said. "You will be safe and well informed in his hands." He lifted his eyes to Tone. "It would be excellent, Mr. Tone, and good for your future well-being, if you can greet Mr. Sprague's arrival with news of at least one kill."

"I'll do my best," Tone said. "In the meantime I need

money and"—he pulled the Enfield from his pocket and laid it on the desk—"a handier piece than this."

Penman's eyes dropped to the big revolver and then went back to Tone's face. "Money is tight right now, but I'll tell Barnabas to give you a hundred from the strongbox. As to guns, since you so carelessly lost yours, the cost of their replacements will be deducted from your first fee."

Penman opened a drawer, rummaged around among papers for a while, then pulled out a card. "This is the name and address of a gunsmith. He and I do business regularly, so tell him I sent you and that he should send me the bill."

The lawyer looked from Tone to Chastity. "Are there any questions?" Neither of the two answered and Penman said, "Excellent. Well, good luck. I'll see you both at the dock when Mr. Sprague arrives."

He rested suddenly hostile eyes on Tone. "One thing, Mr. Tone: please don't disappoint me again."

Penman picked up the Enfield and dropped it into his desk drawer.

Tone and Chastity Christian rode in the rain-lashed cab, close together but separated by a frosty silence. The woman kept her eyes to the front, ignoring Tone, while he, conscious of her warm, shapely body next to his, battled a tangle of emotions.

She was undeniably beautiful, but she had the cool ruthlessness of a born killer that Tone had encountered before only in men of a certain breed. Men like himself, perhaps.

How would she be in bed?

He let his mind wander . . . wondering . . . straying

far from the cold rain of his immediate surroundings into soft, scented, silken places. . . .

The cab rocked to a halt. "Here is it, folks," the driver called from his perch. "Hans Gruber the gunsmith."

Tone helped Chastity from the cab and retrieved the bags that they'd earlier picked up at her hotel. He paid the driver and saw that the woman had already walked into the gun store, a small one-story building wedged between a couple of run-down office blocks within sight of the waterfront.

Stepping inside, Tone took a moment to enjoy the familiar odor of gun oil and leather and the gleam of light on blue metal, then walked up to the counter.

Chastity was browsing display cases of revolvers when Gruber stepped out of his workshop and greeted Tone. The German was a tall man, stooped, with large, capable hands, surrounded by that almost unworldly aura of serenity that all good gunsmiths seem to possess.

Tone explained his needs: something small but hard-hitting and the leather to conceal it effectively.

The gunsmith beamed. "You're in luck, mein Herr. I have the very thing." He disappeared into his workshop and when he returned he laid two beautiful guns and a fancy double-rig shoulder holster on the counter.

"A matching pair of double-action, Colt Model 1877 revolvers, ivory grips, nickel-plated, in .38 caliber," Gruber said proudly. "They have two-and-a-half-inch barrels and I tuned the triggers myself for the gentleman who owned them."

"Why did the gentleman part with them?" Tone asked.

"It was an unwilling parting, I'm afraid. The gentleman was a gambler, now deceased, who was fast on the deal but slow on the draw. Since he owed me money, I claimed the guns from his estate."

Tone picked up the Colts, smiling as he admired their heft and excellent balance. He tried the triggers, which were as smooth as silk, breaking crisp and clean, like glass rods. Chastity looked over his shoulder, nodded her approval, but said nothing.

Deciding to strike while the iron was hot, the German said, "I'll throw in the leather at no charge. Now, the price for the pair of revolvers is—"

"I don't care what they cost," Tone said. "Luther Penman is paying for them."

Gruber looked slightly disappointed. "In the past, Mr. Penman has sent several gentlemen here to be armed," he said. "He always pays his bills, of course, but never on time."

"I'll take the Colts," Tone said. "And a box of cartridges to go with them."

"I load my own ammunition," Gruber said, brightening. "Each round is top quality, mein Herr, and I guarantee that you will never have a misfire."

The gunsmith sacked up the guns, then said, "If you ever need anything else, you know where to come . . . Herr . . . um . . ."

"Tone, John Tone."

It was obvious that Gruber had heard the name before. Men talk of arms in gun shops and of the pistoleros who use them.

"Would you be the John Tone from up Reno, Nevada, way?"

"I would."

"Then this is an honor, Herr Tone. I spent many

hours tuning those Colts and I'm happy that they're going to a man who can appreciate them and use them well. Their last owner was a fine gentleman who fancied himself a gunfighter, but wasn't."

"What was his name?" Chastity asked, speaking for the first time.

"Nathan Black, ma'am," Gruber answered.

"Never heard of him," Chastity said.

The gun shop was within walking distance of the waterfront, but Tone waved down a cab, not wanting to take a chance on being recognized by an early riser, unlikely as that was.

The driver, an elderly man wearing an oilskin coat and a battered top hat, allowed that if it was after dark and not morning, it would take a hundred dollars and a cavalry escort to get him to set foot in Murder Alley, but since the thugs and dance-hall loungers would still be in bed he'd take the chance and be damned to all of them.

As they clattered over the cobbles, Chastity determinedly kept her eyes to the front, saying nothing. But her rounded hip pressed closer to Tone on the seat, whether by accident or design, he could not guess.

Chapter 15

The Barbary Coast's Murder Alley was so named long before the Chinese took it over. So narrow that the rain barely fell on its cobbled street, it was lined with gimcrack stores, opium dens and brothels. Even at that early hour, the alley was thronged with people speaking a rapid language that rose and fell like the call of birds.

Tone stopped men and women, asking for Chang's house. They bustled past him without answering, either not understanding what he said or at least pretending they didn't.

Finally Chastity convinced an old woman sitting in the doorway of a store to point out the house, a rickety, unpainted frame and timber building that teetered alarmingly into the alley as it soared to a second and then an overhanging third floor.

A tiny wizened man, who seemed to carry the wisdom of centuries in his black eyes, opened the door. He had obviously been well briefed by Penman because he looked at Chastity and smiled. "I am Chang, Miss Christian. Welcome to my humble abode."

Chastity and Tone stepped into a hallway that smelled of incense, boiled cabbage and sex. This early in the morning, there were no women in evidence, but nailed to each doorway along the corridor was a framed, well-painted picture of the specialty of the woman inside. It seemed that every facet of men's lust was covered, plus a few even the most perverted of them probably never imagined.

Tone expected to see a maidenly blush on Chastity's cheeks and downcast eyes, but instead she closely studied each illustration and finally gave her verdict to Tone, summing it up in a single word: "Exhausting."

Chang led the way to the end of the hall and opened the door to a sparsely furnished room with a dresser and chair, a rice-paper screen painted with cherry blossoms and, Tone noticed immediately, a single iron bedstead made up with a thick mattress and clean sheets and pillows.

If Chastity took note of the sleeping arrangements, she didn't let it show. "Mr. Chang," she said, her voice brittle and businesslike, "you have clothing for us?"

"Yes, Miss Christian, for you and the gentleman." He looked Tone up and down. "I had his specially made by a seamstress I can trust."

He opened a door that Tone had thought led to another room, but it turned out to be a closet, with a variety of folded pants and colorful tunics on the shelves.

Chastity stepped to the closet, inspected the clothes, then turned to Chang. "Those will do nicely. You will arrange food and drink, should we require it?"

The Chinese bowed. "But of course, Miss Christian."

Chastity sat on the edge of the bed. "Do you have information for myself and Mr. Tone?"

Chang shook his head, his lined face grave. "I have no information to give. I am not an informer, for that is a dangerous occupation along the waterfront. But I can pass on good news. Good news is always welcome, is it not?"

"I like to hear good news," Chastity said evenly.

The Chinese man smiled. "Then here is a good-news story. Once there was a certain bandit who lived with his five brothers in a big house by the great ocean. Now this bandit did not wish to stay home, but left almost every night to visit a fallen woman. The bandit's behavior was so strange that his brothers began to laugh and say that he'd fallen in love with a whore. The young bandit didn't mind; he went on visiting the woman, and still does to this very day. All this was very good news for his enemies, for they hated the young man and planned to cut off his head."

"And this young bandit, do you suppose he is with the woman now?"

Chang shrugged. "If he was a real person, I think he would wait until tonight."

"And where would the woman dwell?" Chastity asked.

"If she was a real person, she would have a room above the Opera Comique at the corner of Jackson and Kearny."

"And this young bandit, does he have a name?"

"He is not a real person, so he has no name." Chang looked sly. "But he was the least of the bandits because his brothers were much more feared and powerful. You can give him a name and, if I like it, I will nod."

Chastity looked at Tone. "There's only one man suits

that description. His name is Mickey Kerr and he strong-arms for the others."

Chang was nodding vehemently and the woman said to him, "A very interesting story, Mr. Chang. A pity it's not true."

"Yes, a pity. But alas, it is just a good-news fairy tale." Chang bowed to Chastity. "If you need anything, Miss Christian, my office is at the front of the hallway."

After the man left, Chastity threw a bundle of Chinese clothes to Tone. "Wear these and get used to them." She took hers behind the screen and began to undress.

"I'm going after Mickey Kerr tonight and start earning my money," Tone said, talking to rice paper and cherry blossoms.

"No, we are," Chastity said. "Both of us."

"It's something I have to do myself."

Chastity screeched in horror and Tone stepped quickly to the screen. "What's wrong?"

"Nothing. I just discovered what Chinese women wear in place of bloomers. They're . . . they're . . . indecent."

"Let me see," Tone said.

"Back off," Chastity said. "I told you, they're down-right indecent." A rustling pause, then, "But comfortable, though."

Tone was having his own problems. Chang had obviously described him to his seamstress as a giant, because his blue tunic swamped him, the sleeves falling over his hands. The baggy black pants were also voluminous, the crotch sagging between his thighs.

Then he remembered his holsters. Sighing, he yanked off the shirt and strapped himself into the harness. A two-gun rig is uncomfortable at the best of times, but the leather and buckles chafed against his bare chest when he moved around.

There was nothing to be done about it. He couldn't wear his guns over the tunic in full view of everybody.

"Ready?" Chastity asked from behind the screen.

She stepped into the room and Tone felt his breath catch in his throat. She wore a pink embroidered tunic that showed off every luscious curve of her body and her dark hair fell in glossy waves over her shoulders.

"You look . . . You look . . ." Tone couldn't find the words.

"Ugly?"

"No! No! You look . . . wonderful."

The woman joined her hands together in front of her breasts and bowed low. "Thank you, kind sir." She studied Tone from his shoes to the top of his head. "And you look—"

"I know what I look like."

"Since you don't have a pigtail, a hat will cover your hair, but the big mustache has to go."

Tone was horrified. "It's taken me years to get this mustache to where I like it. It stays. Rather than shave it off, I'd dress like a sailor again and take my chances."

Chastity shrugged. "Your funeral, Mr. Tone."

"Thanks, but when we're in bed you can call me John."

Chastity gave him a sidelong glance but said nothing.

She picked up her bag off the floor and laid it on the bed. She removed her .41-caliber Remington over-and-under derringer and a strange-looking gun rig that Tone had never seen before.

The woman held it up for him to see. "It's a sleeve holster. Not something I use often," she said. She raised an arm, revealing the wide sleeve of her tunic. "But tonight, this will conceal it."

The holster was finely crafted of soft, thin leather, and two thin straps secured it to Chastity's forearm. The derringer snapped into a leather-covered metal clip.

Chastity let her sleeve cover the rig, then she raised her arm and opened her hand. The derringer sprang into her palm, hammer up and ready.

"I had it made for me in El Paso," she said. "It's uncomfortable to wear, like your shoulder holsters, but, under certain circumstances, quite effective."

Tone smiled as Chastity replaced the derringer in the rig. "I've got to get me one of those," he said.

"Then you'd better wear a coat with roomy enough sleeves or the gun will snag inside and you'll be a dead man."

"A thing to remember," Tone said, immediately losing any passing interest he might have had in sleeve holsters.

He stepped to the window and glanced outside, bending to see the sky. It was still raining, but the dark clouds were splintered with light.

"Long time until dark," Tone said. He looked at Chastity and raised an eyebrow. "What can we do to pass the dreary hours?"

"I'll get Chang to bring you a book," the woman said.

Chapter 16

Night fell along the Barbary Coast and the streets thronged with sailors who rubbed shoulders with drovers down from the hills, bearded miners, rubes from the sticks and respectable businessmen in from the city who knew that any degenerate appetite they possessed, no matter how perverted, would be satisfied, so long as they had money to pay. Amid this bedlam bustled thugs, murderers, thieves, burglars, gamblers, pimps and whores, scuttling through the darkness like cockroaches.

The rain that had promised to stop had lied, and now fell in a light drizzle that added its gray curtain to the veil of the fog. Wet cobblestones gleamed like polished blue iron in the light of the streetlamps and passing cabs threw up cascades of water from their rattling wheels.

A gas lamp burned in the rear room of Chang's house in Murder Alley, the window a rectangle of pale turquoise in the gloom.

Inside, John Tone was not in the best of moods. The

round Chinese hat Chang had given him to wear was, like his clothes, too big for him and kept falling down over his eyes. Irritably, he pushed it back for the tenth time that evening, then growled when Chastity asked him a question.

Getting no answer, she asked it again: "How do you want to play this?"

Tone snatched the infernal hat off his head and glared at the woman. "Mickey Kerr is visiting his lady-love in her room above the Opera Comique. I plan to climb the stairs, kick in the door and gun him. Then I'll turn around and get the hell out of there."

Chastity nodded. "A fine plan, Tone. Just a couple of problems: One, Luther Penman told me the Opera Comique is a concert saloon with a dance hall in the cellar. The front door will be guarded and they won't let you inside. You're supposed to be Chinese, remember? And two, you'd never get out of there alive after shooting Kerr."

Fighting down his irritation, Tone said, "Then what, pray, do you suggest?"

"I'll go inside and take care of Kerr. But when I come out again, I want your guns covering me."

"You're also supposed to be Chinese, you know. Why would they let you inside and not me?"

Chastity stepped to the closet. She settled a straw coolie hat on her head, then picked up a bundle of clothing. Taking small, mincing steps, she trotted toward Tone, carrying the bundle.

"Let pass, please," she said in a high, accented voice, keeping her head down, her face covered by the wide brim of the hat. "Laundlee for missy upstairs. She in velly big hurry." She looked at Tone and said in her

normal voice. "The toughs at the door will let me go.
They'll probably grope my tits and ass as I run past, but
I'll get to Mickey Kerr."

Despite his peevishness, Tone saw the logic in what
Chastity was suggesting. It showed in his eyes, because
the woman said, "What are you worried about, Tone?
You'll still get credit for the kill."

That gave Tone pause. Bounty hunting was a dirty,
sometimes violent and bloody business, but he'd never
bragged on the men he'd killed and considered those
who did to be low-life tinhorns.

Chastity knew his wages depended on gunning Kerr
and five others, and that was why she'd told him he'd
get the credit. But to hear it put so coldly and matter-of-
factly as she'd just done troubled him.

Or was it bounty hunting that troubled him? Had he
ever been completely at ease killing men or tearing
them away from their wives and children all in the
name of supporting his expensive lifestyle in Reno?

Angry at himself now, realizing that having second
thoughts about his profession was a form of betrayal,
Tone shoved the notion from his mind. His reaction to
his self-damning introspection was to tear the Chinese
tunic off his back and yell, "Hell, I'm dressing like a
white man. I've had enough of this coolie shit."

Chastity's voice was controlled, level. "Penman is
trying to save your life, Tone, or at least keep you alive
long enough to fulfill your contract. I suggest you do as
he says and wear the Chinaman's clothes."

Tone threw the round hat across the room. "Penman
is an idiot!"

The woman refused to be baited. In the same controlled voice she said, "He is far from being an idiot. He's possessed of a shrewd, calculating brain that helped make Mr. Sprague a millionaire." She smiled without warmth. "Don't make the mistake of underestimating Luther Penman."

Tone stripped off the shoulder rig and picked up his seaman's jersey.

"Where did you get those shoulders, Tone?" Chastity asked, smiling.

"Down on the farm, when I was a boy."

"Your father was a farmer?"

"Yes, and a good one. Then the British came and burned everything he had. My mother died, of grief, the doctor said, and me dad soon followed."

"I'm sorry."

"Ireland's history is written in sorrow." Tone pulled on the jersey. "Anyway, it all happened a long time ago when I still had songs to sing."

"You don't sing now?"

"No. I can recall the words of the songs, but the music has long since fled."

"How sad that is."

"I don't need sympathy." Tone strapped on the shoulder rig.

"No, I suppose you're not a man who does. But it's still sad."

Tone shrugged into his peacoat, then donned his watch cap. He glanced in the mirror. "There. I look myself again."

"You mean you're a target again," Chastity said.

"I mean I'm a bounty hunter with a job to do and I start doing it tonight." He looked at the woman, a delicate, haunting beauty in the pale blue gaslight. "Are you ready?"

Chastity checked her derringer, then picked up her bundle of linens. "I'm ready."

"Then let's get it done," Tone said.

Chapter 17

The Opera Comique was a large two-story frame and timber building located on what was locally known as Murderer's Corner. The rain had stopped, but fog prowled the streets and alleys. When the sky was visible, the moon looked like a red pool tucked in the clouds and the night air smelled of the shoaling fish out in the bay. Earlier, the crowds had sought shelter from the drizzle in the saloons and there were few travelers on the streets.

To Tone's joy, a fruit and vegetable stand stood opposite the door to the concert saloon, bare and abandoned now that darkness had fallen. The building behind the stand had fallen on hard times and was boarded up. A faded sign above its door said:

THE SEAMAN'S MISSION
Bible meetings at 7 p.m. and 10 p.m. every weeknight

Tone guided Chastity along the docks, well clear of the taverns and brothels, then angled toward the fruit stand.

"I'll be here when you come out," he said quietly. "Run across the road, then keep on going." He pointed down Jackson Street. "That way. A lot of the street-lamps are out for some reason and there will be plenty of dark places to hole up until I find you."

"When I come out, I'll be yelling, 'Murder! Murder!'" Chastity said. "With luck, the guards at the door will ignore a hysterical Chinese girl and dash upstairs."

"If they don't, I'll open up," Tone said. "Then run like hell. Just be sure not to shoot me, because I'll be right on your heels."

In the shadowed night, the woman looked small and vulnerable. "You certain you're up for this?" Tone asked. "You're about to make a grandstand play, you know."

"I'm up for it. I've been in worse scrapes."

"Back!" Tone exclaimed suddenly. He pushed Chastity into the dark doorway of the abandoned mission.

A man had stepped out of the Opera Comique and a match flared as he lit his pipe, casting a brief red glare on his tough, bearded features.

He smoked for a few minutes, then tapped out his pipe on his heel and walked back inside.

"One of the guards," Tone said. "He sure was a big feller."

"You trying to scare me?" Chastity asked.

"He'll be a bigger target, is all."

"No, you tried to scare me, Tone, and you succeeded. I don't know the whore's room, or that Mickey Kerr will even be there."

"Chastity," Tone said, using the woman's name for the first time since he met her, "let me do it. I'll claim to be a friend of Mickey's and say I'm going upstairs to talk to him."

"And if the guards don't let you pass?"

"Then I start shooting."

Chastity shook her head. "I told you before, that won't work." She hefted her bundle of linens. "I'll find her room." She smiled. "Me askee nice mens at door."

Then she was gone, trotting across the street. Tone watched her disappear into the Opera Comique . . . and suddenly he was chewing on his own heart.

He drew his guns, thumbed back the hammers for faster first shots, then crouched behind the fruit stand, his arms straight out in front of him, elbows resting on the rim of a wooden display box.

A minute passed . . . then another. . . .

Tone touched his tongue to his dry top lip. Where was the woman? What was happening? An errant breeze tugged at him, then swirled among the fog. He felt sweat on his palms.

A shot! Muffled by the walls of the saloon. Then one more.

Long moments dragged past. Tone stood, his guns up and ready.

Chastity ran out of the door, screaming, "Murder!" at the top of her lungs. She ran past Tone, grinned at him, then vanished into the gaslit gloom of Jackson Street.

Tone waited a few moments, watching for any pursuit. There was none, and he followed after Chastity. He caught up with her after a hundred yards. She was standing, waiting for him, outside a noisy dance hall.

The woman's face was vibrant, alive, as though illuminated by a strange inner glow. It did not add to Chastity's prettiness; rather, it detracted from it. To Tone, her radiance seemed unearthly . . . unholy.

Her words came out in a rush. "They let me upstairs, and the door wasn't even locked. Mickey Kerr, I suppose it was him, had the woman kneeling on the bed and he was humping behind her, both of them as naked as jaybirds. He tried to go for his gun on the nightstand, but I shot him right between his eyes. The redheaded bitch opened her big mouth to scream and I put a bullet into it."

Chastity held up a hammered-silver bracelet. "I took this off her wrist, then started screaming blue murder. The stupid guards ran past me on the stairs. Can you believe that?"

"Why . . . but why did you take time to steal the woman's bracelet?"

"A trophy—what else? When I make a kill I always take a memento. Mickey probably gave the whore this."

Almost breathless with excitement, Chastity lifted shining eyes to Tone. "Now I've got five kills. Wherever Western men gather, they'll talk about me in the same breath as Hardin, Thompson and Hickok. Think about it: I'm only a woman, but I'm making history."

Tone was too stunned to speak. Was this what a born killer sounded like? And was he disturbed because he was hearing an unsettling echo of his own arrogance?

Chastity Christian enjoyed the act of killing and she was a woman without a conscience. Where was his own conscience? He had always presumed it was dead and buried with Molly O'Hara. But had he killed it himself, much later, when he'd first taken up the gun and hunted men?

Tone had no chance to question himself further. Chastity pressed her body against his, her lips parted, scarlet and glistening, her pelvis grinding into his. "Take me home, Tone. Take me home now, and ride me like an unbroken mare. I feel wonderful!"

They walked back to the alley through the thickening fog and neither of them spoke. But Chastity's shining eyes were everywhere, as though seeing her surroundings for the first time and in a different light. The woman was ecstatic, radiant and as beautiful as a fallen angel.

In bed, Chastity came to Tone willingly, eagerly, but before he could hold her he had to invade her, forced to penetrate a defensive bulwark of elbows and knees.

When Tone woke, Chastity was already out of bed. She sat at the dresser, where she'd just finished cleaning her derringer.

She saw that Tone was awake and smiled at him. "I asked Chang to bring us coffee."

"How long have you been up?"

"About an hour. You were sound asleep and I didn't want to wake you."

Chastity rose to her feet, wearing only the pink Chinese tunic, her breasts unfettered. She sat on the bed and crossed her legs.

"We meet Mr. Sprague later today, remember?" she said. "At least you have good news to give him." She leaned over and kissed Tone lightly on the mouth. "I suspect Luther will also be here to greet his boss."

At that moment the woman looked so desirable that Tone reached for her. She evaded him and got to her feet. "The moment's gone, Tone," she said, smiling. "I needed it last night, but not today. Wait until I make my next kill, huh?"

Tone shook his head, the woman's coldness again shaking him to the core. "Chastity," he said, "there's more to life than killing."

"That, coming from you, John Tone, the famous bounty hunter? How many have you killed?"

"I don't enjoy killing. Every one of those men were notified and I tried my best to take them in alive."

Chastity no longer seemed cold, merely indifferent. "The dodgers on the first three men I killed said, 'Wanted, dead or alive,' so I took them in dead. What was wrong in that?"

"It's the fact that you enjoy killing that's wrong. Can't you understand?"

The woman slowed her speech, as though she was talking to a child. "Tone, when I was eight years old I watched my father beat my mother to death in a drunken rage. He tried to beat me too, but I ran away. I told our local sheriff what had happened and he brought me back to our cabin. The sheriff—I remember his name was Hank Dillbury—looked at what my father had done to my mother. Then he looked at my father snoring in his chair, then at me.

"Dillbury drew his gun, pressed the muzzle against my father's forehead and pulled the trigger. I saw it happen and I smiled and so did the sheriff."

Chastity waved her hand dismissively. "Men kill each other all the time, Tone, and most enjoy it. I can tell you that Dillbury did. Why should a woman be any different?"

"When you killed Mickey Kerr, why did you have to shoot the girl?"

"She was about to scream. She would have told the others what had happened." Chastity shrugged. "Besides, like my mother, she was a whore. Does anybody care about the death of a whore?"

"It seems that Sheriff Dillbury did."

The woman laughed. "Hell, he was one of them who went at Ma every chance they got. Dillbury didn't care about her. He was mad at Pa for killing his favorite poke."

Chastity picked up the hammered-silver bracelet and pushed it onto her left wrist. She held it up so it caught the morning light and asked Tone: "You like?"

He was spared the necessity of answering when Chang scratched at the door. Chastity told him to come in, and the little man entered, a grin on his face and a tray in his hands.

"Did missy sleep well?" he asked.

"Well enough, Mr. Chang," the woman answered.

The man set the tray, bearing a coffeepot and cups, on the dresser, then turned to Chastity again. "Mr. Penman was here. He say he going to the docks, come back later. Seemed very cross."

"Thank you," Chastity said. "That will be all for now."

She poured coffee into the cups. "Better get dressed, Tone," she said. "If Penman really is cross, our good news should cheer him up."

Tone nodded, but said nothing.

Chapter 18

"Mickey Kerr was the least of them," Luther Penman said. "During the late war he wasn't even an officer, just an ordinary seaman with more brawn than brains."

The lawyer opened his briefcase. "Nevertheless, you have a payment coming to you, Mr. Tone, less deductions for the guns you bought and miscellaneous expenses incurred while entertaining whores."

Chastity gave Tone a sidelong look, half annoyed and half amused.

"Penman, I didn't kill Mickey Kerr," Tone said. "Miss Christian did. The money should go to her."

"Perhaps, but Miss Christian has no contract with Mr. Sprague to cover that exigency. The fee is yours, Mr. Tone. You are free to pass it on to a second party as you see fit."

When Tone handed Chastity the bundle of notes, she looked at it for long moments, a triumphant little smile on her lips. She then handed the money to Penman. "Invest this for me," she said. "Opium, whores, slaves, whatever . . . I trust you to make the right decisions on my behalf."

The lawyer nodded and shoved the money into his briefcase. "I declare, Miss Christian, you'll be the richest woman in America one day."

Chastity nodded. "That is my intention."

Penman shifted his attention to Tone. His hard eyes searched the younger man's face but slid away, baffled, as though he'd tried to read a message carved in stone and had failed.

"I have left a man at the dock," the lawyer said. "He will tell us when Mr. Sprague's longboat is in sight. He will have fighting men with him and the war against his five surviving enemies will begin in earnest."

Again Penman sought Tone's eyes, and again he turned away, seeing something in their blue depths that disturbed him. "Mr. Tone, you're not having second thoughts, are you? You know what will happen if you break your sacred oath."

"Don't try to railroad me, Penman," Tone said evenly. "I signed on with the brand to fight, and that's what I'll do."

"Despite your rather colorful frontier language, I'm glad to hear that," the lawyer said. "When the shooting starts, Mr. Sprague will expect you to be at his side."

Tone nodded, his talking done.

"What now, Mr. Penman?" Chastity asked, filling in the silence.

"Now, my dear, we await Mr. Sprague's arrival. In the meantime I suggest that you discard the Chinese garb and dress in your normal fashion. I fear that the time for disguises is past."

The woman nodded. "It served its purpose. This little Chinese girl got close enough to Mickey Kerr to kill him."

"And there's more killing to be done, Miss Christian."

"I'm ready," Chastity said. Her eyes were glittering, like sun-splashed ripples in a brook.

The sun was nudging noon when a man scratched at the door and told Penman that Sprague's longboat was in the bay. The lawyer passed the man a coin, dismissed him, then said, "We will make our way to the dock." He glanced at Chastity. "You look lovely, Miss Christian. The green color of your afternoon dress becomes you."

The woman smiled and dropped a graceful little curtsy.

"You are armed, of course?" Penman asked.

"Of course."

"Then if you are also ready, Mr. Tone, shall we proceed?"

At that time of the day, most of the people in the streets and alleys along the waterfront were Chinese, though a few sightseers from the city were in evidence, elegantly dressed men and women shivering with delight as they passed drinking dives, whorehouses and opium dens, chattering in high, excited voices.

As Tone and the others arrived at the dock, Sprague's longboat was just tying up. Tone did a quick count. Including Sprague and his shadow, the giant Blind Jack, there were thirteen men crammed into the small craft.

Superstitions of childhood coming back to him, he

felt like crossing himself. Thirteen, the number at the Last Supper, was an unlucky omen.

But Tone was reassured by the swaggering confidence of Sprague's men. Each one of his tough, weather-beaten sailors wore a brace of Colt revolvers and had a wicked-looking cutlass tucked into his belt. They looked like men to be reckoned with, and Tone had a sudden premonition that before this war was over, Sprague would need every one of them.

Sprague himself looked as hale and hearty as ever, short, stocky and indestructible. He had not dressed himself from the slop chest, but wore an expensive pearl gray suit, a top hat of the same color and a huge diamond stickpin sparkling in his cravat. He did not appear to be armed, perhaps trusting to the Colts of his men for his protection.

As soon as he set foot on the dock, he beckoned Penman to one side and the two had an animated, heads-bent conversation. When it was done, Sprague stepped to Tone, his hand extended.

"One down, five to go, Mr. Tone," he said. "But there is still much work to be done."

Tone made the appropriate response, and Sprague's attention was drawn to Chastity. His eyes moved over her body from shoes to hat. Then he said, smiling, "And who is this divine creature?" He looked at Tone. "Yours?"

Tone shook his head, then nodded in Penman's direction. "His."

Sprague was surprised. "Luther, you've been holding out on me. I didn't know you'd given up boys, you old rogue."

The lawyer was quick to explain. "I hired Miss

Christian to be Mr. Tone's assistant," he said. "To aid him in any way he deems necessary."

"You mean as a private secretary or something?" Sprague asked, puzzled.

"He means as a bounty hunter," Tone said. "I didn't kill Mickey Kerr. She did."

Sprague was silent for a moment as he took the mental step from puzzled to completely bewildered. Finally he said, "I've never heard of such a thing. There are no lady bounty hunters in the West."

Chastity smiled. "There are now, Mr. Sprague. Well, one at least."

"She's good at her job," Penman said. "Men who underestimate her have a habit of ending up dead."

"In Boot Hill. Isn't that the term, Miss Christian?" Sprague grinned.

"That's the term. And I've put a few there."

"And are you as pure as your name implies?" Sprague asked.

"I'm sure you will very soon endeavor to answer that question for yourself," Chastity said.

Sprague laughed. "Damn my eyes if that wasn't well said! Come alongside o' me, lass, and take my arm. We'll walk together. I keep a fine establishment on Kearney Street befitting a lady like yourself."

"Mr. Sprague, we've got trouble," Penman said, his voice low and urgent.

Tone looked ahead of them and saw two dozen policemen shaking out in a loose skirmish line, guns drawn. At their head, stern as ever, was the broad and determined form of Sergeant Thomas Langford.

Chapter 19

"Langford," Sprague said, "what the hell are you doing out of your scratcher at this time o' the day? I always thought you were a nocturnal son of a bitch, like a bat."

"Ah, Captain Sprague, as pleasant as ever," the cop said, his huge arms crossed over his chest. "What brings you on land? Is the piracy business slow?"

"Is that an accusation, Langford?" Penman said, taking a threatening step toward the sergeant. "I warn you, be respectful now. I could have your badge."

"Respectful, to a well-known pirate rogue"—Langford's eyes roamed over Sprague's toughs—"and as scurvy a group of cutthroats as I ever clapped eyes on."

"I warn you—" the lawyer began.

Sprague talked over him. "Langford, we go back a ways, you and me. You know that the last brave pirate lads hauled down their colors and found berths on the beach twoscore years ago. If you have come to arrest me, then get it done and be damned to ye." He thrust out his hands in a dramatic gesture. "Where are the shackles?"

Langford shook his head. "I'm not here to arrest you, Cap'n Sprague—"

"Then, damn your soul, why did you bring an army?"

"Call it a bait o' insurance, Cap'n. Force is the only thing a blackhearted pirate rascal like you understands."

"Be circumspect, Sergeant Langford," Penman warned. "You're treading on extremely dangerous ground here."

If the big cop was intimidated, he hid it well. "Cap'n Sprague—"

"Mr. Sprague," the lawyer snapped.

"Cap'n Sprague, the three-masted clipper ship *Bonny Leslie* arrived in port yesterday, Captain Oliver McCoy commanding," Langford said. "He reported that the day before, he sailed through the wreckage of a ship seventeen miles south of the Golden Gate. Her logbook was found floating among the debris and identified her as the steam freighter *Benton,* bound for the port of London with a cargo of silver coin and gold bullion."

"And what's all that to me, Langford?" Sprague asked. "Two days ago I was thirty miles nor'west of the Golden Gate strait. Hell roast your guts, man, what are you implying?"

"What am I implying, Cap'n Sprague? Piracy, man! Piracy on the high seas! The *Benton* went down with all hands, but I believe every man jack of them was murdered before the ship was sent to the bottom."

"I've heard enough, Langford," Penman said. "The only place Mr. Sprague will answer your vile accusations will be in a court of law." He looked beyond the officer. "Now, call off your dogs and give us the road."

Langford ignored the man. "Cap'n Sprague, my jurisdiction does not extend to the high seas, but through my superiors I can raise the matter in Washington. I suspect that a naval court of inquiry into the sinking of the *Benton* could go badly for you."

Sprague was taken aback. "Damn you, there's a whiff of blackmail in the wind. Are you trying to shake me down, Langford?"

The cop stared at Sprague, and even from where he stood Tone could feel the force of his anger. Seagulls quarreled noisily over kitchen waste dumped overboard from a ship and a key clanked as a bartender unlocked the door of an early-opening saloon.

"I want no truck with your blood money, Sprague," Langford said finally. "But aye, 'blackmail' is the right word for what I have in mind. The sea is not my jurisdiction, but the waterfront is, and if you start a war, damn you, I'll go to my superiors and demand an immediate inquiry into the sinking of the steamship *Benton*."

Penman yelled, "Blackmail by an officer of the law!" He looked around him. "All here present heard it, my client being threatened with lies and perjury. I will demand—"

"Luther, shut the hell up," Sprague said. He looked at Langford, who was apparently unmoved by the lawyer's rant. "Certain elements along the Barbary Coast are attempting to take over my business interests, and they will use force if necessary. What am I to do if I, or my men, are attacked?"

"You will come to me, Cap'n Sprague. My officers will give you all the protection you need."

Langford's eyes moved to Tone, dismissed him, then settled on Chastity. "Young lady, I fear you are in the wrong company," he said.

The woman shook her head. "No, Sergeant, I'm in the right company."

"I think you may soon change your mind."

Without another word, the cop turned on his heel and waved to his men to follow him. Holstering their guns, the officers did so, and none of them looked back.

Sprague turned to Tone. "That man will have to go, and soon. A two-thousand-dollar bonus for his head, Mr. Tone."

Penman was flustered. "Mr. Sprague, it's no small thing to kill a San Francisco police sergeant. There will be repercussions all along the waterfront."

Chastity smiled. "A police sergeant can die like any other man and it is a small thing."

Tone looked at Sprague. "A full-scale police investigation could be bad for business."

"Then what do you suggest, Mr. Tone?"

"Kill your five enemies quickly enough and there will be no time for a war."

Sprague thought that through, then said, "What you say makes sense. But at least for now, the death of Langford must remain an option." He smiled at Chastity and put his arm around her slender waist. "I like the cut of your jib, young lady. I think you and I are going to be the best of friends—lay to that."

The expression on Penman's face shocked Tone. The man was looking after the woman, his lips peeled back from his long yellow teeth in what was almost a feral snarl.

Was he jealous of Chastity? Hardly that. Penman was a known pedophile who had no sexual interest in women.

Damn it, Tone thought to himself, why does he look at her like that?

The question troubled him and he wished he had an answer.

The man was spread-eagled on the wood floor, his wrists and ankles lashed to iron rings that had been bolted to the thick timber. A fire burned in the room, several iron pokers glowing cherry red in the coals.

There was a single chair, set near the terrified prisoner, and it was currently occupied by Chastity Christian, Sprague standing at her elbow.

When Tone had stepped into the room, Sprague had smiled at him and said, "I wanted you to witness this, Mr. Tone. The information we get from this sniveling wretch could be useful to you."

Now Tone glanced at the man, who was naked, his skin gleaming with sweat.

"That poor excuse for a human being on the floor is Five Ace Johnny Kemp, sometime gambler, sometime pimp and full-time weasel. He works for Joseph Carpenter, one of the five, and he knows where we can find him."

Tone searched his brain, then remembered. Carpenter owned a waterfront saloon and kept a steam yacht at the docks. He was said to be good with a gun.

"Mr. Sprague, I don't know where Joe is. I swear I don't." Kemp groaned, his eyes bulging.

The man was beyond fear, teetering on the verge of hysterical terror. Tone figured Kemp must know his

chances of leaving Sprague's house alive were slim. But
it was the manner of his dying that was scaring him.

"I'll ask you again, Johnny," Sprague said. "Where is
Carpenter?"

Kemp shook his head. "I don't know. I haven't seen
him in days."

"Jack, let him kiss the hot iron," Sprague said.

The blind giant stepped to the fireplace, pawed his
way among the pokers and pulled one from the flames.
It glowed ruby red in the semidarkness of the room.

"Let me," Chastity said, jumping to her feet. "I'll
make him talk."

"Let her have the poker, Jack," Sprague said, smiling. "Damn my eyes, but she's a woman after my own
heart."

Chastity kneeled by Kemp, the smoking iron in her
hand. Her breath was coming in short, sharp gasps and
she had a look of ecstasy on her face, her lips wet and
parted.

"Johnny, where is Carpenter?" she whispered.

"Mr. Sprague," Tone said quickly, "I think the man's
telling the truth. I don't think he knows where Carpenter is."

Sprague shrugged. "Maybe, maybe not. Chastity will
find out with her woman's wiles."

"Where is he, Johnny?" Chastity purred. "You can
tell li'l ol' me, can't you?"

"I don't know," Kemp gasped. The dull scarlet glow
of the poker gleamed in his eyes. "Oh, God help me, I
don't know."

"Too bad, Johnny boy," the woman said, "because
now I'm going to hurt you real bad."

"No . . . please . . . no. . . ."

The red-hot iron moved down Kemp's sweating body, an inch from his skin, then came to rest on his naked testicles. Flesh seared and bubbled and Kemp's shriek was a living thing that ripped its way around the room with claws of sound.

"Well, use my guts for garters, she gelded the son of a bitch," Sprague roared, slapping his thigh. "There's a woman for you!"

Chastity's entire body shuddered convulsively and her head rolled on her shoulders. After a few moments, panting, she said, "Jack, bring me another one."

"No!" Tone yelled. "The man's had enough."

"Keep out of this," Sprague snapped. "I'll say when he's had enough, and that won't be until he talks."

"I can't stand back and watch any more of this," Tone said, stepping toward the shackled man. "He doesn't know where Carpenter is."

"Jack," Sprague said quietly.

The blind man walked quickly across the room and enveloped Tone in his huge arms. Jack's strength was enormous and no matter how he struggled Tone was trapped like a small child in the grasp of a bedroom monster.

"Amazing, isn't it, Mr. Tone," Sprague said, "how he can close with a man. I don't know if it's his sense of smell, if he detects body heat or if he has some kind of third eye. He can ram a cutlass dead center into a man's belly, and I've yet to see him miss."

"What do you want done with him, Cap'n?" Jack asked.

"Hold him. I'll tell you when to let him loose." Sprague turned to Chastity. "I'll get you another iron," he said.

"I'll do it," the woman said. She stepped to the fire and tested the handles of the pokers. Finally she bunched the skirt of her gown in her hand to protect against the heat and slid a poker from the flames.

She walked back to Kemp, who was mouthing whispered pleas for mercy.

"Where is Joe Carpenter, Johnny?" she asked.

"I don't know. If I knew I'd tell you. I haven't—"

Chastity kicked the man in the ribs. "You dirty son of a bitch," she screeched. "You goddamned whore's bastard!"

The crimson poker plunged downward, into Kemp's right eye. Then Chastity pushed hard.

Kemp arched his back in agony and the echoes of his shrieks chased each other around the walls.

Tone struggled, using his elbows as he tried to break Jack's hold on him, but it was impossible, like striking out at an oak tree.

"Jack, let him go," Sprague said. Then: "Is Johnny boy still alive?"

The blind man threw Tone from him and kneeled beside the gambler, who was now silent. "The lady burned his brains out, Cap'n. Five Ace Johnny ain't with us no more."

"Too bad," Sprague said. "I guess he told the truth. He really didn't know where Joe Carpenter is holed up."

Chastity let the poker thud to the floor. She looked at Sprague, her hair wild, her eyes wilder. "Now, Lambert," she gasped. "Take me now!"

Sprague jumped to his feet and grabbed the woman's arm, pushing her roughly toward the door. "Get rid of that mess, Jack," he threw over his shoulder. Then he and Chastity were gone.

Tone sat on the chair, his face buried in his hands as shrieks of a different kind rang through the top floor of Sprague's house—the cries of a madwoman in demented rapture.

Chapter 20

Tone had been allotted a guest room on the ground floor of Sprague's house, ornately and overly decorated in the respectable middle-class fashion of the time.

The only point of interest was a portrait of Lambert Sprague, resplendent in the gray and gold of a Confederate naval officer, that hung on one wall. Sprague, twenty years younger and heavily bearded, leaned confidently against a cannon, posing stiffly for the camera.

Tone looked up at the picture, wondering if it had been taken before or after the gallant captain had turned from blockade runner to pirate.

He turned as someone knocked on the door and swung it open.

Sprague stepped into the room, Blind Jack and a couple of armed sailors backing him.

Tone's guns were on the bed, too far a reach if the man planned a shooting.

"How are you, Mr. Tone?" Sprague asked pleasantly. "Do you find your quarters comfortable?"

Allowing that he did, Tone added, "To what do I owe this honor?"

"Ah, there's big happenings afoot, Mr. Tone, and tonight you and I will be part of them." He moved to the side of the bed, a seemingly casual change of position that nonetheless put him between Tone and his guns.

"But first, I have something to tell you." Sprague shook his head, almost sadly. "By this time you know that I dislike unpleasantness of any sort, but what I have to say must be said. Do you understand?"

"I don't like to see a man, any man, tortured," Tone answered.

"Yes, and there we have the crux of the matter, so I will state my position fairly and clearly." He smiled, but quickly replaced it by an angry scowl. "If you ever try to cross me again, I will have Blind Jack break every bone in your body, one by one, starting at your toes. Trust me, Mr. Tone, it is a most painful death."

Tone realized he was on dangerous ground. Blind Jack and the sailors were alert and ready and he read no backup in their eyes.

"The man knew nothing," he said. "There was no point in torturing him further."

"A simple apology will do, Mr. Tone."

Swallowing his pride like a dry chicken bone, Tone said, "I'm sorry. I shouldn't have interfered."

"There," Sprague beamed. "It's done, and we are perfect friends again."

The man sat on the bed. "Since our friend Johnny Kemp disappointed us, I have a plan to bring the rats out of their holes. Joe Carpenter owns the Bucket of

Blood saloon, and other dives besides, but it is from the saloon that he derives most of his income. Tonight we will put a dent in his little gold mine."

He turned his head. "Jack, the bomb."

The blind man handed a burlap sack to Sprague, who held it open so Tone could see inside. "It's a ten-pound cast-iron grenade filled with lead balls, on a fifteen-second fuse. When this goes up inside the Bucket of Blood it will destroy the whole rotten den."

"And a whole lot of people," Tone said.

Sprague cocked his head to one side. "Mr. Tone, I'm beginning to suspect you don't have the belly for this kind of work. This isn't Dodge City, it's the Barbary Coast, and we do things a little differently here."

"Why kill innocent people? Wait until the saloon closes and then bomb the place."

"Firstly, there are no innocents along the waterfront, and, secondly, the Bucket of Blood never closes." Sprague shrugged. "If people are killed it can't be helped. It's the cost of doing business in San Francisco."

"Cap'n, let me go with you," one of the sailors said. "That man has a yeller streak a mile wide."

Tone's cold eyes turned on the man, a young towhead with blue eyes and freckles. "Sonny, if you want to see your next birthday, I suggest you hobble your lip."

"The devil roast your damned hide, Jim Hunter," Sprague snapped. "I told you I want no unpleasantness. Step outside and wait in the hallway."

The towhead gave Tone a sneer that he obviously hoped made him look tough, then turned and swaggered outside.

Sprague turned his attention to Tone again. "The bomb will bring Carpenter out of his hole and probably the others. Once they're in the open we can deal with them and you'll start earning your money." He hesitated, studying the other man's face, then said, "Well, Mr. Tone, are you for us or against us?"

"I signed on to use my guns. I don't throw bombs."

"And you won't. I'll toss the bomb. You'll stand by and keep a weather eye open for Langford."

Tone didn't say it, but he wouldn't draw down on the big cop. Langford had sand and a sense of honor, traits that Tone respected in a man.

"Well?" Sprague's irritation was growing, and Blind Jack, with his heightened awareness, had sensed it. He moved closer to Tone, his huge hands dangling by his side like meat hooks.

Tone wanted out. But this was not the time or the place.

"I'll ride shotgun," he said. Yet another small betrayal that troubled him greatly.

Sprague nodded. "Good. I need a gun-canny man at my side and I'm glad you remembered the oath you took, Mr. Tone. Remember, I'm the only one who can release you from it and it would go badly for you if you broke it."

Tone nodded but said nothing.

"Then let's get it done," Sprague said. He rose to his feet, the burlap bag in his hands. He looked at the blind man. "Jack, make sure the cook has dinner on the table for me and Chastity as soon as I get back. If Langford shows up it's got to look like I've been here all night. You understand?"

"I'll make sure it's done, Cap'n. Beggin' your pardon, but how long will you be gone?"

"Hell, man, I don't know," Sprague said. He grinned. "How long does it take to lob a ten-pound bomb through a window?"

Chapter 21

Tone walked along Pacific Street with Sprague. The drift of the swarming crowd was toward the saloons, dance halls, opium dens and brothels, and nobody except the bold-eyed whores gave either man a second glance as they passed.

A sense of wrongness at what he was doing gnawed at John Tone.

He had hunted and shot down men in the past and the right or wrong of it had never troubled him. By the very nature of their profession, outlaws were destined to be shot, hanged or imprisoned and all Tone did was hasten their inevitable end.

But a bomb is an indiscriminate killer and a coward's weapon, the choice of a man with no real bottom to him. For the first time, Tone realized that Sprague, despite all his piratical bluster and belligerence, was such a man.

"Stay near me, Mr. Tone," Sprague said. "We're real close." The man thumbed a match into flame, touched flame to the fuse.

"Listen, I—"

The crash of the fizzing bomb shattering the window of the Bucket of Blood drowned out Tone's voice.

"Keep walking," Sprague said urgently, without turning. "Don't run."

Behind them, women's screams. The hoarse curses of frightened men. The sound of pounding feet. A man yelling, "Out! Out!"

An instant later the saloon exploded with a noise like thunder.

A brilliant billow of scarlet and yellow flame erupted through the collapsing wall at the front of the saloon, then the entire second story and higher turret rooms rose twenty feet in the air, only to crash down again into a boiling cauldron of fire.

A man ran screaming into the street, ablaze from head to toe, and collapsed on the cobbles, tinting those around him with crimson light. The screams and shrieks of people burning to death in mortal agony filled the night and a thick column of smoke rose into the red-stained sky.

Walking briskly, Sprague turned and grinned at Tone. "Damn my eyes, but that was even better than I expected. Did you see the whole goddamned roof of the building go sky high?" He made an upward gesture with his hands. "Boom!"

Somewhere behind them bells clanged as fire engines drawn by galloping horses raced to the conflagration.

"That will bring Joe Carpenter out of hiding," Sprague said. "After this night's work he'll come looking for me."

Purposely leaving off the "Mister," Tone said, "Sprague, how many people did you kill tonight to flush a rat out of its hole?"

Now Sprague stopped. He and Tone stood in shadow and alone, the crowds attracted by the spectacle of death and fire.

"What the hell does it matter?" Sprague demanded. "So I killed a few whores, pimps and drunks. Who will miss them?"

"You may have killed hundreds."

Sprague shook his head. "I should have brought Jim Hunter with me. He was right—you don't have the guts for this kind of work."

"You're right," Tone said. "I don't. I'm quitting you as of this moment."

"You can't quit me, Tone. You swore an oath, and it's binding until I say it's not."

Before he walked away, Tone grabbed the man by the front of his coat and pulled him closer. "Sprague," he said, "stick your oath up your ass."

"You're a marked man, Tone, and I doubt that I can save you."

Sergeant Thomas Langford sat at his kitchen table, dressed in his uniform pants, a collarless white shirt and bedroom slippers.

"And thanks for getting me up so early," he said. "I reckon I've had about three hours' sleep."

"Sorry," Tone said. "But I thought you should know."

"How did you find me?"

"I wandered the streets until I found the cop that brought me here."

"His name is Owen Bream and later he and I will have words about him allowing you to disturb my beauty sleep."

Langford poured coffee for himself and Tone. "Will you testify in a court of law that you saw Lambert Sprague throw the bomb?"

"Yes, I will."

"He'll have a dozen witnesses who will say he didn't. Each of them will swear on a stack of Bibles that he spent the night at home, planning charitable works."

"How many people died in that explosion?" Tone asked.

"And in the resulting fire? At last count there were eighty-three dead, about twice that many injured and a third of those are burned too badly to survive."

"Sprague's as guilty as hell. Did you speak to him last night?"

"That I did. He was sitting down to dinner with his new lady friend and she swore he'd been home all night. So did several others."

"You didn't believe her?"

"It doesn't matter. Suspecting a thing and proving it are different matters."

"You always have the sinking of the *Benton* to hang over his head."

"Yes, there's that. Piracy on the high seas is a hanging offense, and sure, I could make things uncomfortable for him. But no one saw him attack that ship, and proving a charge of piracy could be difficult. I know it and, unfortunately, so do Sprague and his lawyer."

Langford rose and took a wooden canister from a shelf. He opened the lid and asked, "Cigar?"

Tone accepted gratefully. "I haven't had one in quite a spell," he said.

"Tell me about yourself, Tone," the sergeant said. "Specifically, tell me why you hated Joe Carpenter."

Tone was surprised. "Who told you that?"

"Sprague and what's-her-name, Miss Christian. They told me that you'd fallen in love with a whore who works at the Bucket of Blood, or did, and that Carpenter stole her away from you. When you began to vow revenge, Sprague said he kicked you out of his house. He says you'd talked about bombing the place."

Langford puffed luxuriously on his cigar. "Did you throw a bomb through Joe Carpenter's window last night?"

"Sprague and Chastity Christian are lying," Tone answered angrily. "I've never even met Joe Carpenter or a whore who worked for him."

The cop let that go and said, "You were born and raised in Ireland, haven't done a day's hard work since and have lived high on the hog up until recently. Way back, maybe in the old country, someone you loved died, your mother maybe or a sweetheart. And you've killed men, in Ireland and here. Am I correct so far?"

"How did you know—"

"I didn't. It's what you call police work. You've lost a lot of your brogue, but it surfaces now and then, especially when you're angry. You don't have the hands of a workingman and you had an expensive manicure fairly recently, so you haven't been hurting for money. No matter how you try to hide it, there's a hurt in your eyes that has been there for a long time. I'd say caused by the loss of a girl who was close to you. But there's also a coldness that I've seen only once before, maybe

ten years ago when I spoke with a man named John
Wesley Hardin down Texas way at Huntsville Prison.
He had a killer's eyes."

"I've heard of Hardin," Tone said. "I'm nothing like
him."

Langford did not respond, and Tone said, "I'm a
bounty hunter and none of the men I've killed have
come back to haunt my dreams."

The cop nodded. "In my line of work, I've learned to
fasten the dead to the earth. I don't search for them in
my sleep either."

He poured himself coffee and motioned with the
pot. Tone nodded and Langford refilled his cup.

"Was I right? Did you kill a man in Ireland and have
to leave in a hurry?" he asked. "Your sweetheart's husband, maybe?"

"British soldiers."

"Ah, it was the Troubles then?"

Tone nodded.

"And the girl?"

"Her name was Molly and she's dead." Tone tried
his coffee. "I used to sing, but I don't anymore. Not
since she was killed." He let out a cloud of smoke and
spoke behind a shifting blue veil. "I've wasted my time
coming here, haven't I?"

"I don't think you threw the bomb, Tone."

"But my eyewitness testimony that Sprague did it
won't stand up in court?"

"Not a chance. Every man on the jury will believe a
sweet young thing with a name like Chastity Christian
over a bounty hunter with death in his eyes."

Langford relit his cold cigar, taking his time. "Where
will you go?" he asked finally.

"Back to Reno, pick up my life."

"What about Sprague?"

"The hell with Sprague. He'll no longer be my concern."

"Men like Lambert Sprague are everyone's concern."

"Yeah, but we can't touch them, Langford. They've got too much money and power."

"There's another way—a long shot certainly, but you might want to consider it."

"Let's hear it."

"Wear a blue suit."

"Huh? I'm not catching your drift."

"Join me, Tone. Become one of San Francisco's finest."

Tone laughed out loud. "Me, a copper? That'll be the day."

"You're a bounty hunter. It's close." Langford leaned forward on the table. "I'm good with a knife and you are a gunfighter. Between us both we can clean up the waterfront and get rid of Sprague and his kind once and for all."

Tone looked at him. "You're serious, aren't you?"

"I've never been more serious in my life."

"Langford, how long does it take to become a cop? Weeks, I imagine."

"We can scrub around that. Especially when I tell them you've volunteered for waterfront duty. Trust me, you'll be one of us in a day or two."

Tone was still amused. "Hell, I'm a big enough target now. Wait until I'm walking up and down Pacific Street in a policeman suit. Every two-bit bushwhacker along the Barbary Coast will be gunning for me."

Langford considered that, then said, "Do you think you'll be safer in Nevada?"

"I'd be fighting on my home ground."

The cop shook his head wearily. "Tone, Sprague won't brace you out where the buffalo roam. His weapons are the bomb, the knife and the garrote and you won't see him coming."

For a few moments the cop was silent. Then he said, "When you signed on with Sprague, did he make you take an oath, an old-time pirate oath?"

"Yes, he did."

"Then you've broken your vow, and he won't rest until you're dead. Sprague's tentacles reach far, and there's nowhere in the entire world that's safe for you any longer. You're also the only man who will swear in court that you saw him throw the bomb. For that reason alone, he can't let you live."

Tone opened his mouth to speak, but Langford held up a silencing hand. "Here's how it will happen: One day a man, or a woman, will leave an envelope for you at the front desk of your fancy hotel in Reno. You'll open it, and all it will contain will be a skull and crossbones drawn on a page torn from the Bible you held when you made your oath." The man shrugged. "After that, measure your life in hours."

"You trying to scare me into that blue suit, Langford?"

"No, but I'm telling you how it will be. No matter how you cut it, hard times are coming down, Tone."

Chapter 22

John Tone sat and considered his options. They were few.

He could head back to Reno, relax for a couple of days, then check through the latest reward dodgers. He could pick up the threads of his life again.

Sprague knew nothing of purple mountains, high mesas, thin-flowing streams and prairie lands that went on and on until grass and sky became one.

The man was a blue-water sailor, a sea-fighter, and Tone could lead him a merry chase.

Unless . . . he'd thought about relaxing for a couple of days, dining well, sleeping with a willing woman again. But suppose the skull and crossbones was delivered during those days? A small sigh escaped his lips. From now on there could be no relaxing. He would have to be on guard at all times, constantly checking his back trail, whether riding out on the long grass or walking down a city street. Until Sprague was dead, he would have no peace.

It was not a way for any man to live.

"The blue suit?" Langford probed, sensing the younger man's troubled thoughts.

Tone smiled. "I shouldn't even consider it, but here I am, like a fool, giving it some serious thought. I don't much like the alternative, hearing a rustle in every bush and wondering if it's Sprague." His smile faded. "Although I could always go back to Ireland and fight the British."

"You have a war to fight right here, Tone," Langford said.

Tone poured himself more coffee. "Let me think about it for a couple of days."

"Do you have a place to live?"

"As of right now, no."

"You can bunk in my spare room. It isn't fancy, but for a hunted man it's the safest berth in San Francisco." Langford stretched and yawned. "I'm going back to bed for a couple of hours. I'll show you the room and you can make yourself to home."

The room was sparsely furnished: an iron cot, a couple chairs and a closet for clothes.

Before he left, Langford looked Tone up and down and said, "I'd say six-four, two hundred and fifty pounds. Right?"

"Close enough."

"Then I'll see you later."

The sergeant closed the door behind him, and suddenly Tone realized he was deathly tired. He pulled off his shoes and hung his guns on a chair. Then he lay on the bed and within minutes was asleep.

He dreamed of screaming people . . . with their hair on fire. . . .

* * *

"Wake up, Tone! Wake up, man, you're having a bad dream!"

His eyes fluttering open, Tone saw Langford standing over him, his face concerned. "Wha-what time is it?" he asked.

"Almost four thirty. I leave for work in an hour."

Tone sat up in bed. "Sorry. I was dreaming."

"I just said you were and that's why I woke you." The big cop shook his iron gray head. "You were back at the Bucket of Blood, watching people die."

"They were on fire.... All of them. The women's hair ..." Tone smiled slightly. "I don't always call out in my sleep."

"Good," Langford said, returning the younger man's smile. "I can't abide a noisy houseguest."

Tone swung his legs off the bed and looked at the sergeant. "Let me walk with you tonight. What do you call it? Doing your rounds?"

"It could be dangerous. You're a marked man, Tone."

"Hell, Langford, so are you."

"The uniform gives me some protection."

"Not from Sprague. If you push him too hard, he'll try to kill you."

"Tougher men than Lambert Sprague have tried that before. They're dead and I'm still here." Langford looked hard at Tone. "All right, but shave and clean up. I won't have a scruffy-looking man patrolling with me."

Tone rubbed his hand over his stubbled cheeks. "I don't have a razor. Recently I seem to be making a habit of losing my luggage."

"Use mine, then join me in the kitchen. I've got supper ready."

When Tone sat at the table, Langford looked him over. "You'll do," he said. "But the mustache needs a trim. Let me see your fingernails."

Tone did as he was told, spreading his fingers out on the table. "Good. I can't abide an officer . . . man . . . with dirty nails. Let's eat."

Langford ladled beef stew onto Tone's plate, then pushed a plate of San Francisco's famous sourdough French bread in front of him.

"The bread was first baked during the Gold Rush," he said. "Now the city ships sourdough starter all over the country. You've probably eaten bread in Reno that was made from it."

"Maybe. But it wasn't near as good as this. You bake it yourself?"

"Hell, no. I buy it from a baker. I can cook bacon and eggs, beef stew and coffee. That's the limit of my culinary skills."

"But you have a fine taste in cigars. I guess that makes up for it."

"Hell, I don't buy expensive cigars. When I'm running low I confiscate a few boxes from the waterfront saloons, on suspicion of smuggling, you understand. Sprague's dives stock the very best brands and his bartenders have taken to hiding them when they see me coming." Langford smiled. "Sometimes they need a little persuading to part with the odd box or two."

Tone was hungry, the food was good, and despite his dreams the sleep had refreshed him. He laughed and it felt good.

Langford was not a man to linger over a meal. He ate quickly and encouraged Tone to do the same. When Tone pushed his plate away and finally declared himself satisfied, the sergeant poured them both coffee and offered cigars.

"I don't feel so bad about smoking these," Tone said, "now I know how you come by them."

Langford winked. "There's a little larceny in all of us."

He looked at Tone, taking his measure. Then he said, "Bring your guns, but when we're out on the street, follow my lead. If there's shooting to be done, I'll tell you when to make a play. Understand?"

Tone nodded. "You're the boss." He studied the glowing tip of his cigar and without looking up said, "You think we'll run into Sprague's men tonight, don't you?"

The cop shrugged. "He wants you dead. It's possible."

Now Tone looked at the man. "No, you think it's probable."

"We'll cross that bridge when we come to it, Tone. Let's not sit here and build houses on it."

Tone drained his coffee cup, then said, "I want to kill Lambert Sprague real bad."

Langford smiled. "Oddly enough, so do I."

"But you won't."

"When I gather enough evidence on him—and I will—I'll arrest him and I'll see him hang."

Tone was silent and the cop said, "I really don't want to know what you're thinking, but I'll ask it anyway: What the hell are you thinking?"

"I've decided to kill Sprague, first chance I get. It's him or me." He smiled. "Hey, did you see that?"

"See what?"

"My policeman's suit just flew out the window."

Chapter 23

At four o'clock that afternoon a thick fog had rolled in from the bay and the crowds of people walking on Pacific Street moved through the mist like gray ghosts. Cabbies allowed their horses to find their own way and the black hansoms loomed out of the gloom, side lamps glowing red as coals. The docks were invisible behind a somber curtain of fog that coiled and undulated like a Chinese dragon. The heavy air smelled of tarry ships, of green seaweed, of the sea beyond the strait and of teeming humanity.

Through this walked Tone and Langford, like everyone else along the waterfront, groping their way like blind men, relying on the feeble light pooled on the street by the gas lamps.

"Damn it, but I don't like fog," the cop said, irritated. "It brings out the most demented of the criminal element. Men are murdered, robbed or shanghaied, and the fog is happy to draw a veil over all of it."

"I haven't seen much fog," Tone said. "But sometimes in the western lands the clouds hang so low they cover the mountains. One time in Nevada I camped in a hanging valley in the Funeral range and got caught by—"

"Police! Oh my God, get the police!"

A woman's voice, screaming into the mist at the top of her lungs.

Langford reached into his tunic and pulled out a whistle on a chain. He blew several loud blasts, then yelled, "Where are you?"

"Police! Police!"

"She's right ahead of us," Tone said.

"Come on," Langford said.

As they walked quickly through the thickening murk, the big cop continued to blow loudly on his whistle. Around them men and women emerged from the gloom, then disappeared again, phantoms in the fog.

Then, "This way, coppers! Over here."

A shadowy figure stood at the entrance of a dark alley and beckoned Langford closer. "It could be a trap," Tone whispered.

"I know. Keep your revolvers handy."

Tone drew his guns and shoved them in the pockets of his peacoat.

A gray-bearded man took a step toward them. "She's dead, ripped. In the alley."

"You, stay around," Langford told him.

"I ain't goin' nowheres," the graybeard said. "I'm a respectable whaling man, a harpooner to trade, and I ain't never seen nothing"—he jerked a thumb over his shoulder—"like that."

The feeble light in the alley came from a single gas

lamp hung over a doorway, the kitchen entrance of a Chinese restaurant. But the dead woman's injuries were terrible enough to be seen in any light.

Her throat had been severed deeply by two vicious cuts and her abdomen had been slashed open. One of her breasts had been hacked off and the other stabbed repeatedly.

Her face was twisted in terror and it was hard to tell her age. Tone guessed she was around forty, but she could have been younger. His eyes moved to the wall behind the woman's body.

"Look at that, Langford," he said.

The sergeant did, and whispered, "That dirty son of a bitch."

Hastily scrawled in red chalk in block letters were the words

I'M DOWN ON WHORES AND WILL NEVER STOP RIPPING 'EM

"Everything all right, Sergeant?"

Two cops, attracted to the alley by Langford's whistle and the press of the gawking crowd, stood at the entrance to the alley.

"No, everything's not all right," the sergeant snapped. "Don't you have eyes, Johnson?"

Then the cop looked and saw what Tone and Langford were seeing. Blood drained from his face and he put out a steadying hand against the wall.

"Wait, I think I know her," the other officer said, a young man with a pink, unlined face. He bent from the waist, peering at the body. "Yeah, that's Annie Forbes. She's been working the waterfront this past twelvemonth, told me she hailed from Chicago originally. Said she wanted to go back one day and walk in the wind."

"I fancy she's never going to walk in the wind again," Langford said. He looked at the gray-bearded man who was standing close by. "How did you find her?"

"I was walking past the alley and heard footsteps," the man said. "Nothing too unusual about that, but I turned to look anyway. I saw a man running toward the other end of the alley, then I noticed the dead woman."

"Can you describe the man?"

"The Ripper?"

"Don't call him that. Yes, damn it, him."

The graybeard shook his head. "Too dark to see much, Sergeant." He hesitated. "I think he was fairly small and slight, but I can't be sure. A well-dressed gent, though. I'd swear to that."

Langford nodded to the end of the alley. "Tone, take a look."

Tone walked into the darkness, past the blue haze of the gaslight. Fog, thinner in the alley, drifted around him, moving aside as he passed. The ground was roughly cobbled with square blue bricks and his boots thudded, a hollow noise in the stillness. He slowed his pace, holding a .38 in his right hand.

The Ripper was probably long gone, but the man may be somewhere, lying in wait for another victim.

The alley opened up into a narrow back street, lined with crowded dwellings that were mostly sway-roofed shacks, their glassless windows covered with newspaper or sheets of cardboard torn from packaging cartons. The place reeked of overflowing outhouses, rotting garbage and abject poverty. Here the Barbary Coast's poor lived, widows, wrinkled whores up in years and down on their luck, abusive, drunken husbands and their slatternly wives who could no longer feel any emotion, not even despair. Despite the darkness and fog, naked, dirty children playing in fetid puddles and skinny dogs with running sores were everywhere.

The stinking slum was separated from Pacific Street by only a single block, but it could have been on a different planet, or an annex of hell.

Tone shoved his gun back in his pocket. A young woman balancing a zinc washtub on her hip looked at him boldly from in front of her shack. A little girl, a thumb in her mouth, clung to her skirts and regarded Tone with wide, uninterested eyes.

"Looking for something, Mister?" The woman asked.

"Did you see a man come past here, small, well dressed?"

The woman shook her head. "Hell, we never see a well-dressed man here." She turned to a toothless harridan who was standing close by. "You see a well-dressed gent pass this way, Peggy?"

"I never seen any gent in Pisser's Alley."

Both women laughed, the strident, wailing screech of the slums.

Tone smiled. "Well, thanks for your help."

If the Ripper had come this way, he was long gone.

He turned and began to retrace his steps, but the younger woman's voice stopped him. "Hey, Mister!"

She had set the washtub down and was holding up her skirt in both hands, her naked crotch a dark triangle in the gloom. "Fifty cents. Poke me as many times as you like."

Tone shook his head and turned away.

"What are you?" the woman named Peggy called after him. "Some kind of goddamned pervert?"

And as both women shrieked again, Tone felt his cheeks burn.

Chapter 24

"See anything?" Langford asked.

"More than I wanted to," Tone said.

"What does that mean?"

"Nothing. No, I saw no sign of him. The Ripper is long gone."

The cop was irritated again. "Damn it, Tone, don't call him that name. If the newspapers get hold of it they will play hob."

But the damage was already done.

Happy to be the center of attraction, the old harpooner had regaled the crowd with his description of the dead woman and her assailant. Now the words "the Ripper" were on every tongue.

"I've sent for the detectives," Langford said, "to see what they make of this." He waved a hand to the young cop. "This officer will stand guard until they arrive." He smiled mischievously. "I told Johnson to tell them they'll have to pick up the body. Detectives love that, getting their nice clean hands dirty."

"Busy night already," Tone said.

"It's the fog," Langford said. "Damn, I hate the fog."

He was silent for a while, taking his time to think, then said, "Let's go talk with Melody Cord. The lady keeps her ear to the ground and generally knows what's happening along the waterfront."

The cop smiled. "Don't get too excited, Tone. Her name's Melody all right, but she's a little out of tune."

"Crazy?"

"You could say she is, a little. She owns a drinking dive named the Jolly Jack that caters to the whaling trade. The only ship that's arrived in port during the last twenty-four hours was the whaling barque *Derwent Hunter* out of New Bedford town. The ship's arrival and the murder of the whore might only be coincidence, but at the moment coincidences are the only leads we have."

"What about the harpooner who discovered the body?" Tone asked.

"It wasn't him. I looked and there wasn't a speck of blood on him. You can't gut a woman and not get bloody in the process." Langford again lapsed into silence for a moment, his face thoughtful. "Unless . . ."

"Unless what?"

The cop shook his head. "It's nothing. I'll wait and hear what the detective branch has to say."

The Jolly Jack was the only single-story building on Pacific Street and hard to find in the fog. Langford told Tone that the tavern was said to be made from the timbers of old whaling ships, but he wasn't sure if that was true or not.

"If it is true, the walls must have some stories to tell," he said.

The big cop stepped inside first, Tone following close behind him.

There were around fifty men in the place, and a dozen women, almost invisible behind a cloud of pipe smoke. A girl, younger and prettier than the others, was sitting on the rough pine bar, showing her shapely legs as she picked out the chords of "Sweet Annie's Blue Dress" on a battered guitar.

Faded prints of sailing ships and whales covered the walls, along with rusty harpoons, splintered oars and an array of flensing tools hanging from part of a massive jawbone. The tavern was lit by lamps fueled with sperm whale oil that provided a soft white light and burned with a pleasant fragrance.

When the girl on the bar saw Langford, her playing faltered to a stop and the buzz of conversation faded, then died away to a few whispers.

"Thomas Langford, you won't find your Ripper in here," a female voice challenged from the blue murk. "Now begone with ye."

A woman pushed her way through the tables, fists on her huge hips. She stood as tall as Tone but outweighed him by at least fifty pounds. Her black hair hung in disarray over her wide shoulders and she sported a mustache that many a man would be proud of. Her breasts were huge, hanging in front of her like sacks of grain, the great V of her cleavage deep enough to hide a bottle of rum.

Her blazing brown eyes bored into Langford. "Are you here to make trouble? Cat got your tongue? Speak up, man."

"It's always good to see you, Melody." The cop smiled. "And may I say you look as beautiful as ever."

"Cut the shit, Langford," the woman snapped. "What do you want? I run a respectable establishment here."

"You heard about the dead woman? Her name was—"

"I know what her name was. I never let Annie Forbes come in here and spread her pox to my customers."

Langford smiled. "Very commendable of you, Melody, I'm sure." He paused as if in thought, then said, "The whaling barque *Derwent Hunter* arrived in port two days ago, then tonight Annie Forbes is murdered horribly. It might only be a coincidence, but such happenstances do bear investigation."

"'ere, copper, are you accusing us o' ripping that whore?" This from a big, belligerent-looking Englishman who sat at a table, a bottle of rum in front of him, a blond woman in his arm. "If you are, then speak plain and be goddamned to ye."

An angry chorus of approval ran around the tavern as Langford held up his hands for silence. When he got it, he said, "I'm not accusing anyone. Did any of you notice a small, slight man, dressed like a gent, come in here tonight? He may or may not have had bloodstains on his clothes."

"No, we didn't," Melody said, stepping forward aggressively. "Now put it to rest, Sergeant Langford. These men have been at sea for three years and they have plenty of uses for whores, but a ripping is not one of them."

The woman waited until the roars of ribald laughter receded, then she said, "Now leave my place, Tom Langford, or I'll play my bagpipes and drive you out." She turned to the girl on the bar. "Fannie, my pipes, girl. I'll give these gentlemen a skirl they'll never forget."

"Such drastic measures won't be necessary, Miss

Cord. Sergeant Langford has been circumspect and has accused no one."

Langford and Tone's eyes met. A small, slight man dressed like a gent had stepped into the middle of the tavern floor.

He was Luther Penman.

Chapter 25

.

"Before you make any wild accusations, Sergeant Langford, I have not left the tavern since late afternoon," Penman said. "Is that not so, Miss Cord?"

"You've been sitting in the nook over there all night," the woman said. "Aye, I can vouch for that, Mr. Penman."

"I do enjoy the Jolly Jack," the lawyer said. "It's a quieter spot than most and I can sit and drink tea and pore over my lawbooks without being unduly disturbed."

His eyes moved to Tone, who had expected to read hostility in them. Instead the man's gaze was mild, without judgment. "How pleasant it is to see you again, Mr. Tone. We've all been quite worried about you."

"I no longer work for Sprague," Tone said.

"Yes, so I heard. What a pity."

Tone struggled to get a read on that last sentence. He decided Penman hadn't spoken out of sympathy. It had been an implied threat.

Langford had been studying the little lawyer closely,

his probing eyes ranging over the man's clothes from his shoes to his shirt collar.

Penman had noticed and was smiling almost imperceptibly. "Can I interest you gentlemen in a dish of tea?" he asked.

Tone was about to refuse, but Langford said, "Yes. I'd like to talk with you."

"About this evening?"

"And other things."

Penman gave a little bow. "I'm at your service, Sergeant. And I have some news to impart that might be of interest to you."

The lawyer led the way to a dark inglenook to one side of the fireplace. The space had been enlarged to accept a small table and bench seats and was enclosed by high timber panels on three sides, providing a measure of privacy.

A candle burned on the table, beside a mutton roast, a dish of boiled potatoes and a gravy boat.

After Langford and Tone were settled, Penman beckoned to Melody Cord. "Tea for three, Miss Cord, if you please."

He smiled at Tone and the cop in turn. "Now, if you will excuse me, I'll finish my dinner as we talk." The smile grew into a death's head grin. "I assure you, gentlemen, I don't speak with my mouth full."

The lawyer picked up a knife and deftly carved slices of greasy mutton, handling the gleaming blade with practiced assurance.

Both Tone and Langford watched with fascinated attention, their eyes fixed on the fat-smeared knife.

Then Tone noticed something that would trouble him later.

Penman was a fastidious little man who was always immaculately groomed, yet the fingernails of his right hand were rimmed with half-moons of what looked like dirt.

For a moment Tone puzzled over that, but Langford's voice pushed it from his mind.

"What time did you arrive at the Jolly Jack, Penman?" he asked.

The lawyer chewed on mutton, swallowed, then answered, "Around four this afternoon, and I've been here ever since."

"Poring over lawbooks and drinking tea?"

"Yes, just that, Sergeant."

"I don't see any books on the table."

"No, you don't." Penman reached beside him and held up a thick tome. "I moved them when dinner arrived. This volume is Mr. Thomas M. Cooley's *The General Principles of Constitutional Law in the United States.* Would you like to quiz me on it, Sergeant Langford?"

The big cop drew back and tried a different tack. "Are you still working for Lambert Sprague?"

"I am still retained by Mr. Sprague as his attorney and business manager, yes."

"Last night Tone here saw him throw a bomb through the window of Joe Carpenter's saloon. What does your client say about that?"

Penman deftly cut a few more slices of mutton, spooned potatoes onto his plate, then covered everything with steaming gravy that pooled thickly on the meat.

"Mr. Tone is mistaken. Mr. Sprague was at home all night, entertaining a young lady. A dozen witnesses who were in his house at the time will testify to that fact."

"Tone is willing to testify that he watched Sprague toss the bomb."

For a moment Penman chewed thoughtfully, his jaw muscles bunching. Finally he looked at Tone and said, "Be circumspect, Mr. Tone. The accusations you hurl at my client could come back to haunt you in the witness stand. The jury would soon realize that you possess neither honesty nor integrity. How can a man who makes his living as a bounty hunter, a frontier gunman and murderous thug convince eight stalwart citizens of his honesty?

"As for integrity, well, we all know by now that you tried to convince Mr. Sprague to bomb a rival's place of business. As a result, he threw you out on the street. Enraged, filled with an insane desire for vengeance, you bombed Mr. Carpenter's saloon, then tried to pin the blame on your former employer. Where is the integrity in that? I wonder.

"Mr. Tone, if I got you on the stand I would chop you up into little pieces and feed you to the wolves."

Penman beamed. "Ah, here is Miss Cord with the tea at last."

Melody set the tray on the table, moving aside the mutton roast platter to make room.

"Miss Cord, do you still say I was in this fine establishment the whole evening?" Penman asked.

"Aye, I do," the woman answered. "You spend so much time here, I'm thinking of calling you Jolly Jack."

"Ah, Jack. Yes, Miss Cord, it would be an honor. For some reason, it's a name I've always liked." He looked at Tone. "Milk and sugar? No? Then I'll just pour tea for you and you can make a trial of it. Sergeant Langford?"

"As it comes."

Tone glanced at his steaming cup, fighting down the urge to reach across and wring Penman's scrawny neck. But he admitted to himself the man was right. A jury would never convict Sprague on his testimony.

He decided to take a small measure of revenge by needling the man. "Penman, you hate women, all women, don't you? Especially whores."

The lawyer shrugged. "'Hate' is a strong word, Mr. Tone. Please be circumspect of speech. I don't like women very much, that is true. I consider them dirty. Any creature that bleeds once a month is an unclean thing."

"Did you know Annie Forbes?" Tone asked.

"No, I never met the lady."

Langford said, "She was the whore who was murdered tonight."

"Yes, I know. Hasn't Miss Cord already alluded to the state of the young lady's health? She had the pox. Such a woman would not be allowed to frequent the Jolly Jack."

The cop pushed away his untouched tea. "You said you had news for us, Penman." He sounded tired, the candlelight casting blue shadows under his eyes and in the hollows of his cheeks.

"Good news, if I may say so." He wiped grease off his lips with a napkin. "Ah, that was an excellent loin of mutton."

"Let's hear your news," Tone said impatiently.

"Sergeant Langford," Penman said, pointedly ignoring Tone, "there will be no war along the Barbary Coast, if such was ever seriously contemplated." He paused dramatically, then added, "Mr. Sprague is extending

the hand of friendship to his fellow businessmen and
hopes that they will accept it most warmly."

"And what brought this miracle about?" the cop
said with a noticeable lack of enthusiasm.

"Miracle indeed, sir!" Penman exclaimed. "My client
is an intelligent man and he realizes just how destruc-
tive a trade war would be for the waterfront. After the
bomb blast at Mr. Carpenter's establishment where so
many were killed and injured, Mr. Sprague decided
that rather than imperil more lives, he would seek a
peace with his five competitors."

The lawyer smiled. "After all, on any given night
you just have to look around Pacific Street and realize
that there's plenty of business for all. As he said to me
only this morning, 'One doesn't have to resort to violence to extract money from another man's pocket.'"

"How does he figure to pull this off, Penman?"

"Through intermediaries, he is sending invitations
to his colleagues, asking that they meet at his house on
a given date. The exact whereabouts of the five men are
not known to Mr. Sprague at this time, but his ambas-
sadors will find them."

"When will this meeting take place?" Langford asked.

"Well, of course, I can't give you an exact date, but it
will be soon. Within a few days, I would say."

"Keep me informed, Penman. I'll have a police presence at Sprague's house."

"Not necessary, Sergeant. This is a peace conference.
I assure you, there will be no violence."

"Still, I'd like to keep an eye on things."

"As you wish, Sergeant. Your officers will be most
welcome."

Langford slid out of the booth and got to his feet. Tone did the same and stood beside him.

Penman's dead eyes lifted to the cop. "The bombing of the Bucket of Blood was a great tragedy." His eyes shifted to Tone, then back to Langford. "I hope you deal with the person responsible very soon."

"I plan to," Langford said. "Very soon."

He said no more, letting that statement lie between him and the lawyer like a duelist's glove.

As they turned to leave, Tone stopped and turned back to the table. "Women aren't unclean, Penman," he said. "It's men who think of them the way you do who are dirty."

He didn't stop to hear the lawyer's response but followed Langford to the door and out into the foggy street.

Chapter 26

Sergeant Langford was waiting for Tone outside. "I want to go talk to the detectives," he said. "See if they've learned anything, though somehow I doubt it."

Then Tone remembered.

"Penman had dirt under the fingernails of his right hand," he said. "He's a fastidious little man and a thing like that is out of character for him."

"Is he left- or right-handed, do you know?"

"Right, I think. He carved his meat with his right hand."

"Penman was rooting around in mutton gravy," Langford said. "It would be easy to get some under his nails."

Tone made no answer, and the cop said, "Still, it's something to think about. It could have been blood, huh?"

"Yes, it could have been," Tone said.

The detective in charge of the murder investigation was an earnest young man who looked hot and uncomfortable in a high celluloid collar and tie.

"Find anything?" Langford asked.

The detective shook his head. "Not a thing. This will go into the records as just another routine prostitute murder. My investigation begins and ends right here."

"I wonder if Annie Forbes thought her death was routine?" Tone asked, irritated.

The young cop looked at him. "Who the hell are you?"

"A friend of mine," Langford said, a hard edge in his voice that warned, "Lay off."

"I can tell you one thing, Sergeant," the detective said, now seemingly anxious to please. "She was strangled before she was cut. She has severe bruises on her neck."

"Would that explain the lack of blood?" Langford asked.

The detective nodded. "Sure. When the heart stops, the blood quits pumping."

"You'll tell me if you come up with anything else," Langford said.

"Of course. But right now I'm investigating a dozen cases, and this one isn't high on my list."

After he and Langford left the alley, Tone said, "That detective feller really burned me."

The sergeant smiled. "Don't blame him. There's too much crime in San Francisco and too few cops. That young man is underpaid and overworked and he's doing the best he can. And he's right. A murdered whore doesn't keep the chief of police awake o' nights."

"Why didn't you mention Penman to him?"

"No point in that. The man has a cast-iron alibi. He was in the Jolly Jack drinking tea when Annie Forbes was murdered. Melody Cord and a bunch of others will swear to that."

"I think Penman did it," Tone said. "He's a sodomite who hates all women with a passion."

"So tell me, how the hell did he leave the tavern without anyone seeing him?"

"I don't know."

"Well, when you do know, we'll talk of this again," Langford snapped.

The big cop was clearly on edge, so Tone closed his mouth, letting him be.

The rest of the evening was taken up by what passed for routine police work on the Barbary Coast.

At the Eureka dance hall two whores, the Galloping Cow and Little Josie Dupree, got into it over the affections of an inebriated whaler. Her talking done, the Galloping Cow, just as drunk as the whaler, summed matters up when she produced a .22-caliber pepperpot and cut loose at Little Josie, missing her with all six shots.

Langford gave the Cow a stern warning and hinted darkly of three days in the calaboose if the offense was ever repeated.

Over at the Last Chance Saloon, a female gambler name Darkie Rose accused fellow cardsharp Banjo Billy Bates of cheating, whereupon the incensed Billy tried to brain her with a whiskey bottle, empty, of course. He swung, missed, and smashed the bottle over the head of a rube who was sitting at the gaming table. However, the rube was a big farm boy who proceeded to pound Billy into a pulp.

Sergeant Langford ended the fracas when he buffaloed the large and enraged lad with his revolver. But the farm boy had a hard head and quickly regained consciousness. After a stern warning from the sergeant, the relieved rube ordered rum punches all round and everyone sang "For He's a Jolly Good Fellow," including Langford and the battered and groggy Banjo Billy.

A person or persons unknown took a potshot at a streetlamp, but no damage was done, and a ferocious dog was reported in an alley off Pacific Street. Tone and Langford investigated, but the aggressive canine was not found.

Two cabs collided in the fog and the drivers argued about whose fault it was and then decided to settle the dispute with fisticuffs. Langford intervened and sent them on their way.

A total of six persons were rolled and robbed. There were eight assaults, one a razor cutting that was serious enough to require hospitalization for the victim and jail for the assailant. Someone stole a walnut ladder-backed chair from in front of Solomon Levy's used clothing store, but despite a thorough investigation by Langford and Tone, neither the chair nor the thief was located.

As dawn broke and Tone and Langford wearily made their way home, the cop declared that apart from the ripping, it had been a quiet sort of night.

Chapter 27

Events escalated the following evening after the Ripper claimed his second victim and Tone was forced to kill a man.

"How it came up, Tone and myself were on routine patrol along the waterfront when the second whore was murdered, then an attempt was made on Mr. Tone's life," Langford told his superior, an inspector named Muldoon.

"Why was a civilian on patrol with an officer of the San Francisco Police Department?" Muldoon asked suspiciously. He looked at the sergeant. "Good coffee, by the way."

"Thank you, sir," Langford said. "Mr. Tone is seriously thinking of joining the department out of a burning desire to reduce crime along the waterfront and I was showing him the ropes."

"What? Is he nuts?"

"No, sir, he wants to dedicate his life to law enforcement."

It was a small lie, or at least a gross exaggeration, but it got him over the hump because Muldoon nodded, squirmed to get more comfortable in Langford's kitchen chair, then said, "Go on."

"Just after eleven o'clock last night, Tone and me were proceeding down Pacific Street when I ascertained that there was a disturbance in an alley between the Dew Drop Inn and Lo San's Chinese laundry.

"Upon arriving at the alley we were informed that a woman had been murdered in her residence. She lived in a shack in a backstreet running parallel to Pacific Street that the locals call Pisser's Alley."

"I know Pisser's Alley," Muldoon said. "I investigated a murder there when I was a young officer, oh, about a hundred years ago." He smiled. "Please continue, Sergeant."

Langford poured more coffee for Tone and the inspector, then said, "The murder was reported by the dead woman's friend, a sometime whore who goes by the name of Peggy French. She led us to the residence and we proceeded inside.

"The woman had given her child into the care of French while she entertained a gentleman caller, so she was alone in the one-roomed shack. She was lying in bed near the stove and was partially naked. As in the previous case, her throat had been severed by two cuts and her abdomen had been slashed open by a long, jagged wound.

"A message had been left in red chalk on the wall over the bed. I wrote it down in my notebook just as it appeared."

Langford pushed the open book across the table. He had neatly copied the words:

The coppers are the boys who won't buckle me

Muldoon pushed the notebook back to Langford and said, "Before I left the precinct to come here, I was told that the victim's left kidney and part of her uterus had been removed."

"I didn't know that, sir," Langford said. He consulted his notebook, flipping up pages until he came to the one he wanted. "The dead woman was a whore by profession, and her name was Elizabeth Jones, but she was known on the street by the alias Jonesy.

"After Mr. Tone saw the body, he ascertained that she was the same woman who had solicited him outside her residence the night before by pulling up her skirt and acting in a lewd and offensive manner."

"Why were you in Pisser's Alley the night before, Tone?" Muldoon asked.

"Mr. Tone was—"

"Let the man answer for himself, Sergeant."

Tone helped himself to a cigar. Outside, the morning was growing brighter and birds were singing in the elm tree in the front yard of Langford's house. He lit the cigar, willing himself to stay awake. He hoped that Muldoon would cut his visit short.

"After the first murder, a witness said he saw a small, slight man run into Pisser's Alley. Sergeant Langford asked me to investigate and I did, but saw nothing."

"That's when you were solicited by the recently deceased?" This from Langford.

"Yes."

"And naturally, you turned her down?" Muldoon asked.

Tone nodded. "She was a fifty-cent whore with a child clinging to her skirt. What would you have done, Inspector?"

Muldoon was lost for words for a moment, then he said finally, "I have no doubt that Elizabeth What's-her-name is the second Ripper victim."

Tone saw Langford wince. "Yes, she was murdered by the same . . . perpetrator," he said.

"It's a bad business, Sergeant," Muldoon said. "The newspapers are already jumping on the story. Did you see the *Morning Chronicle*'s front-page headline? 'The Ripper Strikes Again.' We have to catch this lunatic, Sergeant Langford, and soon. The mayor and more than a few aldermen have commercial interests along the waterfront and a mad ripper on the loose could be bad for business."

"I am pursuing several leads and will continue with my inquiries," Langford lied easily. "I am confident I will have the perpetrator in custody very soon."

"I trust so, Sergeant. As I said, this is bad for business—very bad." He looked at Tone. "Now, to the other matter at hand, the shooting of "—it was Muldoon's turn to consult his notebook—"Silas Pickett, by one John Tone, age thirty-seven, of no fixed abode. Occupation, laborer." There was not a great deal of friendliness in the inspector's eyes. "Enlighten me, especially since the killing was done while said John Tone was in the company of a San Francisco sergeant of police."

"What did you find out about Pickett, Inspector?" Langford asked.

Muldoon consulted his notebook again. "He was a

seafaring man, but for the past few years has worked as a runner, shanghaiing sailors for the New York and Boston ships. He was twenty-nine years of age, unmarried, and was named as a suspect in several murders but never prosecuted. He was reputed to have been a crack shot with the revolver and ... well, that's all I have on him at the moment."

Langford nodded. "After I posted an officer at the murder scene, I proceeded—"

"I want to hear it from Mr. Tone," Muldoon said.

"As Sergeant Langford was about to say, we returned to Pacific Street and proceeded to the Jolly Jack tavern to consult with an informant," he said. He was smiling inwardly at his use of the word "proceeded." It seemed that coppers never walk, they always proceed. And he recalled Langford's caution about telling senior officers as little as possible, so he played his cards close to his chest.

"The informant was not present and we returned to Pisser's Alley. We were proceeding along the alley in a southerly direction when we came under fire."

"At whom was this fire directed?" Muldoon asked.

"I believe it was directed at me," Tone said.

"Aha! Now, please go on."

"I ascertained that my assailant was hiding in the shadows at the corner of a nearby dwelling and I proceeded to return fire. I saw the man stagger and fall and when we examined him we ascertained that he was already dead."

Tone sat back in his chair, looking at Muldoon. It seemed that all his "proceeding" and "ascertaining" had pleased the inspector greatly, because the man was smiling.

"A clear case of self-defense, wouldn't you say, Sergeant Langford?" he asked.

"Yes, sir, indeed. But Mr. Tone somewhat understates his role in the fight. He stood in the open to engage Pickett, and I have never seen anyone draw and work revolvers with such exquisite accuracy and rapidity. It was splendid work, and Mr. Tone's behavior was exemplary."

"Yes, yes, no doubt," Muldoon said. "But one must wonder why he was targeted in the first place."

"He was with me," Langford said. "That was cause enough."

Muldoon nodded. "Policing the waterfront is a hazardous business." He drained his cup, rose to his feet and collected his cap, swagger stick and gloves. "One more thing, before I leave, Sergeant. A little bird told me that following the bombing of Joseph Carpenter's saloon, the various rogues who between them control eighty percent of the Barbary Coast are planning a peace conference. Have you heard anything to that effect?"

"I have heard that same rumor, yes, and my inquiries are proceeding as to time and location," Langford said, his face straight.

"Good. We can't have more bombings, Sergeant. Bad for business. Peace along the waterfront is desired, both by the mayor and his aldermen. I don't have to tell you that the mayor is nothing if not a generous man. It wouldn't surprise me at all to see promotions all round if the peace talks succeed."

"I'll bear that in mind, sir," Langford said. He stood. "Let me show you to the door, Inspector."

Before he turned to leave, Muldoon said, "Good work, Mr. Tone. Keep it up and you'll be in uniform in no time."

"Thank you," Tone said. Like Langford, he did not even crack a smile.

Chapter 28

The next two nights passed without a Ripper murder and there were no more attempts made on Tone's life. But there was a strange tension along the waterfront, as though it were holding its breath, waiting for something to happen.

On the afternoon of the third day, Tone was wakened by the murmur of voices in Langford's kitchen. He rose, slipped into his pants and shirt and padded to his bedroom door, listening.

Someone, a man, was talking earnestly to the sergeant, but Tone couldn't make out the words. For a moment he thought about returning to bed for another hour's sleep. It was Langford's house and he was entitled to entertain visitors in privacy.

But he decided against it. Some instinct told him that this was no ordinary visitor. Perhaps he was a man with information to impart.

Tone walked to the kitchen and Langford turned when he stepped inside. "Take a seat, Tone," the cop said. "Now you're awake, you should hear this."

After Tone pulled up a chair to the table, Langford waved a hand at the tiny, shabby man sitting opposite him. "This unprepossessing character is Willie Sullivan, alias Wee Willie Winkie, for a reason that will soon become apparent to you."

The sergeant sat back in his chair and glared at Sullivan. "Now speak, thou apparition."

Willie winked. "Is there money in it, Mr. Langford?" He winked again. "I'm getting married, y'see."

"Willie," Langford said, "you've got maybe three teeth, no hair and you smell like a sewer. What woman in her right mind would marry a nasty little rodent like you?"

A wink. Then, "You'll never guess."

"No, I would never guess."

"Dago May."

"Willie, she's a whore, and a looker. Hell, man, she won't marry you."

"Yes, she's a whore, and yes, she's a looker, and yes, she's agreed to marry me. Well, as soon as I've got a hundred dollars." Willie winked, winked again, the second slower and more meaningful. "Dago May knows bed stuff, Mr. Langford, if you catch my drift. There ain't nothing she won't do to make me feel reeeal good."

The man winked. "She says after we get hitched, she'll only charge me half price for every item on the menu an' for some I ain't even sampled yet."

"A hundred dollars is a lot of money to pay for information, Willie."

"I don't need the whole hundred, Mr. Langford."

"How much have you got?"

The man dug into the pocket of his ragged coat and spread some crumpled bills and a few coins on the table. He winked. "I'll count it."

It took some time, and Tone and Langford exchanged amused glances as Willie poked at his coins and muttered.

"There, it's done," he said finally. "Eight dollars and fourteen cents."

"You've got a long ways to go, Willie," the sergeant said.

Willie closed a muddy brown eye and tapped the side of his nose with an unwashed finger. "I've got two pieces of information, Mr. Langford. It's valuable stuff."

The sergeant got to his feet. "Stay there, Willie." He looked at Tone. "There's coffee in the pot."

"What about him?" Tone asked, nodding to Willie.

"Hell, no, he's not drinking from one of my cups. You want to catch a disease?"

Tone poured himself coffee and sat at the table again.

"Mr. Langford likes me," Willie said. "I tell him stuff." He winked. "Last year, I was the cove who told him it was Fat Freddie Ferguson who stuck a chiv in that Swedish preacher gal and robbed her. Fat Freddie got topped a month later."

Tone smiled. "Very commendable of you, Willie."

The man winked. "Me, I know a lot of good stuff that happens along the waterfront. I've got all kinds of stories to tell."

Langford returned carrying a small tin box. He opened it with a key hanging from his watch chain, lifted the lid and took out a double eagle.

Placing the coin on the table in front of him, the sergeant said, "This for your information, Willie. If I think it's worth it."

"For half, Mr. Langford, beggin' your pardon," Willie said. He winked. "I have two stories to tell."

The big cop shook his head. "You really are a disagreeable little shit, Willie. I'm only a police sergeant and you know I don't make much money."

"Times are hard all over, Mr. Langford. Information doesn't come cheap no more along the Barbary Coast."

Langford sighed. "Let's hear it, Willie."

The little man winked. "I know where the peace meeting is to be held, the big one, atween them as runs the waterfront. And I know the time." Willie looked at the gleaming gold coin and touched his top lip with the tip of his tongue. "Six men, Mr. Langford, one of them Captain High-and-Mighty Lambert Sprague, who never gave a poor cove like me a nickel in his life."

"How do you know about the meeting, Willie?" Tone asked.

"Dago May is one of the whores Captain Sprague has hired to provide the entertainment after the business is done." He winked. "A baker's dozen whores for six men. That's a lot of ass."

"Where and when, Willie?" Langford asked.

"Not tonight at seven. The night after that. At Captain Sprague's house."

Langford put a forefinger on the double eagle and pushed it toward Willie. When the little man reached for it, he pulled it back. "Now, your other information."

"Cost you one more o' them eagles."

"This is all you get, Willie. I'm a poor man."

Willie Sullivan rubbed his scaly mouth, then said,

"Have you a bait o' whiskey? To wet me voice pipe, like."

Langford looked hard at the man, then rose to his feet. He opened a cupboard door and found an unopened pint of bourbon.

Tone smiled as the sergeant looked around frantically, sick with the notion that he'd have to give Willie a glass. Finally he set the bottle in front of the man and said, "Keep it."

"And a cigar. I'm partial to a good cigar." He winked. "An' I know you only smoke the best."

"Willie," the big cop said, his strained patience thinning his voice, "I don't think you're going to walk out of here with your balls intact. You'll be no good to Dago May then."

"Ah, Mr. Langford, you're a hard man, an unbending, stark officer of the law, an' no mistake." Willie winked. "The cigar?"

Grinning, Tone played peacekeeper and gave him a cigar.

"Light?" the little man asked.

Langford growled as he watched Tone thumb match into flame. Willie sat back, luxuriously wreathed in smoke, and opened the bottle. He drank deep, wiped his mouth with the back of his hand, burped loudly, then said, "It's sailor talk."

"Let's hear it," the sergeant grunted.

"Push the coin closer to me, Mr. Langford, if you please."

Cursing under his breath, the cop did as he was told.

"There's been talk among the seafaring men in the grog shops that Captain Sprague and his pirate rogues sank a ship with all hands off the Golden Gate. I heard that the good cap'n gave her a broadside, then boarded an' cut the throat of every jack on board."

Tone couldn't remember seeing cannons on Sprague's steam yacht, unless they were covered up somehow. He looked at Langford, but the big cop was sitting forward on his chair, interested.

"There were no survivors, Willie," he said.

"Ah, so you say. But maybe there was. Could it be that a certain whaling barque found a man floating in the water on a spar, more dead than alive? Could it be that the barque then lost the wind and was becalmed for three days and the jacks wanted to throw the man back into the sea for a Jonah?"

Willie drank again. "But could it be that the wind finally picked up and they brought the matelot into the port o' San Francisco and that he now lies at death's door in St. Mary's Hospital, raving about pirates and"— Willie hurriedly crossed himself—"being tended day and night by the holy Sisters of Mercy?"

Langford shoved the double eagle toward Willie and he quickly scooped it up.

"I know his name," Willie said slyly, winking. "Cost you, though."

"Willie, you're stinking up my kitchen, drinking my whiskey and smoking my cigars and I'm seriously thinking of killing you." Langford smiled. "If I were you, I'd give me his name."

"Bandy Evans, Mr. Langford, and be damned to ye fer a hard case."

The sergeant rose to his feet. "Get out of here, Willie."

The little man shuffled to the door in his laceless shoes, the dirty old army greatcoat he wore trailing on the floor as he walked.

"Give my regards to the future Mrs. Sullivan," Tone said after him.

Willie winked and nodded. "Thank'ee kindly, sir." He glared at Langford. "It's nice to know that at least somebody in this house is a proper gent."

"Get dressed, Tone," Langford said after Willie was gone. "We have to get to the hospital right away."

"The whaler has been in port for days," Tone said. "Strange we didn't hear about the survivor until now."

"No, it's not strange. The only law that isn't broken along the waterfront is don't tell the coppers anything. I'm surprised a known snoop like Willie Sullivan has lived this long."

He looked at Tone, a worried expression in his eyes. "If Willie's right, and there's been sailor talk, then Sprague might already know about Bandy Evans, unless he's been too busy setting up his peace meeting. Let's hope that's the case and we're not too late."

Chapter 29

St. Mary's Hospital was a grim five-story building perched at the top of Rincon Hill. Around the hospital sprawled a quiet residential area, now deteriorating into lower-middle-class shabby gentility. The new cable cars had helped make swanky but steep Nob Hill the city's most desirable address for the rich and famous, including tycoons like James Flood, the silver Bonanza King, and the railroad robber baron Leland Stanford.

But St. Mary's, despite its increasingly blighted surroundings, still shone as a beacon of hope for the destitute and dispossessed, and the sisters never turned away anyone in need.

As the day shaded into evening, Tone and Langford took a cab to the bottom of Rincon Hill and walked the rest of the way up its abrupt slope. Above them a broken sky promised rain and the trees that lined the street were alive with wind.

A reception desk stood at the center of a large lobby, manned by a nun who pushed her glasses to the tip of her nose and studied Langford over them as he entered. She was obviously interested at a visit from a police sergeant, less so by Tone, who was dressed like the sailors she admitted for medical treatment of one kind or another just about every night.

Langford stood at the desk and looked down at the nun. "Good evening, Sergeant," she said sweetly. "Is this official business?"

Langford was brusque. "I'm afraid so, ma'am. There's villainy afoot and I hope I'm in time to put a stop to it."

"Oh dear," the nun said. "I must confess, I don't like the sound of that."

"We're here to visit a seafaring man named Bandy Evans, Sister," Tone said. "He was brought here a few days ago."

The nun was old, wrinkled, with the glowing yellow cast to her skin possessed by the saintly who have spent much time around smoking candles.

"We have many seafaring men brought to St. Mary's," she said. "Let me take a look in the ledger."

The sister pulled a thick canvas-bound book in front of her and began to flip through the pages, starting at the most recent admittance, then working back.

"Ah yes, here he is, poor soul. Mr. Evans was brought in by Captain Saul Tanner of the whaling barque *Derwent Hunter*. The patient was suffering from exposure, dehydration and a fractured left tibia."

"What's that?" Langford asked. Impatience was clearly gnawing at the man.

"Shinbone," Tone said.

"Then why couldn't she just say that, for God's sake?"

"She's a nurse." Tone smiled. "Nurses say 'tibia.'"

Langford glared at the nun. "Where is Evans? We have to see him right now."

The nun consulted the ledger again. "Because of the seriousness of his condition, he's in a private room." She nodded to her left. "Along that corridor to the very end. Room 20."

"When did someone last check on him?" Langford asked.

"Why, bless you, not more than an hour ago."

"Good, then he's still here and alive."

"Sergeant, because of Mr. Evans' condition, I can only allow you ten minutes."

"Ma'am," Langford said, "he's coming with us."

"I can't permit that—" the nun began. But she was talking to the sergeant's retreating back. The old lady rose to her feet and tottered down the hallway directly behind her. "Mother Superior!" she shrieked. "Murder!"

"This is the room," Langford said when he reached the end of the corridor. He opened the door and stepped inside. Tone followed him.

The room was small and clean and smelled of carbolic acid, soap and the sickness of the man on the iron cot.

Langford stepped to his side while Tone took up a position near the corner where he could cover the door with his Colts.

He heard the cop say, "Evans, wake up," and the cot creaked as he shook the sailor's shoulder.

"Go away," the man on the bed whispered. "I'm sick."

"You'll be worse than sick if you don't come with us," Langford said. "You'll be dead."

Tone looked at Evans and saw the man shake his head. "I can't. Go . . . go away."

The door burst open and Tone was reaching for his guns until he saw it was a nun, stiff, starched and boiling mad.

"What do you two think you're doing?" she demanded. "I'm the mother superior and chief nurse of this hospital."

"This man is going with me," Langford answered. "It's the only way we can save his life."

"He is getting the best medical attention St. Mary's can provide," the sister said, her eyes ablaze with blue fire.

"Sister," the sergeant said, "I'm not talking about medical attention, I'm talking about pirates, black-hearted rogues who will stop at nothing to silence this man's tongue."

The nun threw up her hands in disgust. "What in God's holy name do you mean, man?"

Tone saw Langford fight a battle to contain his always hair-triggered temper. "Mother Superior, Nurse, whatever you're called, if Bandy Evans is not taken from this hospital now, he'll soon be killed, and you will be burying dead nuns."

The sister opened her mouth to speak, but Langford held up a silencing hand. "This man can put a noose around a pirate rascal's neck. Depend on it, when the pirate and his scoundrels come for him your habit won't save you. These are hard, violent men who have made great sport with nuns in the past and they won't hesitate to do it again."

"Sergeant Langford speaks the truth, Sister," Tone said. "They'll come here for Evans and they'll kill to get him."

"Damn it, ma'am," Langford yelled, "murder and

rape are not pretty words, but that's what you're facing if I don't get Bandy Evans out of here."

The nun had gone from angry to thoroughly frightened. "But—but what if the pirates—I mean, what am I to tell them?"

"You will tell them that Evans is now in the custody of Sergeant Thomas Langford, and if they want him, they should come get him. Sergeant Thomas Langford of the San Francisco Police Department. Will you remember that?"

"I'll remember."

"In the meantime, I'll try to convince my superiors to post some officers at St. Mary's until this is over," Langford said. "But the force is stretched mighty thin and I can't guarantee it."

The nun had regained some of her composure. "I recently read *Treasure Island* by Mr. Stevenson and I was of the opinion that pirates were now the stuff of sensational novels and history. I can see I was wrong."

"Yes, you are wrong—more's the pity," Langford said. "The black flag still flies, as many a dead sailor lad could testify, and the California coast has its share of them, damned carrion dogs that they are."

He looked closely at the nun. "Can he walk?"

She shook her head. "That's out of the question. Mr. Evans has a broken leg and he's still very weak."

"We'll have to carry him, Tone," the sergeant said. "To the bottom of the hill and we'll get a cab from there."

"Where are we taking him?" Tone asked.

"To my house. He'll be safer there since one of us will always be on guard."

"Why don't we take him to your police precinct?"

"Ha!" Langford exclaimed. "Those thick-skulled oafs would stick him in a cold cell and he'd be dead within hours. No, we'll keep him alive at least long enough to take his statement, then we'll get Inspector Muldoon in to witness it."

The big cop smiled. "I think we've got Sprague by the balls, Tone." He turned to the nun. "Oh, begging your pardon, Sister."

"I've heard the word before, Mr. Langford, and worse."

The sergeant gleefully rubbed his hands together. "Even Captain Sprague's slick lawyer won't get him out of this."

"Unless Sprague kills us all," Tone said.

Langford shook his head and grinned. "You Irish are such sunny, optimistic folk."

"I know, and we get premonitions of disaster too."

"Do you have one o' them now?"

"Sergeant Langford, pretty soon I think we're going to see the elephant," Tone said.

Chapter 30

Between them, Tone and Langford carried the blanket-wrapped Evans into the street. The man was small and light, but their way down Rincon Hill was slowed by the steepness of the grade and the slick sidewalk underfoot.

A light drizzle was falling and the sky was as black as ink. Lightning throbbed in the clouds to the north and a rising wind tossed the tree branches, throwing sudden cascades of rain against the three men.

Evans' head rolled and he groaned deep in his throat and Langford was alarmed. He glared at the man in his arms and growled, "I swear, if you die on me, I'll kill you."

He turned his head and looked at Tone. "Do you remember any of that stuff the nun told us about his care and feeding?"

Tone shook his head. "I wasn't listening. I thought you were."

"Hell no, I didn't pay any heed to that stuff." Langford was quiet for a while, then said, "We'll feed him plenty of beef stew, whiskey and cigars. That's good food for a sick man."

"I recollect that the sister said something about chicken broth, soft-boiled eggs and custard," Tone said, smiling, knowing what the big cop's reaction would be.

He wasn't disappointed.

"Damn your eyes, Tone, we don't have any of that shit!" Langford roared. "He'll eat what we eat."

"Great, then your vittles will kill him quicker'n scat."

Growling under his breath, Langford retreated into a sulky silence and didn't speak again until they flagged down a cab and had Evans safely wedged between them.

"So far, so good," the sergeant said. He glared at Evans. "Just don't die on me, you son of a bitch."

Evans opened his mouth and his breath smelled like death. "Where are you taking me?" he asked weakly.

"To my house," Langford said. "You'll be safe there."

The little seaman managed to raise his head. "Who wants me dead?"

"The men who sank your ship," the sergeant answered. "Now, don't talk and waste what little strength you have left."

Evans turned pleading eyes to Tone. "The pirates are trying to kill me?"

Tone nodded. "I reckon so, Bandy. You're fast running out of room on the dance floor and we're the only chance you've got."

"But . . . but how did they know?"

Langford laughed. "Hell, man, by this time the whole damned Barbary Coast knows. You were picked up by whalers and like seafaring men everywhere, after they get a few grogs down 'em they talk."

Still smiling cheerfully, he dug an elbow into Evans' side. "Bandy, you're a good man who can put the hemp around the neck of a blackhearted pirate rogue by the name of Captain Lambert Sprague, hell curse him. He'll try to rub you out for sure."

Evans was in a panic, his face ashen. "I know nothing! I didn't see nothing!"

"Too late, Bandy," the big cop said. "Now just relax and enjoy the drive. You're safe and sound with us." He beamed, put his huge arm around the little sailor's quaking shoulders and hugged him close. "Safe as the snuffbox in your granny's apron, my lad."

Three minutes later, as the cab turned into California Street and the rain began in hammering earnest, the horse was shot down in its traces.

The dying Morgan rolled, kicking, to its right and tipped the cab violently over on its side. The driver was sent sprawling into the street and Tone, Langford and Evans were thrown together in a tangle of arms, legs and curses.

Bullets rattled through the thin wood of the cab's bed, followed by a load of buckshot, and Evans screamed. Tone, a sharp stinging in his calves telling him that he'd been hit in both legs, pushed on the door that was now directly above him.

It refused to budge.

He lay on his back, putting all his weight on Evans and the cursing Langford, and kicked out hard. The door splintered off its hinges and thudded into the street. From somewhere Tone heard a woman scream, then another bullet slammed through the cab.

Standing on Langford, who was cursing even louder, Tone shoved his head though the door opening and looked outside, one of his guns drawn, up and ready in his right fist.

The three would-be assassins were already running, weaving their way through the people on the sidewalk, shoving both men and women to the ground as they stampeded toward a nearby corner.

Tone had no chance for a clear shot. There were too many people about. He watched the men disappear around the corner, then climbed out of the cab.

From inside, Langford roared angrily, "Damn you, Tone! You stood on my nose and broke it!"

Ignoring the enraged sergeant, Tone limped to the cabbie. The man's neck was broken, his gray head lying on the street at an impossible angle, dead as he was ever going to be.

"Tone! Get me the hell out of here!"

After he picked up the cabbie's top hat and placed it on the man's body, Tone stepped back to the overturned hansom, pushing his way through a crowd of chattering gawkers. In the distance he heard a police whistle that was soon answered by another.

He looked into the cab. "You all right, Langford?"

"You stood on my nose, damn it! I think it's broke."

Tone smiled. "Take my hand."

The big cop grabbed Tone's outstretched hand and pulled himself erect. His nose was bloody and his mustache was already stained red.

"How is Evans?" Tone asked.

The little sailor was hunched over in a fetal position, whimpering. Langford was standing on him.

"I think he took some buckshot up the ass," the cop said. "But I'll get rid of it when we get him home." He looked at Tone. "You didn't shoot."

"I was too late. I saw three men running for the corner, but there were a lot of people in between."

"Did you recognize any of them?"

Tone shook his head. Langford stooped, and with one hand pulled Evans erect. He studied the man's pale face and asked, "How badly are you hurt, Bandy?"

"I want to go back to the hospital," the sailor whined. "I always told my ma that I'd die in my bed."

"Did you get shot up the ass?"

"Yes . . . no . . . I don't know. Please, I beg of you, take me back to the nuns."

Langford spoke to Tone. "Help me get him out of here."

As gently as he could, Tone lifted the man clear and leaned him against the bed of the cab. "Here, hold on to the wheel," he said. He looked at the little man. "How are you feeling, Bandy?"

The sailor shook his head, his eyes pained. "You two are going to get me killed," he said. "Take me back to the hospital, matey. I'll take me chances with the pirates."

"It was the pirates who just tried to kill you, Bandy," Tone said. "They missed you, but murdered the cabbie."

Evans saw the man's body for the first time and he groaned. "I always said the *Benton* was a bad-luck ship and now I know it for sure."

"What's going on here?"

Tone turned and saw a policeman walking toward him, another at his heels. Rain drummed on their oilskin capes and the steel studs of their boots thumped on the slick roadway.

Langford, who had extricated himself from the cab, pushed past Tone and glared at the young cop. "Where the hell have you been?" he demanded.

The man's eyes moved to the five-pointed sergeant's star on Langford's chest. "We got here as soon as we could," he said defensively. "We were a ways off when we heard the shooting."

"Then you should have come running," Langford snapped, refusing to be mollified.

"What happened, Sarge?" This from the other officer, a middle-aged man with bulging green eyes and a ragged, pipe-stained mustache.

"We were set upon by assassins, that's what happened," Langford said. "Three damned amateurs, if you ask me. If they'd been professionals we'd all be dead by now."

"The cab driver was killed when the cab turned over," Tone said. "His neck is broken."

The sergeant turned to Evans and felt his shoulders. "Soaked to the skin. He's going to catch his death of cold." He pointed at the younger cop. "You, give me your cape."

With marked reluctance, the cop parted with his cape and Langford draped it over Evans. He turned to the two cops again. "There were three assailants, two firing revolvers, the third a shotgun. I have no description of the men, but you can ask around the crowd and see if anybody got a good look at them."

"You've got a bloody nose, Sarge," the older officer said. "It might be broke."

"Don't you think I already know that?" Langford said testily. "Now, get on with your investigation. You'll need written statements from me and Mr. Tone here. I'll bring those to the station later tonight." He glanced at the dead cabbie. "And get that poor man off the street."

Tone flagged down a cab and they bundled Evans inside. The little sailor didn't look good; he was pale and drawn, his black eyes glazed and unfocused.

As they headed for his house through a pelting rain, Langford looked over Evans to Tone. "That ambush back there, was that what you meant by seeing the elephant?"

Tone shook his head. "We caught a glimpse of it, maybe. I believe there's a lot worse to come."

"I hope you're wrong about that."

"I wish to hell I was," Tone said.

He looked at his legs. Both calves were bloody, but the buckshot had been slowed by the floor of the cab and none of his wounds were deep.

Beside him Evans was whimpering again and Tone told him to shut the hell up.

Chapter 31

"I've only got one spare bed, and that's yours," Langford said. "I'll have to put him in there."

Tone shrugged. "I don't mind. I have a feeling that there's not going to be much sleep for either of us."

They laid Evans on the cot and Langford, fairly gently, covered him up to the chin. The man was wailing about being murdered in his bed, begging to be taken back to St. Mary's and the sisters.

Langford poured a glass of whiskey and pulled a chair up to the bedside. "Drink this, Bandy," he said. "It's good for your nerves, like."

He lifted the whiskey to Evans' mouth and the man drained the glass, then coughed, phlegm rattling in his skinny chest.

The sergeant beamed. "That's the ticket, Bandy. By the way, the buckshot missed your ass, and here's some more good news—later you can have some beef stew and a cigar."

"Eggs . . . ," the man whispered. "Soft-boiled . . . with a bait o' toast and butter."

"Yeah, well, we don't have any o' that," Langford said, rising to his feet. "Stew is good grub and it will put meat on your skinny bones." His smile was about as sincere as the grin of a cobra studying a rabbit. "You sleep now, Bandy, and later you can talk about what you saw the day your ship was pirated."

"Nothing . . . I saw nothing." He groaned. "Oh, God help this poor sailorman."

Langford gave Tone an incline of his head and stepped out of the room. When they were in the kitchen, the sergeant said, "I'm on duty tonight. You'll have to stay with Evans."

Tone nodded, but he wasn't really listening. "Smell something?" he asked.

The sergeant sniffed. "What the hell? Is it Evans?"

But his disgusted expression changed to one of alarm when he saw Tone draw his guns. He sniffed again. "Where is it coming from?"

Tone had already stepped from the kitchen into the hallway. Langford's room lay at the end of the short corridor, the door ajar.

"Did you close that when we left for the hospital?" Tone asked.

Langford shook his head. "I don't remember."

Warily, Tone walked to the door. He lifted his boot and kicked the door hard, then as it banged noisily back and forth, he stepped inside.

"Oh my God," he whispered.

Then Langford was at his side. His horrified eyes moved to the bed.

"Those bastards!" he yelled. "Those blackhearted, murdering bastards!"

Willie Sullivan, his face frozen in his last agonized

scream, lay on his back in the bed. Naked, the little man's thin white body was splashed in blood, and his wrists and ankles were tied to the bedposts. The stench in the room was almost unbearable, like an overflowing outhouse in the sun. The source of the smell was Willie's ripped open belly and the guts that had been piled on his chest.

That had been the last barbaric outrage perpetrated on the body, after he'd lost his ears, eyes and tongue.

Tone remembered the small plaster figurine that had stood on the mantel of the cottage where he'd been raised. Three monkeys sitting in a row, one covering its eyes, another its ears, the last its mouth.

See no evil. . . . Hear no evil. . . . Speak no evil. . . .

Langford stepped past him and picked up the note that had been left on Willie's chest. Without a word he passed it to Tone.

Death to traitors

"Sprague?" Tone asked.

"What do you think?"

"I think it was his doing."

"Willie was followed here and Sprague knew what he had to tell us," Langford said. "While we were at the hospital, they were cutting him."

He looked at Tone. "I was wrong. That street ambush wasn't aimed at us. Willie Sullivan was the target."

"Not like Sprague to bungle it so badly."

"They didn't bungle it. The cab tipped over and they didn't expect that. If it had stayed on its wheels, they would have had clear shots at us."

"Then we were lucky."

Langford nodded. "Lucky, yes." He smiled slightly. "Maybe talking to the nuns put God in our corner. I should try to get back on speaking terms with him after this."

He looked at Willie, a wizened wax figure who had died more horribly than any man deserves.

"My damned bed is ruined. I'll never sleep in it again."

Tone said, "Sprague sure spoiled Willie's wedding plans, didn't he?"

"Yeah," Langford said. "Dago May will be heart-broken."

An hour later, summoned by Langford, detectives arrived, stayed for a while, then left. Willie's body was taken away and some profane scavengers dragged out the sergeant's bedding, declaring that it could be washed and reused.

Through all this, Langford was unusually quiet and seemed lost in thought, his normally good-humored face fixed in a troubled scowl.

After feeding the complaining Evans, who demanded, but didn't get, custard, Tone sat at the kitchen table with Langford. They had opened all the windows in the house, but the smell of Willie's death still lingered.

Neither man felt like eating, so they settled for coffee and cigars.

Langford studied Tone's face and it took him a long time to speak. Finally he did something strangely dramatic. He unpinned the silver star from his coat and laid it on the table. Beside it he placed his revolver and bowie knife.

"This has got to stop, Tone," he said. "And the only way to stop it is to kill Lambert Sprague."

"You'll get no arguments from me," Tone said.

His eyes dropped to the items on the table and Langford read the puzzlement in his eyes, because he said, "I'm not speaking to you as a representative of the San Francisco Police Department. Right now, sitting here, I'm a private citizen."

Tone smiled slightly and said, "I'm not catching your drift, Mr. Langford."

But Langford decided not to explain himself, at least not then. "Earlier I spoke to one of the detectives and told him I wish to have a meeting with Inspector Muldoon. I asked that Muldoon be here tonight around midnight. I'll make sure I'm present."

"To witness Bandy's statement, huh?"

"Yes, just that. And now I have a statement of my own to make, bounty hunter."

That last surprised Tone. It was not unfriendly; rather, Langford said it in a very matter-of-fact voice.

"All right, let's hear it," he said.

"Tomorrow night I want you to go to Sprague's house, before, during or after the meeting, and I want you to kill him. The same for as many of the other five as your guns can reach." Langford managed a thin smile. "How you manage it is up to you, but it's in your line of work."

"That's why you called me bounty hunter."

"Yes. Only there will be no bounty, unless you count my sincere thanks."

Tone's eyes dropped to the star again. "Mr. Langford, you're asking me to commit suicide. Sprague's house will be heavily guarded."

"Yes, it will."

After a silence that lasted a slow minute, Tone said, "I guess it could be done. I don't know exactly how, but it's possible."

"I'll leave that up to you, Tone. But stop Sprague and it's over."

"What about Bandy's testimony?"

"A court case, an expensive lawyer, a not guilty verdict. That's also possible. Sprague walks free and resumes his old criminal ways."

Tone was thinking. Absently he said, "I can't shoot my way in. If I could only get inside the house somehow. . . ."

"Will you try?"

Tone looked into Langford's cold eyes, gray as winter mist. "Yes, I'll try. But after I scout the lay of the land I may walk away from it."

"That's fairly spoken. I would ask no more of you."

Langford holstered his gun, shoved the knife into the sheath built into the inside of his tunic and pinned on the badge. He looked at Tone. "What the hell were we just talking about? I've forgotten."

"Me too, Sergeant Langford." Tone grinned. "I guess it couldn't have been too important."

Chapter 32

Langford arrived back at the house in time to greet Inspector Muldoon, who was in a less than convivial mood.

"This better be important, Sergeant," he snapped. "I've got a mountain of paperwork waiting for me back at the station, to say nothing of six—count 'em, six—know-nothing rookies out on patrol."

Muldoon studied Langford's face. "You've had an eventful day, Sergeant. And your nose seems like it's broken. Lucky for you it doesn't spoil your looks. I mean, you being so downright homely to begin with, and all."

"Thank you for the kind words, Inspector," Langford said. "My nose has been broke three times before. A man gets used to it."

Muldoon smiled, removed his gloves and laid them on the table with his hat and swagger stick. "Now, why am I here?"

"I found a survivor from the *Benton*, the freighter pirated by Lambert Sprague."

"We don't know that was the case, Sergeant," Muldoon said.

"A man named Bandy Evans says it was the case. I believe he can identify Sprague as the pirate leader."

Muldoon was thoughtful for a few moments, then asked, "Is this so-called survivor in any way connected to the death of Wee Willie Winkie Sullivan, of hallowed memory?"

"Willie told me where Evans was located, a charity patient at St. Mary's. Tone and me were bringing him back here when we were attacked in the street."

The sergeant's stare moved beyond Muldoon into the hallway. "Sprague's men must have followed Sullivan here, then disemboweled him in my bedroom."

Langford had carefully avoided any mention of the time and place of Sprague's peace meeting, an omission Tone noted and understood.

"You were lucky today," Muldoon offered. When Langford made no answer, he said, "And this Evans fellow, he's here?"

"In my spare bed, Inspector. I want you to hear his statement."

"Before I talk with him, tell me what you know about his miracle escape."

"I don't know much. He was in the water for several days before he was picked up by the whaling barque *Derwent Hunter*, Captain Saul Tanner commanding. It was Tanner who dropped Evans off at the hospital."

Obviously feeling that he was expected to add more, Langford said, "Evans is in poor shape, but he'll survive." He sat back in his chair and looked at Muldoon expectantly.

"All right, let's hear what he has to say," the inspector said.

Tone decided to throw a chip into the pot. "Inspector, as far as I can tell, you don't seem very excited about Bandy Evans."

"I'm not. Again, I don't think we can rely on one man's say-so. How did he recognize Sprague though the smoke and flame of a ship that was sinking under him? Did his days in the water affect his recollection of what happened, and perhaps his sanity? Is he trying to railroad a respectable businessman for reasons of his own?"

Muldoon turned bleak eyes to Langford and then to Tone. "Maybe, when the word goes out that the police have a *Benton* survivor in protective custody, we can scare Sprague into making yet another stupid move."

"Inspector, Sprague doesn't scare worth a damn, and his move against Evans today wasn't stupid. He was just unlucky."

Muldoon smiled. "Good. Then maybe his luck is running out. Now, where do we interview Evans?"

"I'll bring him out here," Langford said.

The sergeant was gone for what seemed a very long while, time enough for Muldoon to comment on the unseasonably wet weather, the rambling roses in his backyard and how the oysters at the Tadich Grill were excellent this time of the year.

The heads of both men turned to look at Langford when he stepped slowly into the kitchen. The big cop's battered face was stricken, his normally quiet hands trembling at his sides.

"Inspector, I've brought you here on a wild-goose

chase," he said. "Bandy Evans won't be giving us any testimony. He's dead. I think every last bone in his body is broken."

Tone jumped to his feet and rushed past Langford. The bedroom was dark and he lit the gas lamp above the fireplace.

Bandy Evans lay on his back, his bulging eyes staring at the ceiling but seeing nothing. His chest looked like it had been crushed by a force so tremendous that a couple of splintered rib bones were sticking through the skin. His head was arched back so far that his prominent Adam's apple looked like it was going to pop out of his throat, and his mouth was black with blood. The unnatural twist to the body told Tone that Evans' back was broken, probably in several places, and the outsides of his upper arms were covered in massive bruises.

"My God, what happened?"

Tone turned and looked at Muldoon. "Inspector, he was hugged to death," he said. "Squeezed to a pulp."

"But, who—"

"The man who came through that window, I'd guess," Tone said. "It wasn't open when we checked on Evans earlier."

He crossed the room to the window and looked outside. "Inspector," he said, "here's how the killer got inside."

A ladder was still propped against the wall, but outside in the shrouded darkness there was no sound and nothing moved but the wind.

Muldoon stepped back to the body. "Who could do that, Tone? I mean, have the strength to crush a man to death?"

"I can take a guess, Inspector. Lambert Sprague employs a giant of a man named Blind Jack. He acts as his personal bodyguard and—"

"Yes, I know," Muldoon said. "Blind Jack is a pirate scoundrel and murderer who should have been hanged years ago." He looked at the broken thing on the bed. "Yes, Jack would have had the strength to do this terrible thing, and he can find his way in the dark like a bat."

Langford came into the room, and Muldoon said, "First Willie Sullivan, now your sailor. It would seem that Sprague is covering his tracks well." He looked at the sergeant and said, without pushing too hard, "One might wish that you'd guarded Evans a little better."

Langford nodded miserably but said nothing.

"Well, what's done is done." Muldoon sighed. "I'll send a detective and later have the body picked up." He smiled, unwilling to sting the sergeant again. "We're making quite a habit of this, are we not? I must remember never to spend the night here."

Langford was not to be cajoled, prodded or coaxed into a lighter mood. A perceptive man, the inspector put a hand on his sergeant's shoulder. "Don't feel bad, Thomas. We're dealing with powerful enemies, and perhaps"—Muldoon struggled to find the right words—"with forces beyond our understanding."

Seeing the confusion on Langford's face, he said, "I walked on your bedroom floor, and every board of it creaks and groans. How could a man as heavy as Blind Jack walk on that noisy floor without alerting Mr. Tone?"

Langford shrugged. "He's light on his feet, I guess."

"Yes, that's a possibility." Muldoon frowned, carefully weighing his words. "Or like the rest of Sprague's bunch, he's in league with the devil."

Tone smiled. "I believe I'll go with light on his feet, Inspector."

Muldoon nodded. "As you wish. But a man doesn't serve twenty years as a police officer in San Francisco without seeing things, evil things, that he can't explain. That creaking floor is one of them."

"Maybe I'm in league with Blind Jack," Tone said. "That would explain it. After all, I was here alone."

"I've considered that already, Mr. Tone," Muldoon said. "I sense recklessness in you, a distant, cold reserve, an inclination to violence certainly, but not evil."

Tone made a little bow. "You flatter me, Inspector."

"None of what I said was meant as a compliment, Mr. Tone."

Muldoon stepped to the bedroom door. "I'll be leaving now, Sergeant Langford," he said. "I'm sure you wish to return to your duties. Tone can handle things here."

After Muldoon left, Langford smiled at Tone. "Recklessness, violence . . . if only he knew what tomorrow night has in store."

Tone returned the sergeant's grin. "I wonder if I can drop the devil with a .38."

Chapter 33

Bandy Evans' body had been removed and Tone was alone in the house.

As the wind hustled around the eaves of the old building he closed his eyes and remembered a cleaner wind, in a more beautiful place. He saw a sea of long grass, swaying gracefully, first one way, then the other, a dance to commemorate the hushed stillness of a prairie that was never still. In the distance, where the lightning gathered, the blue mountains shouldered against the sky and the morning smelled fresh, coming in clean on the breeze, like the first day of creation.

Tone felt a sudden sharp pang of longing for the western lands, where a man could sit his horse and look out and see forever and wonder about his God, who had shaped indifferent matter into such glorious beauty.

His eyes blinked open and he returned to Langford's shabby kitchen and the lingering smell of violent death and its somber handmaiden, the sense of evil that hung in the air like a foul mist.

Tone rose to his feet, coffee cup in hand, and pushed open the window, staring into a night as black as coal, spangled not with stars but with the distant lights of the waterfront.

He turned as three sharp raps beat on the front door. He laid down his cup and slid a revolver from the holsters hung on the back of a chair.

Gun in hand, he stood at the closed door and asked, "Who is there?"

"My name is Lizzie Granger, like that means anything to you."

Without dropping his guard, Tone opened the door.

"Don't look so surprised, Mr. Tone," the woman said. "You're not getting lucky. I'm here to deliver this."

She was small and dark-haired, and possessed pretty brown eyes that peered out from under the brim of a straw boater that was perched atop her curls. She was holding out a long envelope.

Tone took the envelope and saw his name on the front, written in a woman's hand. "Who gave you this?" he asked.

The girl had an impudent grin. "She didn't tell me her name. She just gave me the envelope and told me where to deliver it. 'Give it to Mr. Tone, and no one else,' she said. I figure you have to be Mr. Tone. You look the kind who would know a fancy-got-up lady like her."

The girl waved. "So long, Mr. Tone." Then she turned and walked quickly into the night.

Tone waited until the click-clack of the girl's heels faded before he closed and locked the door and stepped back to the kitchen.

He laid the envelope on the table, then poured himself more coffee. He sat and for a few moments turned the envelope over in his hands. It had probably come from Chastity Christian, perhaps a plea from a lady in distress, designed to lure him into a trap.

Well, there was one way to find out.

Tone opened the envelope.

It contained a single page torn from a Bible. Drawn in black ink on the page was a skull and crossbones, and under that, his name.

Sprague had passed sentence. It was John Tone's time to die.

Tone rose, strapped on his shoulder holsters, and got himself a cigar. He sat at the table again and smoked, thinking.

Langford's house was now a death trap. He couldn't cover the door and every window and the idea of forting up inside a bedroom did not appeal to him. It would take away his freedom of movement.

How many would Sprague send? He knew the answer to that: enough.

And it was only a matter of time before they came calling.

Tone got to his feet and shrugged into his peacoat. He left the page on the table where Langford would see it, then stepped to the back door, a revolver in his hand. The door, badly in need of oil, opened with a loud creak and Tone froze, listening into the night.

He heard nothing but the wind prowling like a cougar among the trees. There were shadows everywhere, dark, mysterious and dangerous, that could suddenly band together and become the shapes of men.

His heartbeat thudding in his ears, Tone followed pavers toward a low picket fence at the rear of the yard.

Even in the gloom, he saw that the garden was well tended, planted with a large variety of desert blossoms and shrubs, bordered by yarrow, iris and red and yellow lupine.

Langford, a hard, unrelenting man who was exposed daily to the filth, degradation and violence of the waterfront, obviously spent time among the flowers for the good of his soul.

Stepping over the fence, Tone found himself in another yard. He melted into the shadows next to a garden shed as he heard roars of anger from the house, followed by the thud of boots and the crash of slamming doors.

Tone smiled slightly. Sprague's gentlemen of fortune had left it too late and were now stumbling around in the dark house, palpitating in every pulse with rage, as they blamed each other for their tardiness.

Getting down on one knee, blanketed by darkness, Tone drew both his guns. No longer the prey, he was now the hunter. His breath coming fast, he watched the house . . . and waited.

Slow minutes ticked by, and then, one by one, rectangles of light appeared in the windows. Tone allowed himself another smile. The idiots were lighting the gas lamps!

A fine rain started to fall and the wind bustled. There was no moon, no stars, only a gunmetal sky that stretched away on all sides forever.

The back door creaked open.

Tone held his breath. A man appeared and was briefly silhouetted against the light of the kitchen. He let the door close behind him and stepped onto the paver path. The iron blade of the cutlass in his right hand gleamed as he walked warily toward the fence.

Rising to his feet, Tone whispered, "Hey, pardner, you brought a sword to a gunfight." He took a step forward, half in shadow, half in the dim light from the house windows. "I guess you're not too familiar with the rules, huh?"

The man froze into an immobile statue. "Mister," he said, his voice a frog croak, "I'm turning around an' weighing anchor. For God's sake, don't shoot a poor sailorman in the back."

He opened his fingers, letting go of the cutlass, and it clanged onto the path. Then he turned and walked back toward the house, stiff and jerky as an automaton, expecting a bullet with every step.

Tone let him go, already changing position. He made his way along the fence and stood behind the trunk of a large live oak, keeping his eye on the kitchen door.

Inside the house, the gas lamps were turned off and once again the building was a rectangular block of inkier darkness against the sky.

The kitchen door creaked. . . . Moments slowly passed. . . . Creaked again.

A hoarse whisper. "Billy, you lay athwart o' me and pay me mind. You others, spread out. If you find Tone bring him to me. By God, I'll hear him squeal. I'll gut him like a hog."

Another man's voice, a grin in the words. "You're square, Jack. You got no lights, but you're square as they come."

"Belay them pretties, and find Tone, damn you, or more than one cove will be cut this night."

Blind Jack's voice, a man who could sense through darkness like a bat.

Tone rubbed the back of his hand across his dry mouth. How many of them were out there?

Then the shadows started to move. . . .

Eight of them at least. Maybe more.

Sprague sent an army, Tone thought to himself. I must be a mighty dangerous hombre.

And he was, that night or any other.

The quiet nerves, muscle and tendon speed and the hand and eye coordination required of a top-rated gunfighter were a gift given to few men, perhaps one in ten thousand or even a hundred thousand. Named men like Hickok, Thompson and Allison were few and rarely encountered. Such men were sudden, sure, dangerous beyond all measure, and best avoided.

Sprague's doomed sailors were just seconds away from finding this out for themselves. And those who survived this night would, years later, wake in the shrieking darkness, eyes wide, hearts clamoring . . . hearing footsteps.

The shadows drifted closer, crouched men, holding revolvers.

Tone stepped out from behind the oak.

His guns hammered out a harsh, rapid staccato, like an iron bedstead being dragged across a rough pine floor. Tone aimed low. He did not want to hit Langford's expensive windows or have his bullets crash through nearby houses.

Screams . . . the sound of falling men, then a wild stampede for the kitchen door.

Men jammed in the doorway as they frantically battled to get into the house, away from the deadly gunfire. Tone, his teeth bared in a snarl, fired into them. A man dropped, then another.

And, as suddenly as it had begun, it was over.

Tone moved again, back to the garden shed. He took time to reload his guns from the loose ammunition in his peacoat pocket, then stood still, heeding the sounds of the night.

Around him sudden lights were showing in nearby houses, and a window opened in an upper story and a man yelled, "Hey, what the hell's going on down there?"

"Police!" Tone called out. "It's all right. Go back inside."

Out in Langford's garden someone groaned in pain. By the kitchen door another coughed, the bubbling hack of a gut-shot man.

Tone waited . . . one minute . . . then another. The lamps in the surrounding houses were being extinguished and a window slammed shut, followed by the click-click of a lock being pushed into place.

He jumped over the fence and walked directly to the kitchen door, stepping over dead men. He lit the gas lamp and went outside again, where elongated rectangles of bluish yellow light stretched across the yard.

It took a while, but he finally located three dead men and two wounded. Blind Jack was not among them. The gut-shot man died as Tone looked down at him. The second wounded man lay with his face in a tangle of yarrow. Tone pushed him over with his foot. The man had a gaping hole in his chest, another in his left shoulder.

He looked up at Tone, his eyes feverish and bright. "Have ye done for me, matey?"

"You can lay to that, sailor."

"Then damn your soul, John Tone. I wish I'd never set eyes on ye."

"Lie quiet," Tone said. "Your time is short."

"I sail along o' Cap'n Sprague," the man said. "He'll see you tangle your feet in your own guts. That's what I'm sayin'."

Tone nodded. "Well, he hasn't done very well so far, has he?"

"Get away from me," the dying man said. "I've got a course to lay I never charted afore, an' I'll be damned if I want you to watch me do it."

Tone glanced toward the now silent house and when he looked back, the sailor was dead.

He prodded the man's still body with his toe and shook his head. This would be the third time in one night that the police had taken dead men from the house at 141 Stuart Lane.

It might not be the last.

Chapter 34

"Mr. Tone, this is getting tedious," Inspector Muldoon said. "Seven dead men carried from this house in one evening is, to say the least, most unusual, and unfortunate to boot."

He looked at Sergeant Langford. "Well, Thomas, what have you got to say for yourself?"

"Those were Sprague's men," Langford said. "Tone was defending himself."

"Yes, I recognized Billy Charbonneau out there with the dead. He was a bad one and he'd been one of Sprague's right-hand men for years."

Muldoon sighed. "I'm going down to the waterfront to speak with Sprague, see if I can get to the bottom of this. He'll deny everything, of course."

"Please give him this, Inspector," Tone said. "Tell him it's from me."

Muldoon looked at the Bible page in his hands. Tone had scored out his name and has substituted "Lambert Sprague."

"He'll know what it means," Tone said.

"I've heard of this, but never seen one before," Muldoon said, looking hard at Tone. "It's given only to those who break the pirate oath."

"I know," Tone said.

"Did you take such an oath, Mr. Tone?"

"I did, before I fully knew what was involved."

Now it was Langford's turn to feel the full force of Muldoon's icy stare. "I must say, Sergeant, for an officer of the law you keep some strange company, Mr. Tone included."

"It's all part of the job, sir," Langford said defiantly. "And I believe John Tone will make a fine police officer one day."

Muldoon was unimpressed. "That remains to be seen, doesn't it? No one knows better than you, Sergeant, that the standards of our department have become very high in recent years."

Langford seemed to consider that a conversation stopper and said nothing.

The inspector seemed to enjoy the pause his words had caused, then said finally, "Well, I'll root out Sprague and perhaps scare him into letting go of this foolish pirate-oath business. And perhaps I can get him to name the date and time of his peace meeting."

Muldoon smiled. "We might be able to work with that, Thomas. Catch all the scoundrels in one place." The smile slipped a couple of notches. "Of course, catching is one thing, charging with a criminal offense is quite another. It seems that when it comes to the police, the entire population of the Barbary Coast is blind, deaf and dumb."

"Indeed, sir," Langford said, his face betraying nothing.

Muldoon sighed again, this time more deeply. "Well, then, I'll be on my way."

"Let me accompany you, sir," Langford said.

"Sergeant, I've worked the waterfront before and I have an escort of two burly officers, so I'll be quite safe." He shook his head. "No, you stay here and keep an eye on Mr. Tone. There's mischief afoot and those brigands could come back in force."

"Muldoon won't find Sprague," Langford said, pouring coffee for him and Tone. "He'll sound the bugle and charge all over the place like Custer at the Little Bighorn and get nowhere. Sprague will be holed up ahead of his meeting tomorrow."

"Tonight," Tone corrected. "It's almost three in the morning."

"Yes . . . tonight." The big cop was silent for a while, thinking. Then he said, "Are we doing the right thing, Tone?"

"You mean are *you* doing the right thing? I plan to kill Sprague, with or without your consent."

"Damn it, man, the law—"

"I care only about one law, and that's the law of survival. I have to kill Sprague before he kills me, simple as that."

Langford was fingering the star on his chest, and Tone said, "Take it off if you want, but on or off, it won't change a thing. A couple of hours ago Sprague came close. Next time he might do a lot better."

"You did well, Tone. Five men dead, shooting in the dark like you did. You burned Sprague real good."

Tone made no answer and the sergeant lifted bleak eyes to his face. "It's the only way, isn't it?"

"Yes, the only way. I kill him, Langford, then you live with it."

"Live with it . . . ordering a man's death. If you think about it, I'm no better than Sprague."

Tone smiled. "I don't need to think about it. On your worst day, you're a better man than he'll ever be. Why should it bother your conscience to kill a rat?"

Langford nodded. "He's a man who deserves killing."

"Then let it go and sleep content."

The sergeant laughed. "On the floor? I don't have a bed any longer." He groaned. "Hell, I'm getting too old for this."

Tone woke as the thin dawn light bladed through the kitchen window. Outside, birds were singing, but the wind drove rain against the glass panes with the sound of a kettledrum.

He pushed the blankets aside and rose to his feet and worked out the kinks in his back. From the parlor Langford's soft snoring provided a homey counterpoint to the rain. The big cop had stretched out between a couple of chairs and seemed comfortable enough.

They'd heard nothing from Inspector Muldoon.

After he put the coffee on to boil, Tone stepped to the window and glanced outside. The garden looked peaceful, the flowers delighting in the rain, and there was nothing to suggest that it was where five men had died in a gunfight a few hours before.

As the coffee boiled, Tone cleaned and oiled his guns, then reloaded. The .38s were double-action revolvers, but by long habit he left an empty chamber under the hammers. If he couldn't do the coming night's work with ten shots, an extra two wouldn't make any difference.

He poured coffee, lit a cigar and relaxed at the kitchen table, allowing the new morning to become one with him and him with it.

Ten minutes later, as Tone was pouring himself a second cup of coffee, someone burst violently through the front door of the house.

Tone grabbed his guns from the table, stuck his cigar in his teeth, and waited.

A few moments later, Inspector Muldoon staggered into the kitchen. Behind him a worried coachman stood in the doorway, wringing his hands.

"I offered to take him to the hospital, but he fair insisted on coming here," the cabbie said. "He'd brook no argument, you can set store by that."

Laying his guns on the table, Tone helped Muldoon into a chair. The front of the inspector's tunic was covered with blood.

"Shotguns," the man whispered, grabbing Tone by the front of his shirt, "up close. Officers Tom Tibbles and Henry Ward . . . both dead."

Suddenly Langford was in the room, holding up his uniform pants with his left hand, his revolver in the other. "In the name of God, Inspector, what happened?"

"I'm done for, Thomas. They've done for me at last."

"What happened?" Langford demanded again.

"I bungled it. Two officers dead because I bungled it."

Langford looked at Tone. "Get him a glass of whiskey."

"No, no whiskey," Muldoon said weakly. "I'm a temperate man."

"It will do you good," the sergeant said. He turned to the agitated cabbie. "Go find a doctor, any doctor, and bring him here. Don't just stand there gaping, man. Go!"

The cabbie touched his hat and quickly left.

Tone put the glass to Muldoon's lips. The inspector drank a little, then coughed and pushed the whiskey away.

"I've sent for a doctor, Inspector," Langford said. "Now tell me what happened."

Tone unbuttoned Muldoon's tunic and the shirt underneath. One look told him all he needed to know. The man had taken a shotgun blast full in the chest and his life was measured in minutes.

"We searched for Sprague for hours," Muldoon said, his eyes already glazing as death stepped closer to him. "Couldn't find him . . . anywhere. His taverns . . . house . . . no one knew anything. 'Gone away,' was all they'd say. Then . . . just before first light, we heard a woman scream in an alley. We investigated . . . three men . . . shotguns . . . fired on us."

Muldoon was struggling to stay alive, but his face was gray and he suddenly looked old. "Woman . . . in a cloak . . . she fired at us. Laughed . . . Thomas, she laughed. . . ."

"Try some more whiskey, Inspector," Tone said.

This time the dying man drank deeply. He managed a pained smile. "Very good. Maybe I should have tried that . . . earlier." He looked at Langford. "Thomas, I crawled out of the alley after . . . they were gone." His eyes took on a wild look. "The devil . . . the woman is the devil . . . cloak . . . laughing . . ."

Muldoon's mind was starting to wander along a misty roadway that led to eternity. He struggled to talk. "Sprague's work . . . didn't want me to get close to . . . to what he's planning. . . ."

He reached out a hand to Langford and the big man took it. "You . . . you're a good officer . . . Thomas. . . . Fine . . . officer . . ."

Then he smiled and died.

Langford held his inspector's hand for a long while, as though trying to help him along the road he had to take. Then he gently laid Muldoon's hand in his lap.

Tone searched his mind for the right words, couldn't find them, and let his silence do his talking. There were tears in Langford's eyes, a strange thing to see in that tough, rough-hewn face.

Finally the sergeant said, his voice thick as molasses, "He was the most useless inspector in the San Francisco Police Department—didn't know his ass from his elbow." He dashed the tears from his eyes with the back of one huge hand. "Rest in peace, Muldoon. My friend."

A young doctor arrived a few minutes later. He could only say what Tone and Langford already knew, that the inspector had died from a shotgun wound. But then he said, "A secondary bullet wound to his left shoulder hastened, but did not cause his death."

Tone was surprised. He had not seen that injury. The doctor pointed it out to him, a round, inflamed hole made by a large-caliber bullet. "I'd guess a .45 or .44," the doctor said, "fired from fairly close range."

Chastity Christian's derringer was a .44. She was the woman in the cloak who had shot Muldoon, then laughed as men died.

Tone vowed to himself that after tonight she would never laugh again.

Chapter 35

Night came to the Barbary Coast and the old round of business, pleasure, folly, vice and violent crime went merrily on.

Already, and still before six o'clock, two Frenchmen got into a duel with rapiers over the favors of a whore. The fight ended with a skewering, a dead man and the sobbing victor dragged off to the calaboose. In the basement of the La Scala Hotel on Drum Street, a man named the Shanghai Chicken, who fancied himself a prizefighter, took on a pugilist by the name of Soapy McAlpine. Before a well-heeled crowd, the Shanghai Chicken was defeated in eighteen rounds. Minus part of his nose and right ear—the other was badly chawed—he later claimed he lost the fight because Soapy landed an illegal low blow that "damn near exploded my balls." But all would have ended peacefully enough had not the Shanghai Chicken's sweetheart, perhaps fretting over possible damage to a part of her lover dear to her, obtained a revolver from behind the bar of the Sailor's Haven tavern and proceeded to demonstrate her annoyance at Soapy by pumping three bullets into his brisket.

As John Tone prepared to leave Langford's house, Soapy was languishing at death's door in St. Mary's Hospital while his unrepentant assailant sat in her police cell and sang the latest hit ballad, "After the Ball," to all who would listen.

"I'll walk with you, Tone," Langford said. He seemed uneasy, a man who was not at peace with himself. "When we reach the waterfront, we'll go our separate ways."

Tone shouldered into his peacoat. "Pity, isn't it, how things work out. We know who the criminals are, what they've done, yet we can't just go and arrest them or rid the city of their shadows permanently."

"It's how the law works."

"I know, and as I said, it's a pity."

"What we face is the scum of the earth, rich enough to hire expensive lawyers and have friends in high places," Langford said. "It's a stacked deck."

"Tonight we'll get rid of one of them, and maybe a lot more," Tone said. "By midnight, Lambert Sprague will be burning in hell."

"It has to be done, Tone. Isn't that right?"

"We've already gone through that. Yes, it has to be done."

Langford tugged at his tunic irritably, his face haggard, fighting his own private war. "Damn, my uniform doesn't fit. It's uncomfortable, like it was made for somebody else."

Smiling slightly, Tone said, "Yeah, and your tin star has lost its luster."

The big sergeant's eyes were bleak. "I'm hurting here. Inside me, something's hurting real bad, like the croup."

"It's called a conscience. All good men have one." Tone pulled on his watch cap. "Walk with me, Thomas."

Tone and Langford parted ways on Pacific Street, where there was now a large police presence following the death of Muldoon. They had spoken little to each other. All the words they might have exchanged had already been said.

The sergeant had contented himself with a handshake and a whispered "Good luck," which Tone had acknowledged with a slight smile and a nod.

Now he made his way toward Sprague's house, walking through a noisy throng of people under a cloud-streaked moon rising slowly in the sky.

Keeping to the shadows, Tone strolled past Sprague's house. The front door was shut and he saw no sign of guards or any other activity. He felt a pang of unease. Had the meeting been cancelled?

Tone walked another fifty yards, then stopped. Across the street an alley was a beckoning rectangle of darkness. There were few people about this far from the waterfront dives, and he sprinted across the road and into the narrow passageway.

After standing still for a few moments for his eyes to become accustomed to the alley's deeper darkness, Tone followed the passage until it fed into a dusty gravel lane. He turned to his left to get behind Sprague's house, his way lit by the waxing moon. Here no tumbledown shacks lined the lane; in their place were large houses with well-cared-for yards that ended in white-washed fences.

Every room in Sprague's house was ablaze with light. Tone stepped over a fence and warily walked closer to the rear of the building, gun in hand. He found a circle of shadow under a tree and studied the windows one by one. Nothing moved behind them. Then a man in a white chef's coat and tall hat appeared at a window to the left of the rear door. He opened the window wide, breathed deeply, and disappeared again.

Tone smiled. If the window stayed open, it would provide his access to the building. But now was not the time. Let the guests arrive and get settled; then he'd make his move.

His eyes searched the house again, hoping for a glimpse of Sprague. But the man was nowhere in sight.

Crossing the street again, Tone took up a position in a doorway where he could cover the front of the building without attracting too much attention.

For an hour, people came and went on the street; then, just as Tone was giving up hope, a cab pulled up to the door and stopped.

Three men got out, two of them making an elaborate show of deferring to the third, a large man with a brutal face and a neck as thick as a ship's hawser. All three were welcomed into Sprague's house by a pretty girl in a maid's uniform and then the cab pulled away.

Over the next ten minutes, all five of Sprague's guests arrived and Tone recognized the banker and slave dealer Edward Hooper, who pulled up in his own private carriage.

He looked up and down the street. There were no

police in sight, since most of them were concentrated in busy Pacific Street. Two Chinese men, bamboo poles over their shoulders, weighted at each end with heavy wicker baskets, were trotting toward him, their faces hidden in the shadow of coolie hats.

Tone ignored the men and plotted his next move. He would return to the lane and then—

The razor-sharp knife edge pressed against his throat numbed Tone's brain into immobility.

"Do not move, Mr. Tone," a Chinese voice whispered in his ear. "You stay away from Sprague house tonight."

The second man stepped in front of Tone and unbuttoned his peacoat. Tone tried to struggle free, but the knife dug deeper. "Very sharp, cut throat real nice," the voice in his ear said again.

The second man removed Tone's guns from their holsters, then raised his head to the moonlight.

Tone recognized the handsome features at once. It was the Tong leader, the man who called himself Weimin.

"Come with me, Mr. Tone," he said. "We must get away from here."

The pressure of the knife edge lessened on his throat enough for Tone to say, "I'm here to kill Lambert Sprague."

Weimin smiled. "Sprague is not at home. We must go now."

Seeing Tone's reluctance, he said, "Why would Lambert Sprague buy half a ton of gunpowder in Chinatown? For fireworks, you think?"

The knife blade scraping against his skin, Tone turned his head and looked at Sprague's house. From inside he heard music and talk and the languid laughter of heavy-lidded whores.

Now the full impact of the danger dawned on John Tone.

"Let's get the hell out of here!" he said.

He and the Chinese men had only gone a few steps when the ticking time bomb that was Sprague's house exploded into thunderous flame.

The force of the blast slammed Tone onto his face and as he lay stunned on the sidewalk, fiery debris rained down on him like molten lava from an erupting volcano. A heavy steel I beam, about ten feet long, torn loose from its mountings, clanged onto the road just inches from his legs. The beam bounced high into the air, then crashed, cartwheeling, through the front window of a house opposite.

Above the roar and crackle of the flames, Tone heard women and children shriek inside the building, then nothing.

He climbed to his feet and looked back. Sprague's house was gone, and the others on each side of it, leaving only blackened, smoking spars of wood on which a few scarlet flames still fluttered.

Weimin, his face blackened by smoke and debris, stepped to Tone's elbow. "No one could have survived the explosion," he said. "They're all dead."

Tone, still numb from shock, nodded to the house opposite, the front window a shattered nightmare of glass and wood. "I saw a steel beam go through—"

"Yes," Weimin said, "I know. I saw it too. That was the front parlor where families gather. We'll find nobody still alive."

In the distance, Tone heard the clamor of fire engines

and saw that there were bodies lying in the street near the destroyed house.

Bitterly he reflected that Sprague had eliminated his five rivals and the fact that he had killed innocent men, women and children in the process would not trouble him in the least. Inside his house, now all dead, had been whores, musicians, waiters, cooks and others trying to earn a rich man's buck. People had been killed in the neighboring homes, and women and children had been slaughtered, scythed by a whirling steel beam in their own parlor.

"Sprague is indeed a formidable adversary, a man without a conscience," Weimin said, as though he'd been reading Tone's thoughts.

Tone nodded. "It's going to take a lot to kill him," he said.

The Chinese man's smile was as brief as a lightning flash. "Yet I will kill him very soon."

Reading the question on Tone's face, Weimin said, "We must leave here." He handed the other man his guns, then added, "Walk with me."

As they headed for Pacific Street, several fire engines passed, bells clanging, their big Percheron drays at full, ponderous gallop. Gaping crowds were already clustered around the blasted buildings and cursing firemen yelled at them to get the hell out of the way. The rain was still falling, turning the cobbled streets into thoroughfares of polished iron.

Walking under the blue cone of a streetlamp, Tone turned to Weimin and said, "I didn't know you had a beef with Sprague."

"I don't, not with him personally. But I am Tong and we are moving to take back what is rightfully ours.

With five of our enemies dead, the time for us to strike is now. Sprague has two choices: Stand, fight and die or run for his life." The man smiled again. "He can always go back to his old profession, piracy on the high seas."

Tone stopped, looking down at Weimin, who seemed small and frail next to his wide-shouldered bulk. "You plan on getting rid of Sprague and taking over the whole waterfront?"

"Yes. At first it was Sprague's plan, now it is the Tong plan."

People jostled past them, and Weimin pushed a reeling drunk away from him. "Mr. Tone, half the whores on the Barbary Coast are Chinese. The opium and slaves that make men like Sprague rich are from China. We Chinese will no longer step back and let white men reap the rewards. If there are Americans along the waterfront who wish to keep their saloons and dance halls, they can do so, but only by paying tribute to the Tong. That is how it will be."

"Do you even know where Sprague is?" Tone asked.

Weimin shook his head. "No, but he will crawl out from under his rock quickly enough when we start to take over his business interests."

Tone looked at the Chinese man. "Right now, Weimin, my fight is with Sprague, not you. But later we could become enemies."

"Better the Tong than Sprague, Mr. Tone. We are only taking back what is rightfully ours."

"You really think you can fight him?"

This time Weimin's smile was genuine. "There are twelve hundred Tong in Chinatown, Mr. Tone. I will bring every one of them here to the waterfront if I have to." He looked into Tone's eyes. "You did me an honorable service not long ago. I would not like it if we became enemies." Weimin looked around him. "We must part ways now. Good luck, Mr. Tone."

Before Weimin turned to leave, Tone said to him, "You saved my life tonight. Your debt to me is settled."

The man smiled and shook his head. "No, I will always be in your debt, Mr. Tone. That is the way of the Tong."

Chapter 36

Whiskey glass in hand, Sergeant Thomas Langford stood back and admired his new mattress. "Beauty, isn't it?" he asked Tone. "Genuine goose down. Look as hard as you like, you won't find a corn shuck in that bed."

"I reckon it's comfortable."

"Sure is, and the salesman said it's good for the rheumatisms. He said Queen Vic sleeps on that very same mattress and she hasn't had an ache or pain in her poor old bones this twenty year." As though he felt remiss, Langford turned to the younger man, flustered. "Of course, I plan on getting one for your bed, just as soon as I have the extra cash."

"No hurry," Tone said. "I've spread my blankets on granite ten thousand feet above the flat, so I don't mind the floor."

Langford sipped his whiskey, then said what he'd been planning to say: "Bad business, Tone. First Sprague blows up his house, killing two dozen innocent people in the process, and now the Tong are moving in all over the waterfront."

A week had passed since Tone had talked with Weimin, and the gang leader was now making good on his threat.

Sprague was being pushed hard. All but one of his late rivals' businesses had been taken over by the Chinese, and they had begun to corner the opium and slave trade. So far there had been only two casualties. The owner of a gin mill on Pacific Street who had objected to paying the Tong protection money was gunned down behind the bar of his saloon. One of Sprague's whores, a woman named Ella Alden, was murdered on Washington Street in broad daylight. It was suspected that it had been a Tong revenge killing, but there were rumors that Sprague himself had ordered the woman's death. Ella's sister had died in the explosion at Sprague's house, and she may have tried to shake down the man by threatening to tell the coppers what she knew.

But the day Langford bought his mattress, the war had come right to Sprague's doorstep.

"The way I heard it," Langford said as he led the way to the kitchen, "Sprague was at the docks, speaking to Wilson Tyler, that captain of his, a man who's sailed under the black flag a time or two, the damned villain."

He watched Tone light a cigar, then said, "The two were deep in conversation when six or seven rifles opened up on them from the top floor of a rooming house. If my sources are correct, a couple of Sprague's men were killed in the first volley and"—Langford

sipped his whiskey, smiling, savoring the moment—
"Sprague got a bullet burn in the shoulder."

Tone slapped the table in front of him. "Damn, I
thought the man was indestructible, bulletproof!"

"So did he, apparently," Langford said. "I'm told
he's back in hiding, nursing his wound, and that the
Chastity Christian woman is caring for him."

"You reckon he's running scared?"

"I'd bet the farm on it. I believe he was talking with
Tyler about making a fast getaway back to his ship if
things suddenly go bad. And they are."

Tone poured whiskey for them both. Outside the
day was shading into evening and a mist was creeping
like a thief into the garden. Somewhere a bird greeted
the arrival of the night and among the flowers small
creatures scurried.

Langford raised his glass, stopped it halfway to his
mouth and said, "Sprague is learning the hard way that
you can scare white men into backing off for a spell, or
for good, but the Tong keep coming at you. The Chinese Exclusion Act of '82 made the Celestials mad as
hell when it took away what little rights they had. Now
they want their slice of the pie and the Tong will give it
to them, for a price."

"Weimin told me the Tong plans on taking over the
entire waterfront," Tone said.

Langford smiled. "Here in San Francisco your friend
Weimin *is* the Tong."

"I'm in his debt. He saved my life."

"Yes, I know." Langford looked out the window,
staring into the gathering darkness. When he'd collected his thoughts, he turned to Tone again. "We let

the Tong get rid of Sprague, then we get rid of the Tong. It's a simple solution to a complex problem."

"No matter what, you're in for a long war."

Langford smiled. "Nothing in this city ever comes easy." He set his glass on the table. "Look at me, Tone. What do you see?"

"Huh?"

"Describe me."

Tone smiled. "I see a tough-looking man wearing a stained old shirt, baggy pants, and"—he bent over in his chair and glanced under the table—"a smelly pair of slippers that should have been thrown out years ago."

"No police uniform in sight?"

"No. Just the rags I described."

"Good. Then talking as Mr. Langford, I think I might know where Sprague is holed up."

Now Tone was interested. "Where?"

"According to my source, and she's reliable maybe half the time, he's taken rooms at the Victory Hotel on Steiner Street. My source says her best friend works at the hotel as a chambermaid and she recognized Sprague and his fancy woman. He's got no more than half a dozen men with him."

Tone nodded. "You want me to go get him . . . Mr. Langford?"

"No. I want you to keep your hands clean on this one. Find your Chinese friend and tell him what I've just told you. Tell him the odds on my information being correct are about fifty-fifty."

"You want me to do it tonight?"

"Is there a better time? Sprague is out of it for now and what men he has left are with him."

Langford pushed his glass away from him. "Damn this rotgut. It makes a man forget things. What the hell were we just talking about?"

Tone smiled and rose to his feet. "The weather, Sergeant."

"Ah yes, the weather. My night off and it's raining hard. Still, I'm glad I'm not out on the street. On rainy nights the wind coming off the bay chills a man to the marrow."

After he was dressed, his guns in place, Tone said, "Langford, I think I'll take a stroll before bed."

"Be careful. The streets can be dangerous at this time of night."

"I'll keep that in mind."

"One other thing, Tone: be careful around Weimin. He's a mighty dangerous man. There's an old Chinese proverb that says you can hardly make a friend in a year, but you can easily offend one in an hour." Langford smiled. "For pity's sake don't offend him. For now at least, we need him."

Tone picked up his glass from the table and drained it, then looked at the big sergeant. "I'll step carefully, but Weimin is all growed up and he doesn't offend worth a damn."

Langford nodded. "I'd say he doesn't scare worth a damn either. That's good for us, bad for Sprague. Get it done, John."

But when Tone left the house and walked into the rain-lashed street, destiny was about to take him in another direction—one that would force him to follow in the footsteps of a monster.

Chapter 37

The rain had swept Pacific Street clear of people, but every drinking den and dance hall was bursting at the seams. Six English clipper ships had come in during the week and were tied up at the docks, leaving their crews with time and money to spend.

A damp, patchy mist hung over the road, drifting in the wind. Rain ticked from the eaves of the waterfront buildings and formed wide puddles on the sidewalks that captured the blue light of the gas lamps.

The collar of his peacoat turned up around his ears, Tone stepped into Murder Alley, but it seemed that even the hardworking Chinese had taken refuge from the rain. The passageway was deserted and its tossing paper lanterns were shredding in the wind-driven downpour.

An old woman opened a door as Tone passed and he stopped and asked after Weimin. The woman shook her head, let go with a torrent of Chinese, then bent and shooed him away from her, as though she was chasing a trespassing rooster.

There were other alleys where brothels and opium dens prospered, and Tone resigned himself to trying each and every one of them.

After an hour, he was ready to give up. Weimin could be anywhere, even back in Chinatown, where it would be impossible to find him.

Irritated by a sense of failure, he retraced his steps along Pacific Street, head bent against the sheeting rain. A man stumbled from a saloon, spotted Tone and staggered directly toward him.

The man bumped into Tone and immediately launched into a string of apologies. "Sorry, Mister, real sorry. Sorry that. I didn't watch where I was headed. . . ."

But his fluttering hands were in constant motion, now and then landing lightly on Tone's chest and hips.

It was the oldest trick in the book, and Langford had once told him how to spot it, even from a distance. The dip's plan was to keep the mark preoccupied with a fast string of patter while his searching hands picked his pocket.

Tone smiled, quickly reached down, grabbed the dip's forefinger and bent it backward. The man squealed and his feet did a little jig on the wet cobbles.

"Does that hurt?" Tone asked.

"Yes! Yes! Damn you, it hurts! Let me go!"

"Sure," Tone said. He bent the finger back until he heard bone snap.

The dip screamed and clutched at his mangled hand. Tone smiled. "Mister, I'm too old a cat to be played with by a kittlin'. Now get the hell out of here or I may take it into my head to break some more of your fingers."

The man cast a single horrified glance at his tall assailant, then lurched back toward the saloon, groaning.

Tone's smile grew as he watched the dip scamper. He didn't like pickpockets. It had served the man right.

His mood considerably lightened, Tone walked along Pacific Street, his eyes searching everywhere, hoping to catch a glimpse of Weimin.

The Tong takeover of the waterfront was not apparent and every dive seemed to be doing business as usual. Drunken sailors lurched from saloon to brothel and back again, bold-eyed whores stood in doorways, welcoming customers, and gaunt, pale-faced addicts patronized the opium dens.

Most of the owners had capitulated easily, deciding that paying protection money to the Tong was better than being forced out of business.

The only holdout seemed to be Sprague, and Tone could spot his establishments easily. They were the ones with a half dozen Chinese *boo how doy*—hatchet men—standing outside their doors, discouraging customers from entering. Judging from the silence in Sprague's saloons, not many had been willing to run that particular gauntlet.

The Tong takeover of the opium and slave trade was even less obvious, but Tone guessed that it was now completely under Chinese control.

He recalled what Langford had said about letting the Tong get rid of Sprague, then routing out the Chinese gangsters. He would have his hands full. The way it was now, with the Tong firmly entrenched along the waterfront, it would take a citywide fire or an earthquake to cleanse the Barbary Coast, and neither was likely to happen.

Tone made one last check of Murder Alley, saw no one, and stepped back to the street. With few people about, a movement to his right caught his eye. He turned and saw a man and a young woman walk into another alley about fifty yards away.

He wasn't sure, but the small, frail-looking man in the long gray coat looked familiar.

Could it have been Luther Penman? With a whore, of all things?

An alarm bell rang in Tone's head. A small, thin man in a gray coat ... the eyewitness's description of the Ripper.

Tone headed toward the alley, his heart thumping in his chest.

Was he about to walk in the tracks of a monster?

Fog had drifted into the alley and, sheltered from the wind, hung in the air like an empty shroud. There were no lights, no sound, only a vast quiet that so unnerved Tone he slowed his pace as he began to clothe every shadow in a coat of gray.

Alert for any noise, he walked to the end of the alley and stopped. There was no sign of Penman, if it had really been him, or the woman.

The cross lane was as he remembered it, the rear walls of Pacific Street buildings to his left, a collection of reeking outhouses and piles of debris of all kinds littering the ground. To his right were the tumbledown shacks of whores, saloon workers and tinhorn gamblers, all of them in darkness.

Tone glanced toward the far end of the lane. A light burned in a shack about a hundred yards away, the pale blue glow of a gas lamp. He walked in that direction, gun in hand.

Gravel crunched under his feet and the rain drove into his face and the darkness around him was inky black. A tiny calico cat glared at him from the shadows and hissed, arching its back, tail puffed in alarm.

Tone walked on, his mouth dry as bone.

There were no curtains in the windows of the shack. He stopped and stepped wide, where he could see inside the house. A woman stood in the middle of the floor and she lifted a small child, then turned her head and as though speaking to someone in another room. A man appeared at the doorway, said something in return, and walked out again.

Penman was not there.

A growing sense of frustration in him, Tone retraced his steps. He had just passed Murder Alley when he saw a window in a shack ahead of him casting a rectangle of lamplight on the wet ground.

There had been no light there a few minutes before.

Tone quickened his pace. He was a few yards from the shack when a noise from inside made him pause . . . a loud cry followed by a long, sighing gasp.

Had it been an outburst of passion—or a shriek of pain?

Tone didn't wait to figure out the answer. He ran for the door of the shack.

The door was locked, but he put his shoulder to it hard and it burst inward, its frail timber splintering.

The room and what it contained hurtled toward Tone, as though he was seeing it from the cab of a speeding locomotive . . . fleeting, vivid, scarlet and white impressions that took time to register on his overwhelmed brain.

A naked woman propped again the wall, slashed wide-open like a gutted deer . . . the woman's crimson-painted mouth agape in her last, frantic scream of agony . . . Luther Penman, bloodied knife in hand, staring at Tone with demented eyes . . . Penman snarling, like a wild beast at bay . . . then . . .

"Wait, Tone, it's not what you think. I was passing by and—"

Suddenly a gun in Penman's hand . . . a shot . . . beside Tone the gas lamp shattered and went out. . . .

Tone fired, fired again, flashes of harsh orange light slamming into the darkness.

The back door crashed open, then slammed shut. . . . The sound of running feet . . .

Taking a moment to turn off the hissing gas, Tone went after Penman, sprinting into the open ground behind the shack. Where was the man?

A bullet split the air beside Tone's right ear. He saw the flare of the gun and fired in that direction. Then he was running again, stumbling around in the littered gloom.

Ahead of him rose the ominous black bulks of several tall warehouses and scattered outbuildings, including one with the sawdust smell of a carpenter's workshop. Beyond the buildings to his right lay Mansion Avenue, its streetlamps winking in the distance, and to his left the back of the waterfront dives.

Gunshots were not rare in this neighborhood, and nobody was paying any attention.

Tone stepped warily, his restless eyes searching the darkness. From somewhere in front of him, a bottle clinked. He stopped. "Penman, you son of a bitch, show yourself!" he yelled. "You're heeled, so let's have this out."

A strange laugh floated into the night like black gossamer. "Everything is going to shit, Mr. Tone. But Jolly Jack is still having fun. If you want me, come looking." A pause, then, "Be circumspect, now. I'm pretty good with a revolver."

Stepping toward the sound of the man's voice, Tone banged his knee on a rusted plate of sheet iron and bent to rub it, cursing.

The stooping motion saved his life.

A bullet whipped through the air where his head had been a moment earlier.

"Did I get you, Mr. Tone?" Penman cackled. "Are you dead, dead, dead, like the filthy whore back there?"

Tone made no answer, crouched behind the plate, probably part of an old ship's hull, and waited for Penman to show himself.

"She smelled, Mr. Tone, like a perfumed fish." A pause, then, "Jaunty Jack still thinks all women are dirty, Mr. Tone, and that their only real purpose is to breed pretty boys." Another moment passed. "Are you dead, Mr. Tone? I'm quite the gentleman, you see, and I shouldn't be talking to the corpse of a low person like you."

Tone made some quick calculations. The warehouses would stop his bullets from reaching the street and he had a fair idea of where Penman was located. It was now or never.

He drew his second revolver, stood up and cut loose. He hammered his guns dry, a rolling thunder that lasted only a couple of seconds. Wreathed in smoke, he waited, listening into the darkness.

A few moments ticked past . . . then came the hollow clap of mocking applause.

"Nah, nah, nah, nah, nah nah! You didn't even come close, Mr. Tone!"

"Penman!" Tone roared, his anger a fearsome thing. "I'm going to tear you apart."

He ran in the lawyer's direction, cursing through teeth clenched in an ungovernable fury . . . and he charged into emptiness.

Luther Penman was gone.

John Tone searched the darkness for thirty minutes before he finally admitted to himself that Penman had made a clean getaway.

He returned to the shack and established that all was as it had been before, only now there was a haunting quiet that only the presence of the noiseless dead can bring to a house.

Chapter 38

"So the search is on for Luther Penman," Langford said, refilling Tone's whiskey glass. "I never did like that man."

"The detectives seem convinced that he's the Ripper, and they're bringing in more officers for the search, starting tomorrow morning."

"Who's in charge?"

Tone thought for a minute. "A young inspector named . . . I think it's Anderson."

"Pete Anderson?"

"I didn't catch his first name."

"It's got to be Pete Anderson." Langford looked pleased. "Well, at least he's got a lick of sense."

"Sorry about not finding Weimin." Tone paused, smiling. "Hey, who am I talking to?"

"Mr. Langford."

"Then I'm reporting failure all round. I didn't contact Weimin, I did nothing to prevent the woman's death and I missed her killer with ten shots."

Langford shrugged. "In the dark, it happens." He sat

back in his chair and studied Tone thoughtfully. "How do you feel about joining in the hunt for Penman? I want that man real bad."

"Do you think it will do any good? He could have left town by now."

"Maybe he's skipped, but he likes fog."

"I'm not catching your drift."

"Penman will stay where there's fog to cover his tracks and a plentiful supply of whores to slaughter. The man is insane and the waterfront is his happy hunting ground. He won't move on unless he has to."

"Now he calls himself Jack."

"Jack the Ripper." Langford shook his head. "Tone, we've got to keep that name quiet or the damned newspapers will be all over it like flies on shit."

Smiling without a trace of humor, Tone said, "It does have a ring to it." He drained his glass. "When do you want to start?"

"Now. Right now. I don't want to sit here at home any longer while big doings are happening all around me. Inspector Anderson isn't stupid, but he's not that clever either. We can do better." He took his watch from his pocket. "Hell, it isn't even midnight yet. Penman might be out looking for another victim, since you interrupted his fun."

"That's possible, I guess. Say, who am I addressing now?"

"Give me five minutes to climb into my uniform and I'll be Sergeant Langford. In the meantime, help yourself to another drink. It could be a long night."

This time Tone's smile was genuine. "Thomas, I have a hunch you've just spoken with the voice of prophecy."

* * *

The rain that had been teeming earlier had settled into a sullen drizzle as Tone and Langford reached Pacific Street.

It was now a few minutes after midnight, and all the respectable folks in San Francisco were already in bed. Only the cops and denizens of the waterfront were awake, prompting Langford to remark that, despite the rain, everything was "full up and rarin' to go."

Word of the latest Ripper slaying had gotten around, and the whores walking the streets seemed wary, their eyes less bold, and the more concerned pimps stood in the shadows, keeping a watchful eye on their meal tickets.

For two hours Tone and Langford patrolled the alleys and dark backstreets, but apart from the usual drunks and a few brawls, they saw nothing.

"Wild-goose chase, you think?" Langford asked as he and Tone stood in the meager shelter of a saloon front.

"Seems like." Tone turned and looked at the sergeant, who seemed to be nursing a vague, unfocused anger. "We could try the Jolly Jack. It's Penman's favorite hangout when he's on the coast."

"Not a chance. Why would he go there in full view when every police officer on the waterfront has his description?" Langford was silent for a few moments, thinking. "Hell, we'll give it a try," he said finally. "Maybe make us feel like we're doing some useful police work."

Melody Cord's welcome was even less warm than it had been the first time Tone entered her establishment. In fact her mustache positively bristled when she caught sight of Langford in his blue uniform.

"If you're looking for Mr. Penman, he ain't here," she snapped. "I haven't seen him all evening." She struck a belligerent stance. "Now, be on your way, Thomas Langford, and leave decent Christian people alone."

Looking around him, Tone decided that the crowd was considerably less than Christian. The whalers were gone, but they'd been replaced by what seemed like the entire crew of an English clipper ship, a weather-beaten, tough-looking bunch. A dozen whores were entertaining the sailors and over in one corner a young brunette had unbuttoned the front of her dress and two men were each fondling a breast, sharing.

"Melody, me darlin', you keep a classy place and no mistake," Langford said, his eyes on the preoccupied trio.

"Don't you speak to me of class, Tom Langford," the woman said. "You who has sent many a brisk sailor lad to an early grave, and never has a word of remorse escaped your lips."

"Damn rozzers, they're all the same," a man growled. He looked around him. "You can lay to that, mates."

"Aye," said another, "ye have the right of it, Billy." His eyes lifted to Melody. "Many a brisk sailor lad, says you?"

"What I say, I say," replied the woman.

"Then throw him out, damn him. We want no blue-coats 'ere."

Langford's eyes sought out the man who had just spoken. Standing square and solid as a brick wall, his eyes blazing, he said, "Why don't you come over here and do it yourself?"

The sailor was big, with a seamed, tough face that had seen its share of brawls, but he obviously wanted no part of the sergeant, that night or any other. He looked away, muttered under his breath and went back to his rum.

Langford showed his disappointment, his chance to work off some of his growing frustration gone. He turned to Melody. "Are all your girls accounted for?"

"You see them, all of them."

"Then keep them close. I have reason to believe that Luther Penman is the Ripper."

The sergeant was rewarded by the look of horror that crossed Melody Cord's face. "That can't be true," she gasped.

Tone said, "I'm afraid it is. Earlier tonight I caught him in the act. Red-handed, you might say."

"You saw him murder Pattie Johnson?"

"No, I saw him just after he murdered Pattie Johnson."

Melody turned and said to the bartender. "Rum, and quick."

She drained the glass and rubbed the back of her hand across her mouth. "He was here. Penman was here earlier this evening. The Ripper was right here at the Jolly Jack and I never knowed it."

The bar had suddenly become hushed, and even the busy threesome in the corner were intently studying Melody's stricken face, the delicious word "Ripper" capturing their undivided attention.

"What time was that?" Langford asked.

"Early, just after I opened around four. He had tea, then he told me I wouldn't see him for a while, that he was going on a long sea voyage for his health." The horror in the woman's eyes grew. "He—he must have left here and then murdered Pattie."

Tone and Langford exchanged glances. Did a long sea voyage mean that he was planning to fly the coop with Sprague?

"Who is this Ripper, then?" a sailor asked.

Langford answered. "He's a monster who enjoys working on whores with a knife."

"What's 'e look like, then?"

"Small, thin, and he could be wearing a gray coat that may be bloodstained."

The sailor looked around him, half rising to his feet. "What do you say, lads? Should we go hunt for him?"

"Aye," said another. He winked at Melody. "If we find him, he's as good as pork, lay to that."

Except for the amorous pair in the corner, the sailors, bottles in hand, streamed out of the Jolly Jack. Langford stood back, a benign expression on his face, and let them go.

"They'll be back soon enough," he said to Tone. "But in the meantime they'll charge around and make a lot of noise. If Penman is still about, three dozen drunken sailors on a rampage might change his mind about doing more business tonight."

"Walk with me over to the inglenook," Tone said. "I want to scout around."

"I told you, he's not here," Melody protested.

"I know, but I still want to take a look."

The woman sighed and led the way. She said over her shoulder, "Tom Langford, you've run out all my customers and now you're going to scare the few that are left."

Melody spotted the three in the corner and directed her irritation at them. "Hey, Lucy, you slut, button up and take it outside."

"But it's raining, Melody," the girl whined.

"Yeah, well, give them two a quick knee-trembler and then come back inside. And when you do, make sure them cheap swabs buy rum. That's what I'm selling in this place, not ass."

Tone and Langford stopped and let the whore and her admirers pass. She led the way to the inglenook, but walked behind it to a narrow, recessed door. The girl fumbled in her purse, found a key and turned it in the lock. Then she and the two men walked outside, closing and locking the door behind them.

"Did Penman have a key for that door?" Tone asked Melody.

The woman nodded. "Yes, he did. I only give them out to my regulars. The rest who want to use the outhouse have to walk around the front. If the door is unlocked it's too easy for bummers to sneak out without paying their score."

"Can you see the door from the bar?" Langford asked.

"No. But since only regular—" Melody's face changed, as the implication of what the sergeant had said dawning on her. "Oh, I see. . . ."

"That's how Penman managed it," Langford said. "He slipped out the door, did his dirty work, then sneaked back inside, and nobody the wiser."

"He told me to leave him strictly alone unless he asked for something," the woman recalled. "He said he didn't want to be disturbed while he was studying his lawbooks."

"So he had time enough to do what he had to do," Tone said.

"Damn it, I'm going out there and dragging that slut

Lucy Barnes back in here by the hair," Melody said, alarmed. "The Ripper could be out there laying in wait for her."

Once they were in the street again, Tone said, "What do you think about Penman's sea voyage? Was he just covering his tracks?"

"I've been studying on it," Langford answered. "Lambert Sprague has been pushed to the wall by the Celestials. It could be that he's given up on the Barbary Coast and planning to set up somewhere else. He'd want to take his faithful lawyer and business manager with him."

"Now I remember something," Tone said. "When I went after Penman he yelled to me that everything had gone to shit. He must have been talking about Sprague's enterprises along the waterfront."

"Sprague is getting weaker while the Tong is growing in strength. They already control most of the Barbary Coast and are looking for more." Langford glanced at the black sky. "At heart, Sprague is still a pirate and it's not in his code to stand and fight when the odds are stacked against him. He'll haul down his flag, make a run for it and hope for better times."

"It seems to me that a man with his money could hire all the gunmen he needed and make a better fight of it," Tone said.

"He'd need hundreds, an army, and even then the Tong would outnumber him. There are a lot more Chinese in San Francisco than guns for hire in the western lands. Besides, it would take time to recruit the kind of force you're talking about, and by then Sprague knows he could be dead. The Tong have already come close to killing him once, and by now he must be afraid that every coolie carrying a bundle of dirty laundry on his head is a potential assassin."

The big sergeant nodded to himself. "No, he'll cut his cable and run. Gentlemen of fortune know when they're outgunned."

"Where to now?" Tone asked.

Langford sighed. "Do some more searching for Penman, I guess."

Tone smiled. "Like you said, it's going to be a long night."

"Some nights," the cop said, "are longer than others."

Chapter 39

Dawn came slowly to the waterfront. Out in the bay a gray mist hung over green water and the sky had cleared, shading from scarlet to violet, adorned with ribbons of jade. Gulls squawked and quarreled around the topgallants of the tall ships at the docks and the morning smelled of salt air and timbers worn by wind and sea.

A sorry procession of hungover sailors and miners, exhausted by rum and whores, made their way to their bunks in the brightening light, seeking sleep or a merciful death.

Tone and Langford sat in Tilly Tucker's Tea Room off Pacific Street, watching the world go by as they yawned over coffee and Tilly's famous hot rolls and unsalted Wisconsin butter. There were few other patrons at this time of the morning and the three men and two women who were present sat pale, silent and numb.

Tilly was a little old lady, bent and wrinkled, with lively brown eyes and hands mottled with the same color. She stepped to the table, opened the lid of a cigar box and displayed them to Langford. "A morning cigar, Sergeant?" she said. "You look all in." Then to Tone, "And so do you, young man."

"It's been a long night, Tilly." Langford sighed. "A man gets tired."

He selected a cigar and the woman reached into the pocket of her pinafore, found a match, thumbed it into flame, and lighted his smoke.

She did the same for Tone, who marveled at her expertise. He'd been around Texas drovers who lit matches like that, but none of them had possessed the old lady's casual skill.

He told her so, and Tilly smiled. "Young man, I've been lighting cigars for gentlemen since I was fourteen. That was when these"—she slapped her flat chest— "were out to here." She cupped both hands an exaggerated distance in front of her. "Back in those days, on the riverboats, they called me Tits Tucker."

The last was so unexpected, coming as it did from the prim mouth of a little old lady, that Tone laughed, his first real bellow in a long time, and it felt good.

Tilly toddled away to wait on another customer and Tone and Langford smoked and drank coffee, letting a comfortable silence stretch between them.

After a few minutes a police whistle warbled in the distance. Tone looked at the sergeant and raised a questioning eyebrow.

The big cop shrugged. "Ah, let him get his head kicked in. I'm off duty."

Then more whistles, strident and urgent.

Tilly was at her far window, craning her neck so she could see the waterfront.

"What's happening out there, Tilly?" a man asked.

"I don't know. Some kind of disturbance at the docks. Policemen running . . ."

Langford sighed and got to his feet. He looked at Tone. "I guess we'd better get down there."

"Is Sprague making his run, you think?"

"Could be. Or they caught a drunken sailor pissing off the dock."

There were two dozen policemen milling around the dock area when Tone and Langford arrived, the sergeant with a cigar in one hand, a half-eaten roll in the other.

"What's going on?" he asked the nearest cop. "And where's Inspector Anderson?"

"He's escaping, Sergeant!"

"Damn it man, who's escaping?"

"The Ripper! Look, out there in the boat."

Langford's eyes moved to the bay, where the boat was a dark dot in the distance, almost lost between a shoaling sea and the flaming sky. Desperately he turned to Tone. "Can you see anything?"

Tone's far-sighted gaze searched the bay. "I think maybe six, seven men. Is Sprague's longboat still tied up?"

Langford hurried to the edge of the dock, glanced down, then yelled, "No, it's gone."

Agitated, he tossed away his cigar and roll and walked back to Tone. "It's got to be Sprague and Penman must be with him." He looked around at the milling cops. "Who saw the boat leave?"

An officer stepped forward. "We did, Sarge, my partner and me. We were proceeding to relieve the two officers on duty here and that's when we saw the rowboat pull away."

"How do you know it was"—Langford hesitated—"the Ripper?"

"One of the individuals on board answered his description: a slight, small man wearing a gray coat."

"Did you recognize any of the others?"

The officer shook his head. "No, but one of the men at the oars was a real giant." He jerked a thumb at Tone. "Even bigger than him."

"That could be Blind Jack," Tone said.

"Sergeant Langford!"

Langford turned to the voice. "Inspector Anderson, I was wondering where you were."

"I've got two dead officers back there, hidden behind the stack of whale oil barrels yonder. Their necks are broken." He looked into the bay. "I believe the men who murdered my officers are in that boat, and quite possibly the Ripper is with them."

"And Lambert Sprague," Langford said. "If he's harboring a fugitive from justice we could put that damned pirate away for years."

Anderson was a young man with a full, spade-shaped beard and intelligent blue eyes. At that moment he looked both frustrated and helpless.

"Inspector, I'd bet my pension that they're heading for Sprague's steam yacht anchored off the Golden Gate," Langford said.

"Then we'll never catch them," Anderson said. "We don't have a steamboat or any other kind of boat. And even if we can find a rowboat they have too much of a start on us. We're police officers, not expert oarsmen."

Suddenly Tone recalled his conversation with Simon

Hogg, the night the man described the six men Tone had been contracted to kill.

"Langford," he said, "Simon Hogg once told me that Joe Carpenter kept a small steam yacht." He looked at the crowded rows of sailing ships lining the docks, a forest of masts stretching away in the distance. "If we can find it and get the thing going we have a chance of catching them."

Anderson was willing to clutch at straws. He yelled to his men, "Spread out and search for a small steam yacht. It must be anchored around here someplace."

"How will we know which one it is, Inspector?" an officer asked.

The inspector was on edge and he let it show. "Damn it, man, find any steam yacht. How many can there be?"

Fifteen minutes passed while Anderson fretted and fumed, pacing up and down, occasionally throwing a long-suffering glance at Langford.

Finally he glanced at Tone, then said to the sergeant, "I don't believe I've met this gentleman before."

Langford made the introductions, then, anticipating a possible objection from Anderson, he said, "Mr. Tone plans to join the department soon."

"Excellent, but still, he's a civilian and—"

A whistle sounded and a policeman waved frantically in the distance.

"By God, they've found it!" Anderson yelled. Then he was running.

Tone and Langford pounded after him, their tiredness forgotten along with Anderson's lowly estimate of civilian status.

Chapter 40

The yacht was moored at a jetty in front of an unused warehouse, well away from the main shipping channel.

Tone calculated she was about seventy feet long with a ten-foot beam. The boat was built low and racy, her single funnel raked for speed, and her foredeck was covered with a white canvas awning. She looked ship-shape and ready for sea. A man in Joe Carpenter's profession would be expected to keep her that way. There was no one on board.

Tone, Anderson and Langford stood on the jetty, admiring her lines, and the inspector said, "She'll do." Then his face fell. "Wait, does anyone know how to make the thing go? I expected there would be a crew on board her."

"For a start, she'll need to get up a head of steam," Tone offered. "I would imagine that takes hours."

Anderson cursed out his frustration. "Hours! The Ripper and the others will be long gone by then."

He turned to his men, who were grouped together among rusting machinery in front of the warehouse.

"You men, find me sailors who know steamboats!" he yelled. "Empty the brothels if you have to, shanghai them if you must, but get me seamen."

"Begging the inspector's pardon," said an older officer, stepping forward, "but I was a boiler man on the old *Wabash* during the late war. If that tub's wood-fired, I can get her started nice as you please."

"Come forward, man," Anderson said. "How long to get her going?"

"Let me take a look below, sir," the man said. Gray hair showed under his helmet and peppered his thick mustache. "I have to see if she's stoked with wood or coal."

"Then do it, man," Anderson said, tapping out an impatient little jig on the jetty timbers. "Time is a-wasting."

The officer disappeared down a hatchway and was gone for a couple of minutes. When he came back on deck he said, "Aye, she's wood-fired right enough. One boiler, single screw, but she'll be fast through the water."

"How long to give her . . . what do you call it? A full head of steam?"

"From a cold boiler, using a fire of split pine logs saturated with oil, five or six minutes."

"That's all?" Anderson asked incredulously.

"Yes, sir," the cop said. "There's only one problem."

"What's that?"

"The boiler could blow up."

It took Anderson only a few moments to consider that warning and dismiss it. "There are barrels of whale oil on the dock. Get a few on board and soak that wood as much as you need. Let's get her started."

Tone angled a glance at Langford. "The boiler could blow up," he said mildly.

"Yeah, and us along with it."

"It do fill a man with confidence. Don't it, Thomas?"

After ten minutes Anderson sent a couple of his men belowdecks to feed the boiler and he ordered the *Wabash* veteran to the wheelhouse, since he was the only man on board who had some knowledge of steering.

As Tone and Langford joined the inspector, Anderson was asking his officer how the boiler was holding.

The man shook his head. "Hard to say, sir. When you rapidly heat a cold boiler, some parts expand faster than others and it causes internal strains. At best you get seams in the metal, at the worst, boom! and the whole shebang goes sky-high."

Anderson had suddenly developed a twitch under his left eye. "What's your name, Officer?" he asked.

"Charles Benson, sir. Originally of New York town."

"Good man, Benson. You aim this scow at the Golden Gate full speed ahead. If we catch up with the rowboat I'll see you get a sergeant's star in ten years or so."

"Thank'ee kindly, sir," Benson said, smiling, as he opened the throttle and eased the yacht away from the jetty. "Not so much for me, you understand, but the little lady would appreciate it."

Tone, who had been thinking, said, "Officer Benson, that boat you were on—"

"The old *Wabash*, sir."

"Right. Did she have guns?"

"She was a fifty-four-gun frigate, sir."

"I believe if we tangle with Lambert Sprague's pirate ship, she'll have cannons on board."

Benson's face stiffened and he was silent for a moment. Then he smiled. "Well, sir, maybe our boiler will explode before that happens."

"Good man, Charlie," Tone said. "Always look on the bright side."

"Yes, sir. It's me nature, you might say."

But Anderson was obviously worried. His eye twitching, he said to Tone, "How many cannons?"

"I don't know, Inspector. I never saw them. But about a month ago he used cannons to shoot up a freighter, so he's got some big guns, all right."

"He could blow us out of the water before we even get close," Anderson said.

"We could always turn back and leave it up to the Navy," Tone said, testing what the young inspector's reaction would be.

"No!" Anderson said, the word almost a shout. "I've left two officers dead on the dock back there and I plan to bring their murderers to justice." He turned to Benson. "Full speed ahead!"

"And damn the torpedoes," Tone added.

The inspector allowed himself a slight smile. "Yes, indeed."

Tone was no sailor, but it seemed to him that the yacht was fairly racing across the water and he said as much to Benson.

"Yes, sir, she can fly. I'd say we're doing twenty-three knots. We should catch the rowboat before it clears the strait, if the boiler holds."

"Yes," Tone said, "if the boiler holds."

"Take the wheel, sir, if you will. I'm going below to see how she's bearing up."

Benson vanished and Tone gingerly took the wheel, concentrating on keeping the bucking boat aimed for the strait.

White water was crashing over the bow and two dozen cops were huddled under the canvas awning, soaked and miserable, several already leaning over the side, retching.

Tone's face was grim. Could they depend on seasick men to fight when the time came? Revolvers against cannons?

Beside him Anderson was pacing anxiously, his eyes constantly measuring the distance between the yacht and the Golden Gate. Langford seemed composed, almost resigned to his fate, but when Tone caught his eye he could read a troubled mind in their blue depths.

Langford knew the odds they were facing and, like Tone, he apparently did not rate their chances very highly.

As soon as Benson reappeared, Anderson snapped, "Report!"

"She's opened a seam, sir. We're losing steam, but so far not too badly."

"Will the damned boiler hold, man?"

"I don't know, sir."

Anderson looked out toward the strait. "We should have found that rowboat by now."

"They had a fair start on us, Inspector," Langford said mildly.

"What if they've already reached the steam yacht?"

"Then we're in a heap of trouble, sir."

Anderson swung on Benson. "Go tell the stokers to push it! I want every scrap of speed I can get from this tub."

"Sir, the boiler!"

"I don't give a—" Anderson fought to remain calm. "Carry out my order, Officer Benson."

"Yes, sir."

The inspector looked at Langford. "What do you suppose will happen if the boiler blows?"

"I don't think we need worry about that, sir. There will be sudden vacancies in the police department for an inspector, a sergeant and two dozen officers, that's all."

Chapter 41

The boat was shuddering violently by the time she reached the strait and more officers were sprawled sick on the deck. There was a hammering noise from below and Tone noticed that Benson's face was ashen.

He read the question on Tone's face and shook his head. "She's shaking apart. We're up to twenty-five knots and she was never built to sustain that speed for any length of time."

"The boiler?"

"She'll blow; lay to that."

Anderson was trying to appear calm. "Full throttle and keep her steady, Benson," he said. "We'll come up on those murderers soon."

But Sprague's longboat was nowhere in sight and a rolling fog bank had reduced visibility to a few yards.

"See anything?" Anderson asked. "Anyone?"

"No." Tone answered for the others. "We're sailing blind."

"Damn it," the inspector said, peering through the wheelhouse window into the mist. "Where are they?"

"Sprague would have told his crew to keep the yacht close to the strait," Langford said. "We'll find them."

"Or they'll find us," Tone said.

A few minutes later the fog betrayed them.

As suddenly as it had appeared, the bank shredded into curling wisps of mist and suddenly the little boat was visible and vulnerable, charging through a blue sea spangled with sunlight.

Sprague's steam yacht lay half a mile ahead, and men were scrambling up her starboard side from the longboat.

"We've got them!" Anderson yelled, smashing his right fist into the palm of the other. "We can board 'em, by God! Full speed ahead, Benson."

But as men rushed around her deck, the big yacht was already turning to port.

"She's showing us her ass," Anderson said, perplexed. "Damn it all, she's running."

"No, sir!" This from Benson, who looked sick. "They're uncovering a chase gun on the stern." He peered through the window. "Oh, dear Lord, help us! It's a Hotchkiss revolving cannon."

"Look!" Langford called out, pointing.

Now the others saw what the sergeant had seen: the terrifying flag of the pirate ship fluttering from the *Spindrift*'s mainmast. Against a black background, a grinning white skeleton held a cutlass in one bony hand, an hourglass in the other.

"They'll stand and fight," Anderson yelled, grinning, his eyes wild.

As Tone recalled it later, those were the last words the inspector ever said.

Smoke puffed from the stern of Sprague's yacht, followed by a bang that rolled across the flat sea.

A tall column of white water suddenly erupted on the little boat's port side, and a moment later a second, vicious exclamation point of surf exploded to starboard, this one closer.

The yacht's third shell crashed through the wheelhouse window, neatly decapitated Anderson, then detonated against the rear bulkhead with an earsplitting roar. Tone saw a flash of crackling silver and scarlet light around him and he was thrown headlong into the shattered window in front of him.

He lay stunned for a few moments and staggered to his feet as more shells crashed into the boat. He heard men scream and over in a corner Benson was groaning.

Through a drift of acrid smoke, Tone saw Langford lying on his back. The sergeant was bloodied but alive. Stepping over Anderson's headless corpse, he kneeled beside Benson. He could see no apparent injuries and helped the man to his feet.

Tone took time to glance outside. The boat had turned broadside to Sprague's yacht and was taking punishment, though she still had steam pressure and the screw was turning.

"Benson," he said, staring into the cop's face, "can you understand me?"

A shell crashed into the side of the boat and exploded. Abruptly she listed heavily to port and the wheelhouse reeked of cordite.

"Benson!" Tone yelled, shaking the man.

It took a few moments, but finally the cop's eyes focused. "We've still got steam. Ram the yacht's stern. You understand me? Ram her stern."

Benson nodded and grabbed the wheel, spinning it fast, turning toward the big steam yacht.

Supporting himself on a shattered timber, Langford was on his feet, his face bloodied from a deep gash on his forehead.

"Are you all right?" Tone asked.

"I'll survive."

"Sprague's boat rides high in the stern and they can't depress the big gun much lower," Tone yelled above the roar of yet another hit, this time well behind the wheelhouse. "We can sail under her line of fire and ram her."

He studied Langford's face. "We'll go forward. Get your men ready to board her."

"Where's Anderson?"

"Dead. Now let's go!"

Slipping on the blood and brains of dead men, Tone made his way to the bow. He heard Langford trying to rally his surviving officers. "Use your revolvers and then go to the knife, boys. Pirate scum can't take cold steel in the guts."

A thin, ragged cheer went up from fewer than a dozen throats. When, and if, they managed to board the pirate yacht, they could be badly outnumbered.

Tone looked behind him, across a deck torn by shot and shell. Despite his bloody face, Langford looked eager and ready, like a mighty, unmoving rock defying a sea storm. He had only ten officers around him, and one of those was favoring a wounded right arm.

Tone knew that his guns would have to make up for their weakness in numbers, a realization that thwarted his immediate plans.

The little boat was still plowing forward, though at a

much-reduced speed. Smoke was pouring from the boiler room and she was shuddering so badly that Tone heard the screech of iron plates buckling. She was also settling lower in the water, wallowing like a sow in a sty.

Fifty yards separated them from the *Spindrift*.

A couple of shells from the Hotchkiss exploded far to their stern. Then the shooting stopped. The cannon could no longer be brought to bear. Slowly, the yacht began a turn to port to give the gun a clear field of fire.

In the shattered wheelhouse, Benson, his blood up, was screaming obscenities like a madman.

Thirty yards . . .

One of the officers sent to tend the boiler fire scrambled on deck. There was only a ragged stump where his left hand had been. He spotted Langford and yelled, "Sarge! She's gonna blow!"

Twenty yards . . .

Langford looked back to the wheelhouse. "Benson!" he roared. "Ram her, damn your eyes!"

In reply, the man screamed louder.

"Sergeant Langford," Tone said. "Your revolver, if you please."

The big cop understood instantly why Tone would not fire his own guns. He passed over his revolver.

Ten yards . . .

The Hotchkiss cannon had been abandoned, but now the boat was coming under small-arms fire from Sprague's deck. Tone aimed at a towheaded man who was leaning over the rail aiming a rifle and fired. The towhead threw up his hands and vanished from sight. Tone kept firing and, for the moment at least, cleared the rail.

With a tremendous crash, the little boat, now a splintered wreck, hit Sprague's yacht on her port side just forward of the stern. Her bow failed to penetrate the *Spindrift*'s stout iron plates, but she rose up and climbed onto her, like a stallion mounting a mare.

The bow rose higher, tumbling Tone and everyone else head over heels along the deck until they collided hard with the base of the wheelhouse. Now almost vertical, the boat hung there until her weight forced her downward again. The bow crashed onto the deck, breaking apart *Spindrift*'s timbers as it buried itself deep.

A smoking, shot-riddled hulk, the little craft groaned, as though completely spent by this final effort, and stuck fast.

Tone scrambled to his feet and clawed his way up the crazily slanted deck. A bullet chipped wood a few inches from his face, a second sang a whining death song past his head. Behind him, Langford was exhorting his cursing men as they sought footholds on blood-slick planking.

Tone reached the bow and clambered over, aware how dangerously exposed he was to marksmen on the deck. He jumped onto the *Spindrift*—and was immediately skewered by a snarling sailor wielding a wicked-looking boarding pike.

Chapter 42

The sailor had aimed for a killing belly thrust, but Tone saw the danger and turned at the last moment. The foot of razor-sharp steel missed Tone's guts, but scraped bone, skidded and buried itself an inch deep into the flesh of his left hip, just below his belt.

Feeling as though he'd just been branded by a red-hot iron, Tone grabbed the wood shaft of the pike with his right hand and aimed a roundhouse left at the sailor's head. His punch connected with the man's jaw and he went down hard.

Tone let the pike fall to the deck and quickly glanced around him. Led by Sprague, a dozen men were charging toward him, armed with pikes and boarding axes.

A bullet crashed into Tone's left shoulder and sent him reeling. His back slammed hard against the Hotchkiss cannon and he cursed wildly. They were cutting him to pieces!

"No! I want that one alive!" someone yelled. It was Sprague's voice.

Suddenly Langford stepped to Tone's side, huge

bowie knife in hand. Guns were firing and a pirate went down, screaming. The cops were swarming onto the deck, revolvers blazing.

"Stay right there, John!" Langford yelled above the battle din. "You're out of it!"

Tone shook his head and elbowed himself erect. His .38s were in his hands and he was firing. Even lightheaded as he was from loss of blood, at a range of less than ten yards Tone's fire was devastating. Five of Sprague's men immediately dropped dead or wounded to the deck, and the rest turned away from the deadly hail of lead.

Langford roared and led his men in a charge after the fleeing pirates.

His revolvers shot dry, Tone indulged in a grandstand play, a showy bit of bravado that he would marvel at later. He spun his guns fast, then, in one slick motion, did a border shift, reversed the .38s and slid them into his belt. It was his way of showing the pirate riffraff that he was still alive and eager for a fight. He would assure himself afterward that it seemed like a good idea at the time.

The battle had moved forward toward the bow of the *Spindrift* and the deck around Tone was deserted, except for the dead and wounded, several of them wearing blue uniforms.

Suddenly Tone became aware of the trim of the yacht. The deck was tilted away from him at an odd angle, and a marlin spike rolled toward him and vanished under the chase gun.

The *Spindrift* must have suffered below-water damage from the collision and was settling by the stern.

A sense of urgency in him, Tone stooped, picked up

the boarding pike at his feet, and got ready to move forward to rejoin the fight. He felt weak and dizzy, though neither of his wounds pained him. If he survived, the pain would come later.

Seagulls, attracted by the scent of blood in the water, wheeled and swooped, calling out to each other. From horizon to horizon, the sky was a deep azure bowl and the sun was fair up, wedding itself to the sea with bands of gold. The pirate flag, black as a crow, still flapped from the mainmast, the skeleton dancing a jig in the breeze.

Tone started to make his way across the slanting deck, then stopped in his tracks. Blind Jack, huge, intimidating and dangerous, emerged from the narrow deck passage between the main cabin and the port rail. He grasped a bloody cutlass in his hand.

But it was the three people behind Jack that gave Tone pause.

Sprague was in the lead, holding a boarding axe. Behind him, dressed in a split canvas riding skirt, black vest and white shirt, was Chastity Christian. And behind her, thin and white as a cadaver, was Luther Penman, who caught sight of Tone, reared back his head and hissed his fury like a snake.

"Jack," Sprague said, taking the giant by the arm and pointing him in the direction of Tone, "take him. Throw him into the longboat." He turned. "You two, get in as well, or I'll leave you to drown like rats."

Blind Jack had lost the black band from around his eyes, revealing empty sockets networked with scars. He shuffled toward Tone, leading with his left foot, the scarlet-stained cutlass chopping at the air in front of him.

"Come to me, little rabbit," he whispered. "I'm a rough-and-ready man, an' no mistake, but I won't hurt you—lay to that. See, matey, Cap'n Sprague wants you for his own, to gut at his leisure, as you must surely understand."

Jack was only yards away and Tone had no intention of fighting him hand to hand. That was a battle he could not win. He bounced the boarding pike in his hand, finding the balance, then drew the weapon back and hurled it with all of his waning strength at the grinning giant.

Tone's aim was true.

The lance-shaped blade drove through Blind Jack's chest and stuck out a span-length between his shoulder blades. The giant staggered, dropped his cutlass and tried to tear the pike free. He failed and his knees buckled, sending him crashing onto the deck. A pool of blood, as black as Blind Jack's heart, spread around him.

Sprague had been watching from the rail. "Stand by," he yelled to Chastity and Penman, who were already in the longboat. "I'll be right back."

Now he looked across the deck at Tone, the axe slanted across his chest. "I'm going to cut you into collops, you traitorous dog."

Wearily, Tone picked up Jack's cutlass. Suddenly he wanted it over with. He needed rest . . . a place to rest. . . .

Sprague, knowing that the last grains of sand were trickling through the hourglass, charged, the axe poised for a tremendous killing stroke.

He was counting on Tone to step back, vainly trying to parry his attack with the cutlass. But Tone stepped into him. The axe swung, too wide. But the lower edge of the blade cut deep into the thick meat of Tone's left shoulder, staggering him.

Cursing, Sprague sprang back. He eyed Tone and readied the axe again. Circling. "I've got ye now, Tone," he snarled. "By God, I'll chop you up and feed you to the sharks."

Tone thrust with the point of the cutlass, stepping into it. Sprague easily avoided the other man's clumsy rush and Tone stumbled and fell facedown onto the deck, the cutlass clattering away from him. He rolled over quickly. Sprague, grinning, had the axe raised above his head, ready to drive the blade into Tone's brain. Knowing it was over, Tone threw up his right arm in a futile attempt to ward off the blow.

Sprague tensed, the axe swung. . . .

With a thunderous roar, the abused boiler of the little boat exploded.

The gigantic blast staggered the *Spindrift* like a terrier shaking a rat and she immediately listed crazily to starboard. Sprague was knocked off his feet and his head struck hard on the deck.

As debris thudded and clanked around him, Tone rose, his red-rimmed eyes searching. He spotted what he'd hoped to find, a securing rope neatly coiled at the base of the Hotchkiss cannon.

As Sprague groaned and rose to a sitting position, stunned, Tone made a loop in the rope. He stepped behind Sprague, dropped the noose over the man's head, and tightened it around his throat.

Suddenly aware of what was happening, Sprague tried to scramble erect. Tone kicked him viciously in the side of the head and the man fell on his back.

"I'll kill you, Tone," Sprague croaked. "As sure as my mother is roasting in hell, I'll kill you."

"After I hang you for a damned pirate," Tone said.

The *Spindrift* was sinking fast. Tone heard Langford yelling to get boats launched and, forward, feet pounded on the deck.

"You can't hang me, Tone." Sprague grinned. "I'll take you down with me." He grabbed the rope and rose to his feet, his face a twisted mask of hate. "Damn you, we'll feed the sharks together."

Tone felt unsteady and sick. His head swam and the slanting deck, sea and sky reeled around him. Sprague was closer, a taut stretch of rope in his hand extended in front of him like a garrote. The man's eyes looked as though they were made of iron—flat, pitiless, eager to kill.

Letting go of the rope, Tone dropped to one knee and picked up the axe. Sprague was almost on top of him. The man ducked behind him and dropped the rope over his head and around his neck. Immediately the hemp tightened, crushing into Tone's throat.

Gasping, his mouth a strangled O of pain and fear, Tone summoned his last reserves of strength. As pirates had done for hundreds of years before battle, Sprague had taken off his shoes for a better grip on the slippery deck. His bare right foot was extended in front of him to Tone's side.

As blackness threatened to envelop him, Tone raised the axe and chopped down hard on Sprague's unprotected toes. The man screamed and the pressure on Tone's throat immediately stopped. Sprague had left four bloody toes on the deck.

Unable to stand on the stump of his right foot, the

man dropped to a sitting position. Tone rose to his feet, swung the axe in a roundhouse arc, and Sprague's head jumped a foot into the air, then rolled like a ball on the deck.

Roaring, teeth bared in a savage snarl, Tone lifted the gory, grinning head by the hair and held it aloft, an ancient Celtic warrior ritual as old as time, a throwback to a more savage age that still ran strong in his blood.

It was Langford who took the head from him and threw it into the sea. "John," he said gently, "you must get into a boat. We're sinking fast."

Tone looked at the big sergeant, but neither heard nor understood.

Then, at long last, the blackness took him.

Chapter 43

"I woke up and saw this nun bending over me, smiling," Tone said. "I thought I'd died and had gone to heaven, and that pleased me. I always figured I'd end up in the other place."

"Give it time, Tone," Sergeant Langford said solemnly.

Tone sat higher on the creaking St. Mary's Hospital cot. "I killed Sprague, didn't I?"

"You killed him." Langford shook his head, his eyes bleak. "The butcher's bill was too high, John, all those dead officers. I talked to nine widows, and twice that many orphans, telling them how gallantly their husbands and fathers had died." He sighed deeply. "It didn't help much. Sprague was not worth one of those officers' lives and they knew it." The big cop managed a smile. "Benson was promoted posthumously to sergeant. His wife is very proud of him."

Tone nodded. "He deserved it. The man had sand."

He let a silence stretch between them, then said, "How long have I been out of it?"

"Nigh on three weeks. A few times we thought we'd lost you, but the nuns always pulled you through. Surprising, I guess, because when we brought you in you were at death's door, all shot and cut to pieces."

"Chastity Christian and Luther Penman got away clean, huh?"

"They did. But the woman didn't last long. We found her body in a room at the Imperial Hotel. She'd been gutted and her tongue had been cut out because Penman had wanted to take his time with her."

Tone shook his head. "Bad as she was, she didn't deserve that. No human being should die that hard." He looked at Langford. "And Penman? Did you get him?"

"He's long gone, cleaned out the safe in his office and vanished. I'd guess he's out of the country by this time."

Langford closed his eyes, as though trying to get rid of an image he had not wanted to bring to mind, then opened them again. "On the wall above the bed where Chastity Christian's body was found, he'd written, 'Now jaunty Jack is off to have a jolly good time.'"

"Jolly good time . . . that's an English expression, isn't it?" Tone said.

The cop nodded. "Penman will go where there's fog and whores, and what city fits the bill better than London town?"

"Jack the Ripper in London," Tone said. "There's a harrowing thought."

"He won't escape justice for long. Scotland Yard has an excellent detective branch and after his first murder they'll catch him and hang him."

"The sooner the better," Tone said.

Langford pushed his chair away from the cot and got to his feet. "It's been quiet around the waterfront since you've been gone, Tone. But you'll be out in a couple of days and we've got another war to fight. We have to put the crawl on the Tong and run them out of the Barbary Coast." The big sergeant smiled. "I'd like you to be at my side."

"I'll give it some thought." Tone sighed. He looked around his tiny, bare room. "I've got nothing better to do."

Three days later Tone lay on a new mattress in Langford's spare room. Outside, rain lashed through the darkness and a keening wind tossed the trees, but lost in a volume by Mr. Dickens, Tone paid it no mind. He felt relaxed, perfectly at ease and comfortable, since the sergeant had spared no expense in his choice of bedding. There was a glass of whiskey at his elbow and a cigar waiting to be smoked, and Tone was eagerly anticipating both.

There was a tap on his door, and Langford, his hair much grayer since the sea fight, stuck his head into the room. "I'm going to bed now, Tone," he said.

"Pleasant dreams, Thomas." Tone smiled.

"I've brought you something." Langford stepped inside and hung a blue uniform on the hook behind the door. "Later I can have it altered to fit you better," he said.

After Langford was gone, Tone stared at the uniform for a long time. Finally he rose to his feet and padded to the door. He ran his fingers down the blue wool serge and lightly touched the patrolman's copper badge.

It was a fine uniform, and one he'd be honored to wear.

Tone sat back on the bed and silently studied the blue tunic for many minutes, lost in thought.

He knew he'd never wear it.

The time of the bounty hunter was almost done and would soon go the way of the buffalo and the Indian. He realized that. The growth of cities, better law enforcement, the telegraph and the newfangled telephone were shrinking distances even across the vast western lands and, like his own, the days of the roaming outlaw were surely numbered.

But the West was a beautiful, mysterious woman singing her siren song to Tone. She was calling him home to the aloof mountains, the quiet forests and the limitless plains, seductively reminding him what it was like to watch the smoke of his fire rise like incense to pay homage to the stars. He recalled the play of sunlight on a trout stream, the rustle of aspens and the sigh of tall pines in the wind.

He could not turn his back on her. Not now, not ever. To do so would be to spit on his life.

The path he had chosen was one of flame-streaked violence and sudden death. He knew that one day he would end up with his face in the sawdust of a sod saloon in a one-loop town somebody had named Who-Gives-a-Damn. But that was his choice and he would accept its consequences.

Tone rose and dressed in his peacoat and watch cap. Langford had cleaned and loaded his guns and he dropped them into his pockets. He stepped quietly to the kitchen, hearing the cop's soft snoring from the other bedroom.

Tone found pen and paper and wrote: *Thomas, if you're ever in Reno . . .*

He had no need to write more. Langford would know.

Tone walked to the front of the house, stepped outside and quietly closed the door behind him.

Acknowledgments

The author would like to thank the City of San Francisco and its police department for their valuable insights into the life and times of Sergeant Thomas Langford and his role in policing the crime- and violence-ridden Barbary Coast in the 1880s.

I'm indebted to Thomas Asbury for his wonderful book *The Barbary Coast*, published by Alfred A. Knopf in 1937. Also to Colonel Albert S. Evans' *Sketch of Life in the Golden State* (1871) and to Frank Soule and Dr. John H. Gihon for *The Annals of San Francisco* (1855).

According to a 2005 article in Britain's *Manchester Guardian* newspaper, Jack the Ripper may have been a merchant seaman who arrived in England aboard the cargo vessel *Sylph* in July 1888, just before the murder of his first victim, Mary Ann Nichols. The *Sylph* returned to the Caribbean on September 22, two weeks after the gruesome killing of prostitute Mary Kelly. In January 1889, six prostitutes were murdered in Managua, the capital of Nicaragua. Police later said the victims "were mutilated beyond all recognition, their faces horribly slashed."

Jack may have returned to England and murdered Whitechapel prostitute Alice McKenzie on July 17, 1889. Although never officially listed as a Ripper victim, the woman was strangled, her throat slashed and her body mutilated.

Jack may have then left England and murdered and mutilated a woman in Hamburg, Germany, on October 18, 1889, before vanishing into the fog for the last time.

Was Jolly Jack a seaman or a paying passenger, say a rich lawyer? In the Ripper saga, all things are possible.